PART 1

Hell 1982

To T, D and J: You are my Heaven.

CHAPTER 1

NERO

Of all the horrible jobs to be assigned in Hell, coal was the worst. Nero scraped endlessly at the wall and tossed the bits of loosened rock on the flames. His hands felt magnetically attracted to the shovel, nearly impossible to remove, and occasionally blood swirled down his forearms from the constant friction. The ironic part was that if he did manage to let go of the shovel, the fires stayed just as hot. They didn't really require his little additions at all. Sweat stung his eyes and his muscles ached, but the compulsion to shovel outweighed everything.

Brut and Nero had shoveled coal side by side for eons. Then Brut, a silent and horrible companion, began speaking one day, telling tales of Hell's minions crawling to Earth. He said that upon touching the soil, minions lost their mandates, their compulsions, and they could just *be*. In Hell, the Devil saw to it that there was a constant flow of fresh flesh and endless, impossible-to-refuse activities for the damned. As Brut continued to tell his tales, day after day, finding the opportunity to simply be free for a bit became, in a way, its own compulsion.

Working one day (or was it night?) Nero hit the wall with his shovel, but instead of finding solid rock, the blade sunk right through, revealing an open space. At their next respite, Brut and Nero looked through the hole to find a crude tunnel. After that it took them months to explore the passageways that ran like veins through Hell, while still doing their jobs.

When they finally found the one that led to the surface, they had to power through their compulsions and *force* themselves to crawl through and stand on solid ground. But once they'd done so, the implications were amazing. Minions *could* be on the surface. All the security measures and traps were rendered useless by this one, perfect escape hatch.

They weren't the first to get out, but it had been so difficult, there couldn't have been more than a few others. Brut took off running, wild and free. Nero took deep breaths of the fresh, clean air. The last time he'd seen the stars, his humanity barely made him different from the animals. But now he looked around to see houses, cars, lights...so much had changed.

He was out of Hell. He didn't know what to do first. He wanted to just lay back and curl his fists in the green grass. He'd crouched to run his fingertips over the soft blades when he saw her. She was playing with a tiny dog, which started growling the minute he saw Nero. The minion curled his lip, and the animal yipped like he'd been bitten.

But she was something. Her brown hair had been basking in the sun and, even in the darkness, bits of sunlight threaded between the strands. Her eyes were brown as well, but ringed in gold. She followed her dog's line of sight, and then she saw him.

Nero stood, his leather pants and rippled chest marked and burned from the flames in Hell. He couldn't imagine what she thought of him.

"Who is it?"

She asked the question like she thought he might be intimidated into providing his résumé in response. Instead he walked slowly toward her. The poodle jumped up, and she caught him in a well-practiced move. She watched Nero as he came closer.

"I'll call the police. They can be here in less than two

minutes."

"I do not seek to injure you, woman." Nero stepped into a white pool of illumination. The cabin's lighting offered him a stage. He was still as she assessed him. He watched as the understanding that he wasn't human reached her eyes.

"Oh...*Oh.*"

"Your police?" He said the words as if they were a foreign language. "What will they do? I wish only to breathe fresh air, but your beauty has stopped me from enjoying nature."

She cleared her throat and brought her poodle closer. "Flattery won't stop me from calling the authorities."

"I speak only the truth as I feel it."

"Well, you better go back to where you came from. Don't step any closer."

Nero could tell she was trying to stay angry, but his body — clad only in torn leather pants — had mesmerized her.

"I will not step closer. For you, I will stay here. But I would like to touch your hair and see if the different colors have distinct textures. I would love a cool drink of water, and after that, I will touch my lips to yours in appreciation of your kindness." He remained fixed as a statue as he spoke.

"You know what? Why can't a guy like you — wearing all his clothes, for that matter — approach me in a bar? If you said that to me on a Friday night I'd hand you my panties in surrender. Instead you have to be a thing that emerged from the dark of my backyard. My luck sucks."

She moved slowly and carefully to the side of the cabin, never taking her eyes off of him, and turned a small wheel. A hose puffed up with a rush of liquid, and soon there was a cold, clear stream pouring onto his feet.

He growled at the sight of the water and knelt quickly, dipping his mouth into the stream and lapping it hungrily like an animal.

She sighed and set her poodle down. The nervous canine scampered away as she picked up the hose to demonstrate. "Look.

Here, you can pick it up and drink." She held it to her lips and took a small sip, wiping her mouth when she was done.

He rose and took the hose carefully, not touching her. He felt her eyes on him as he drank his fill. Then he held his hand under the stream and reveled in the silk of the water covering his fingers. He turned the hose toward his chest and closed his eyes. The sensation was too pleasurable to bear.

"You're smoking." She took a step back.

He smiled at the cloud of steam around him, and she bit her lip as he sighed and scrubbed his chest. "Can I have your lips now?" he asked suddenly. He let go of the hose, and the stream drenched the leg of her jeans on its way to the ground. When she gasped, he stomped on the green rubber to stop the watery assault.

"Maybe we should know each other's names?" she shot back, recovering quickly. "And no, of course not. I don't want to be a slut."

But he could see her looking at his mouth. "I'm known as Nero. What do you go by?" He pushed his dark hair from his forehead.

"Um, Jenny. I go by Jenny." Her poodle peeked around the house and barked.

"Your beast is tiny and angry." He pointed to the shaking poodle. "Spike's afraid of everything. But in this case I think he has good sense to be afraid of you. Where do you come from?" She turned and shushed the whimpering dog with an impatient wave.

"So I cannot have your lips?" Nero touched his own.

"I can't believe I'm going to do this. Fine. If I give you the lips, will you leave?" She stepped closer and stood on her tiptoes. She pursed her lips and pecked him on the mouth.

"Thank you." Nero smiled his dimpled smile as he looked over his shoulder. *How long do I have?*

"You know, I've found a few things in my backyard — a mole, a crapload of squirrels that steal from my birdfeeder, a baby copperhead snake — but you're the first thing I've kissed." She threaded her fingers together anxiously.

"When you give me your mouth? That's kissing? I would like to kiss you again." Lust put a sparkle in his eyes.

She took a step backward. "Why are you acting so strange? Did you just escape from prison or something?"

"Or something. It's like a prison. Nothing of beauty is found there. You are beautiful. I'm glad you didn't kiss the copperhead snake." Nero's hands began to shake just a little.

"Are you a drug addict? I just can't figure you out." She took another step back.

"It's better that you don't." His voice had longing in it. The shaking grew more pronounced. "May I drink from your hose again, taste a kiss again, if I return?"

She rubbed her face with both hands. "I guess you could drink from the hose. You could do that. The kiss...I'm not so sure. Tell me where you're from."

Behind her, Nero caught movement in the shadows. Brut was returning — his whole body shaking as he ran as fast as he could.

"I'm from the worst place, and the compulsion to return? It will overtake me. Do not follow. Never, never follow me, Jenny." His shaking traveled from his hands to his arms, and he stepped into the dark so the beautiful girl would not see how his mandate controlled him.

"Maybe. Maybe on the kiss, Nero."

He heard those words as he was claimed by his desire to shovel. His run was not human, but he made time to secure a large rock in front of their exit.

Back at his post, Nero began shoveling quickly to make up for time lost. His muscles groaned as they returned to the job they'd done for so many, many years. He turned to Brut, eager to plan their next outing — he needed to see Jenny again — and for the first time he looked closely at his companion. The minion's face and arms were covered in blood. The only break in the color was a strong, white smile of pure joy.

CHAPTER 2

JENNY

Jenny wished she'd never met Nero — never touched his lips, never spoken to him. And then with the next breath she wished she'd kissed him properly, felt his ridiculous biceps. She wished she'd handed him a flower so he could have something beautiful to take with him.

The little conglomeration of rocks that had materialized at the site of his disappearance didn't seem to include a door. After it had been a few months and Spike had stopped growling at the spot, Jenny poked around. She was drawn to it and often sat there. She read books near it as if it were the grave of a dear friend. Eventually, she planted flowers around the rocks, imagining that Nero would return, drink his water, and see the blooms — if he came in the right season.

But a year passed and Jenny mostly gave up, or that's what she told herself. And anyway she wasn't sure if she hoped he wouldn't come back or that he would. She dated and went out on the town with girlfriends, but at night in her dreams — her spectacular, blood-boiling dreams — she lay with Nero and touched his thick, black hair. His eyes had been so black they were almost glowing.

She finally began to work from home, writing a romance advice column, of all things, and her waiting became an obsession.

Building a shed over the site gave her something to do. She told herself she was protecting him by sealing the entrance with a door. Then she told herself she was protecting the world by locking that door to keep things in.

Two years came and went. It was fall when she rose from her bed to get a drink of water, which she always needed after her dreams of him, and peeked in the backyard out of habit. Her shed was glowing orange and red, like it was on fire. She was transfixed watching — scared, hopeful, and scared again. "Nero," she whispered.

Just then the door blew off, and Jenny flinched. When she looked again, a thing that was *not* Nero looked back at her with the sick, demented smile of a jack-o-lantern, one carved to scare. Fear climbed over her skin like a swarm of bugs. The thing in front of her was death put on legs, vaguely in the shape of a man. It broke their stare to look over its shoulder. From the shadows Nero walked with purpose and authority, pointing at the thing with what seemed to be angry words.

When the thing scampered away, chastised, Nero looked to her window.

He was back. He was here. Jenny ran downstairs to meet him in the driveway. By the time she got her door open, he was already feasting on the water, letting it run over his face and chest as he gulped.

When he saw her he dropped the hose, and water spilled on the driveway, spreading like clear blood from an open wound. "Jenny. The maybe kiss? May I have the maybe kiss?" He looked from her mouth to her eyes and back. "I've been thinking of you, only you, all this time. I didn't even stop to breathe, just imagining your lips over and over again."

The fear she should have felt was washed away by his words. She'd been dreaming of this man minutes earlier, and she wanted to go to him — whether or not he was even a man. "I know how you feel. Yes to the maybe kiss. Please."

Minding her bare feet, she stepped toward him, watching the

passion gather in his face. Her long, white nightgown swept through the gathering puddle, and she felt it heavy behind her as she reached him. Her memory was faulty. He was so much more handsome than she'd been allowed to remember. She touched his face, her thumbs outlining his lips before she whispered his name.

He bent and she offered him her lips, sliding a hand into his hair as she gave him his maybe kiss. His whole body tensed as she added her tongue, letting her dreams become reality, in her nightgown on her driveway.

In a rush he gathered her in his arms, hugging her tightly. He gave her a look she should've had enough sense to fear, but instead she tipped her head back as he kissed her throat. Nero laid her on the soft grass near the driveway. Then he left her for a moment, and she shivered. He dragged the hose over and let the water cover her. Her white gown became just a hint of a whisper. Her nipples hardened, and their pink bloomed through the now-translucent fabric. And then there was his hot mouth, warming her chilly skin. Nero wet her down completely and with his hands and tongue and lips saw to it that she was thoroughly heated. As the steam rose, its swirling sensations almost stealing Jenny's humanity, she could only moan and writhe. Through the barrier of the cloth, he pressed against her.

The weight of Nero on top of her was worth the nights without him. She lifted her head to watch when he slid down to run the water between her legs. He drank the water and licked her at the same time. In the moonlight he looked amazing, the muscles in his back flexing and urgent. Jenny wanted the gown and panties gone.

Out of the corner of her eye she saw movement, and she had to fight through her pleasure to focus on the spot in the distance. The thing she'd seen first, the horror that had preceded Nero, was standing in her shrubs, watching their passion. She didn't even think to cover for modesty's sake as it smiled at her and mouthed, "Want."

By the time Nero looked where she was pointing, it was gone, disappeared back into the shed. Nero pulled Jenny from the ground and shook his head as he gathered her again.

His embrace was like being wrapped with a towel warm from the dryer. "That thing," she asked. "What is it?"

Nero's voice was low and rough. "Brut. He is like I am. A minion. From Hell."

"You're nothing like that!" Brut had evil etched in his very essence.

"Let's not think of him now. Jenny, my maybe kiss was everything I hoped for and then some." Nero touched her lips and smiled.

His dimples and strong arms almost made her forget. Almost. "Let's go inside." Jenny pulled the beast from the center of the earth into her house and into her heart.

NERO

Nero walked into Jenny's cabin and immediately wanted to stay. He never wanted to see another shovel, never wanted to sweat next to Brut again. This woman, this house. It was everything Hell wasn't.

He turned to look at her again. He had warmed her, but she was still damp. She led him into a room and turned on more water. Water was such a luxury — to drink, to wash in — but putting water on Jenny was so amazing it was painful.

She looked shy as she stepped out of her gown. It fell around her feet like a sopping halo. Blushing, she covered her mouth as he fell to his knees. She was entirely available — to him, of all creatures. He crawled until he could touch her and licked his way up her leg, the skin so very soft. He slid her panties down.

She put her hands in his hair and stilled him. "How long do we have?"

He held out a hand to show her the tremors that had already begun. "Not long, Jenny. I will submit to the compulsion. Brut has already returned."

"I need you inside me. Be warm inside me." Jenny stepped into the shower, and Nero stepped out of his pants to follow her. She took the soap and a washcloth and rubbed him down between kisses and strokes.

By the time he'd lifted her and pressed himself into her, the shaking, the vibrating of his damnation made her tremble too. Before his release he stopped. "Jenny, we are not the same. I cannot fulfill myself in you."

"Nero, I don't care." She wiggled, and the soapy shower wall allowed her to slide down.

He couldn't speak. His manhood had entered her as far as he could go. She was so much colder than he was, pure bliss and silk and release. She tossed her wet hair and screamed, and he was done, the sight of her panting with pleasure emptied him. Her nails dug into his skin, and he gently nipped her shoulder.

He wanted to stroke her again. He wanted to lay with her and watch her hair dry, but he was done. His power to fight had left him as his arousal washed out like a tide. There was no goodbye, no words of caution. He had nothing to say to her as he returned to the shed.

When he arrived, Brut was already working, but he greeted Nero with a deadly smile. Nero took his place, naked, and began to shovel.

"Want her."

Mid-shovel, Nero lifted his blade and slapped Brut with all his might.

He staggered and laughed. "You cannot fight the minion who knows all your secrets, can you?"

Working again, because he must, Nero shook his head. Brut

was right. If he wanted to see Jenny again, he'd have to endure Brut's taunts. The last thing he needed was his escape hatch revealed. So with every shovelful of coal, Nero endured Brut's new, steady cadence: "Want her. Want her. Want her. Want her."

CHAPTER 3

JENNY

Jenny washed his pants, so she could get the Hell out of them, but they disintegrated in the machine. She sat down and cried when she discovered that she had nothing to remind her of their night.

It was stupid, she knew, to think a folded pair of pants beside her bed would be a promise he'd have to keep. He was a minion — or else she was stark raving mad with a very pornographic imagination.

At night she still dreamed of him, but now, instead of just Nero and their passion, Brut's eyes always watched. She often woke with the crystal-cold sensation of not being alone, and it scared her. She now knew loving Nero came with a price greater than being alone for great lengths of time. Brut was another burden.

After a month, Jenny had a much bigger problem. When her period did not arrive, she felt a new sense of dread. Soon she realized why Nero had not wanted to come inside her. Jenny was about to bring a life into the world, and she had not one clue what sort of life it would be.

The pregnancy was a nightmare. Between the sweats and the fevers, Jenny had her doctor in a panic. She continued to write, but inspiration came at odd times during the day and night. The thought of having to provide for a new baby gave Jenny mild panic attacks. If Jenny lived. If the baby lived. If it would even be a baby.

As the months added together, Jenny made a will and arranged for her aunt to raise the baby if she didn't make it. But nine months came and went with no labor pains, no signs of an impending birth. Jenny's doctor wanted to induce her, but Jenny just had a feeling her baby wasn't done. So she avoided the ringing phone and the letters from her gynecologist asking for an update, an appointment...anything.

Then, thirteen months after Jenny had made passionate love with Nero against the tile wall of her shower, the first pains came. Unlike the textbook description of pain after pain with some sort of rhythm, some sort of pause in between, a freight train of agony ripped through her. She knew she wouldn't survive. She was positive. And despite her concern that whatever she gave birth to shouldn't be seen by the outside world, she struggled to the phone and dialed 9-1-1. As she slipped down the wall and into her own blood, Jenny knew there was too much. So much blood. She whispered her address and was unconscious when the operator asked her to repeat her words, saying she could barely make out what Jenny had said.

NERO

Time slipped by above Nero and passed below him, but he could never tell where he was in it. There was only the shoveling. At one point he was given pants, at another he was whipped. Such was the nature of Hell, and it both soothed and disgusted Nero that he'd been there long enough to make some sense of the place. He now knew there were two different ways to become ruler of the damned. The first, and most common, was to systematically challenge everything in the underworld and fight your way to the top. When there were no more in the way, you went toe-to-toe with the Devil, winner take all.

Alternately, Heaven sometimes put their own candidates into the ring. Jack, the current Devil, was the best of the best. The Devil before him had never been bested in a challenge, but Jack — fresh from Heaven with glitter still falling from his skin — had dispatched him so quickly that the minions called to be witnesses instantly granted him their respect.

And the changes Jack implemented in Hell after he came to power had made a difference. There were jobs to be done, and Hell became a well-run business. The minions could even come to him and suggest changes — within reason of course, and they were usually granted only if Jack could see something in it for himself. But he often observed the tortures (the jobs, the compulsions) and tweaked them just enough to make them reasonable.

Hell was still horrible, but there were now measures in place to keep the beings there sane enough to do their work. Thus, Nero and Brut's occasional brief respites from the shoveling. Maybe it had been the knowledge that Jack was evil, but fair, that gave Nero the balls the take the out when he saw it.

Whatever his motivations, Nero knew his chances to go to Jenny were few and far between. Brut had to be ready, he had to be strong, and time had to be slow — just a bit so they could find a break in it and escape. Nero also found it increasingly hard to ignore the fact that his desire for pleasure unleashed Brut on an unsuspecting world. And he'd also noticed the minion was fixated on Jenny. Nero warned him often — told him to find his own woman — but he doubted Brut was even listening.

When finally the moment came again, Nero knew it had been longer than last time. But how much time had whisked by was a mystery as he and Brut lifted the stone into their brief escape. The bright sun paralyzed them both the moment they broke through the lock on the shed door.

Brut began panting like a dog, and Nero instinctively covered his eyes with his hands. Why he'd just assumed it was always dark, it would always be night, he didn't know. But the sun was crippling. Both minions returned to the shed and waited for their eyes to adjust, unsure if they even would, until finally they could see clearly.

In the light of day, Brut looked even more unstable. He was a bit shorter than Nero, but he was so muscled. The crazy in his eyes might just make him stronger in a battle. If it ever came to that. Brut took off first, and Nero stood in the shed doorway to ensure that the minion did not force his way into Jenny's cabin. He waited for Jenny to come to him, but there was nothing.

After a time, he broke open her backdoor and let himself in. The house had little punches of square sunlight streaming in from the windows and leaving a patchwork of stepping-stones on her brown carpet. He avoided them. She wasn't in the shower, still wet and waiting for him. He walked into another room and for a moment he didn't see her, his Jenny. Then he found her lying on a couch, smaller then he remembered. He went to his knees next to her, touching her cool face until she opened her eyes.

Jenny smiled weakly. "I love this dream. If only Brut wasn't watching."

Nero left her to check the premises, returning only when he knew they were safe. "We're alone," he told her. "He is not here. I am not your dream. When I came through I expected night, and instead there is day. But there is still you, and that is all that matters." He kissed her lips. "You look so tired. What has befallen you?"

Jenny sat up and ran her hands over his chest. "My love, you are back. I'd given up."

"Never give up. I'm always coming back to you — in my head if not with my feet." He uncovered her, sliding the worn, brown blanket to reveal her clothes.

"Before that I have news to share." She swung her legs around and drew him between her thighs, pressing them against him as if to make sure he were real.

He listened with his whole body, stroking her hand all the while.

"We made a child, my love. She's so beautiful and smart and healthy."

"A child? A daughter? From me — from this? I cannot be so lucky." He kissed her again, deeply. "Where is the babe?"

"She's no longer a babe. Kate's five years old. My aunt just left to pick her up from kindergarten. Somewhere I have a picture..." Jenny searched the room with her eyes before becoming distracted. "Ironically, today is Bring your Daddy to Tea day," she continued. "She was asking me about you."

"Kate. Kate. You chose well with a name. This is so much. Thank you. Thank you, Jenny, for making a child. My child. What did you tell her?" Nero moved to sit next to Jenny, and the couch groaned with displeasure at his immense size.

"I tell her that her father is a good man. A true man. And that you love her. Will you stay? Will you meet her?"

Nero saw caution in his love's eyes. The wariness of a mother. "Can I go to the tea? I will proudly claim my daughter at the kindergarten." Nero touched his chest with his fist.

She covered his fist with her hand. "I think that's more than kindergarten is ready to handle. She'll be home soon."

"I missed the tea. Will this make her sad?" Nero spotted what must be Kate's picture and rose so he could lift it from its spot on the wall. "This is her. I see you, and I see me. Look at her eyes. Was it terrible, Jenny? All this time alone?"

"She has been a gift, but seeing her growing and not knowing when you would return, if you would return, that was terrible." His vibrant Jenny didn't rise from the couch.

Nero's hand began to shake, the image of his daughter trembling with her father's damnation.

"Will you make it, Nero? I don't want her to be scared. She's just a little girl."

Nero closed his eyes briefly as a lightning bolt of jealousy soared through him. Jenny loved this girl more than she wanted him in her world. And in the next beat he respected her. This strength and possessiveness of her young was as it should be.

"I'm not positive. I will leave immediately if that's what you wish, Jenny." He loved calling her by name. He returned to her side, hugging her close and kissing her hair. "You smell like goodness." He touched her chin, turned her face to his, and kissed her. He slid his lips to her neck, whispering, "And you taste like perfection."

She felt frail in his arms, and he was about to ask her about her health when Kate skipped through the open door wearing a T-shirt with a puppy on it. She filled the whole room with her sweet voice.

"Mommy, that door is so broken! Where are you? I brought cookies from the tea." She stopped cold and stared at her mother and Nero. "Get away from my mommy."

Nero felt his whole being swell with sheer pride. He loved Kate at first sight. Her long black hair and dark eyes made her look like a doll. And her quick temper was probably a trait from her minion father. Her cheeks flushed, and she pointed at him as she repeated her warning.

Nero slid away from Jenny on the couch and sat on his shaking hand. The picture of Kate lay between her parents. Then Jenny's aunt came in the door with concern all over her face, which was quickly replaced by confusion at the sight before her.

"Sweetheart, I'm so glad you're here because this man is important to me," Jenny said, her voice soothing. "He's nice. It's okay." She waved her daughter over.

Kate kept her eyes on Nero as she came to sit gently on Jenny's lap, as if her mother was made of glass.

"Remember how I said your daddy was a good man and that you might not get to meet him, but he loves you? Well, today you *do* get to meet him. This man is your father."

Jenny cuddled her daughter as she spoke, her calm voice

belying the tension in her eyes. Nero could tell she would never have rushed an announcement like this had their circumstances been better or even the slightest bit normal.

Nero tried to make his voice less scary as he drank in the sight of her, creating the memory he would picture while he shoveled. "Kate, I'm happy to meet you. I'm sorry I didn't make the tea. I would have loved the tea."

Kate stood, an act of bravery Nero admired instantly. "Did you break our door? You're going to have to fix the door because my mommy's sick, and my aunt is old. You better get a hammer."

"I will fix your door, Kate." Nero turned to search Jenny's eyes for more information. Shaking her head, dismissing his concern, she motioned toward Kate.

"Can we have the tea now?" Nero asked. "Do you have tea?" He folded his hands, though he desperately wanted to hug the girl.

"I guess — if you're going to fix the door. I have a tea set! Mommy, can I use my tea set? I'll set it up right here, and we can all have tea!"

Excitement began edging out the wariness in Kate's eyes, and Nero's heart cried silently. That just having a drink at the same time as her father was a treasure...it was almost too much.

"Katie-Belle, go get your tea set and your favorite bear." After the girl's footsteps faded, Jenny turned to her aunt. "Bess, this is Nero. He won't be staying long."

Nero rose and bowed formally. Jenny hissed softly and touched her fingers to his whipped back. Aunt Bess nodded, not seeming particularly impressed, and raised her eyebrow as she spoke. "I do believe Katie will need a kettle of hot water. I'll see to it." She gave them a semblance of privacy, but no doubt remained within earshot.

"She is so brave and strong." Nero returned to Jenny and hugged her carefully. "Sick how? What has robbed your vitality?"

She was sparing him pain with her words, he could tell. "They're not sure yet. Don't worry. Kiss me again."

He complied, and she moaned against his lips. The clattering of the little girl's footsteps returning parted the lovers. Nero still held Jenny's hand, and she allowed it.

"Well, I brought Fuzz Bucket, and here's my tea set." Kate set down the small wicker basket with a thump, the porcelain inside threatening to crack with the force.

Nero knelt and watched as Kate opened the gold hook and set out tiny plates and cups. "One for you." She looked at Nero and smiled a bit, just a little — enough for him to know he was a special guest.

"Thank you, milady." Nero gestured with a flourish.

Kate giggled. Nero looked from her to Jenny and back again with unabashed delight.

"One for Fuzz Bucket. He's my bear. He sleeps with me at night." Kate straightened the bear and propped him against an ottoman so he could sit up straight.

Nero waited as she set the table. Aunt Bess brought napkins and a teapot. He tucked his shaking hands between his legs and nodded as Kate poured his tea.

"Oh, wait. Let me get the cookies from school. That'll make this party perfect!" She stood and rushed to her backpack, her own hands trembling like her father's, only from excitement. She kept picking the wrong pocket to unzip.

Jenny knelt slowly in front of her designated plate and whispered, "Leave if you must. I'll explain."

His arms were shaking now. "I'll make it through the tea and cookies. It's the very least I can do...for her."

Nero was sure the strain in his neck made his fight apparent, but Kate was too busy handing out iced sugar cookies shaped like a necktie. Nero nodded when she offered him sugar, and Kate happily added three heaping spoons.

Nero looked over to see Jenny's face blooming with love and pride, but as he watched, it was transformed by fear and horror.

"Oh, God. Nero, he's here."

Nero followed her eyes to find Brut smiling through the mesh that separated him from the sweet scene. Horrifically, he was covered in red paint. Or was it —

And the scene changed. The sweet memory Jenny and Kate should have had was altered, now to be engraved with terror as Brut simply walked through the door.

Nero stood, his tremors so violent that that he could hardly see straight. "Go." Nero charged toward Brut, knocking Kate out of the way. Their tiny tea party cracked and splintered as Nero slammed straight through the table.

JENNY

Jenny had no idea if Nero was telling Brut to leave or the women to run, but her body was hardwired to react to this particular fear. She'd practiced nearly every time her eyes closed.

"Bess, get Kate downstairs." She didn't feel her sickness now. Jenny felt only the adrenaline pumping through her system.

Bess grabbed Kate from her place crying on the floor and ran for the kitchen. Jenny followed them into the room and paused to grab her carving knife. She stepped back out and kicked the door shut, sealing in her daughter and aunt. "Lock the door, Bess. Lock the door, damn it!"

There was a satisfying click. Jenny turned her back to the door and stood guard. An epic battle was destroying her living room. She couldn't tell which minion was hers, but their noises reminded her of wild animals. Close, close animals. Finally Nero's body slammed into the wall and gravity pulled him to the floor. He was motionless. And Jenny knew she was about to face her nightmare with her eyes wide open.

Brut began singing a high-pitched, deranged song. "Where once there was one, now they are two. I'm going to eat you and your daughter too."

The minion cackled with laughter as he rounded the corner. His shaking made him look like stop-gap photography. He moved frantically in quick bursts, pausing to shake in place for a few hurried breaths.

"I like skin the best. It has a crunch." He was so close she could see his mania. It seeped from his pores.

First, fear pooled in her stomach, and her heart froze in disbelief. But then there was rage. Rage from a primal place. She *would* protect her daughter. Jenny growled and showed her teeth, making a claw with one hand and gripping her knife with the other. Reason would have made her sit right down and cry. Nero had been so strong, and this thing had bested him. But Jenny didn't invite reason to this fight.

Brut laid his hand on Jenny's arm, squeezing her muscles like Play-Doh. She slashed her knife first for his hand, then changed it up at the last second to fake him out and stab him right in the eye.

His screams were so loud Jenny thought her head might crack from the sheer noise. She raised her fists and was disappointed when only one came to her call. The arm Brut had injured remained limply at her side.

The minion pulled her knife from his skull and closed the distance between them. He put his hand around her neck and showed his teeth. Jenny wet her pants.

This was the sacrifice for loving a minion. The price was so very high. Jenny only hoped the shaking would force Brut back to Hell before he could get to her daughter and her sweet aunt. She hoped Brut would relish her death, get carried away, take too much time. She closed her eyes, not wanting to see this thing in front of her, his mangled eye marring his horrible face.

"Want. Want. Want." Brut hissed his favorite word all over her body, and the knife traveled a painful path, their blood mingling, hot and wet, on its blade.

And then his hand was gone from her neck, along with the knife, the hissing. Jenny had to try three times to get a decent breath. She opened her eyes to see Nero's whipped back and Brut crushed in a bear hug-like hold. And then the minions were gone, shaking strong and crazy, and there was just a cabin around Jenny. She was still alive.

After a moment Nero returned, pulling himself along the wall and clutching his side.

"Where is he?" Jenny's words were vocal tears, clogged with so many emotions.

"Hell. He's gone. I've just a moment." Nero fell to his knees in front of her.

Jenny wrapped her good arm around his head.

"Nero, he wanted her too. Just now. He wanted Kate too." Jenny loved this man, but all she wanted was him gone now, and her daughter in her arms.

Nero looked up at her, his dark features serious. "I promise you, he will not get her. Either of you."

And then he was gone. There had been movement — Jenny felt the air move around her, a hint of a kiss on her lips. But Nero was returned to the fires of Hell.

Jenny staggered away from the door and called to Kate and Bess, letting them know it was safe. She sank to the tile floor, so cold and afraid. The door unlocked and Bess came out cautiously before she let Kate come too. Her daughter couldn't stop crying. Her special day, her tea with her father, was ruined.

They waited for an ambulance to take Jenny to the hospital.

CHAPTER 4

NERO

Hell wasn't ever pleasant, but being bound next to a seriously disturbed minion made Nero's sentence seem that much longer. Brut's eye had healed from its horrific injury at an alarming rate, and he bore no marks from his battle with Jenny. But he certainly hadn't forgotten it. Between singing and promising horrors, any sound he made was to taunt Nero. Jenny and Kate were Nero's ultimate weaknesses now, and Brut had to know he was wearing him down.

Nero was desperate for her — the touch of Jenny's skin, the smell of her hair. And even more than that, he was concerned. Why was she sick? Had Brut injured her and made things even worse? And Kate. Just the thought of her name stirred such immense pride. He had made a child, and that was something to exist for. Another person to protect.

As much as he loved them both — and he realized now that the intense, deep longing he felt for them was love — he could not go back. Bringing Brut to the surface again was impossible. But his sweet Jenny was scared, and he needed to ease her mind.

Mid-shovel, an answer came to Nero. He needed to let more minions know of his escape route. Immediately he knew this was the wrong way to accomplish his goal. But like a seed, the idea grew and changed until it was a rational choice.

He'd need at least three accomplices: two to hold Brut down and one to help him back through the tunnels and traps to get to Earth. At his next brief respite, he ran, rather than sitting to catch his breath. He searched for minions who weren't serving violent sentences. It wasn't a fool-proof plan — after all, Brut was only shoveling, and he was sickening. Minions weren't a trustworthy bunch.

He passed the stretching carousel, and the screams drove him farther away from the shoveling. Alcove of evil after alcove of evil slipped past Nero until finally he came to a small cave where a group of minions waited.

He slowed and approached the closest female. "What is this sentence?"

At his words, all the minions turned their attention to him. They looked mildly annoyed.

"We wait here. That's the sentence." Her wild yellow eyes drank in his form.

"May I ask what you wait for?" Nero could see no apparatuses, no tortures evident.

She gave a shallow laugh. "Well, damn it, if I knew what I was waiting for, it would be a whole lot easier. No, I just wait. For what's next."

Nero thanked her and left, tearing off at a dead run to get back to his shoveling. Some of the waiters were likely his best choice of accomplices. He could offer them a result, a conclusion for their wait. On the soil they could pick anything, watch a bird fly, and see it land. They could wait for a car to pass and, more than likely, one would. They didn't seem particularly dangerous.

It took two more trips to the waiting cave before Nero had three minions willing to help, each for their own reasons. The first was the female who'd answered Nero's question. Her name was Sin. Her yellow eyes and matching sunshine hair could be spotted from three miles away, which Nero thought was good for when they were above. Others would know to watch out for her, like a vibrantly colored poisonous frog.

The second female went by Velvet, and she had deep skin and a bald head. She was easily taller than Nero. The last one Nero wasn't sure about, but he needed three. Ransom had shifty blue eyes and close-cropped brown hair. He was lanky, but he looked plenty strong. He'd assured Nero he could hold Brut easily.

It was stupid, showing three more minions the way out. Nero knew trust wasn't a gift any of them had given him. They each wanted to see something else. Sin wanted to see a sunset, Velvet wanted to see fireflies, and Ransom had answered simply, "Boobs."

Nero told them Jenny's house was off limits, and that he'd rather rat any of them out than have them wreak havoc on the soil. When finally they had an opportunity, when the time slowed and became flexible enough, he whistled. At the sound, Brut cocked his head and placed his demented eyes on Nero. Fortunately, the waiters were much faster than Nero expected. He guessed their nerves were so frayed from their punishment that actual action excited them.

Brut didn't even sense Ransom, and the tall man quickly folded the unsuspecting minion into a restrained pretzel. Velvet sat on Brut's legs as Ransom held his arms. Brut began screaming, cursing, and begging for justice, but in Hell none of those cries was unusual enough to raise an alarm.

Sin hopped from one foot to another, seemingly ready for anything. Nero nodded at the pile of minions once and ignored the many things he could see going wrong in his head: Brut getting loose, the minions being reclaimed by their compulsions and having to return to the waiting cave. He powered through his doubts and lead Sin through the hole.

It had been easier to transverse the traps, gates, and beasts with Brut. The crazy minion had just enough sense to outwit them. He was clever, but Sin did a good job for a first-timer. However, by the time Nero got to the rock, his hands were already shaking. Sin helped him move the boulder out of the way. It was almost twilight, and that boded well for his companion.

"Head that way, and you will see the sunset," Nero told her. "Your patience will be rewarded this time. When you can stand the shaking no longer, meet me at this spot. Hurt no one."

Sin waved Nero away with a frustrated hand and ran toward the descending sun. Nero watched her for a moment, then slid the boulder back in place. If Brut got loose, Nero hoped he would be unable to move the boulder alone.

This plan was ridiculous and unstable, but right this minute he could see Jenny's house, and he had to remind himself to use the door, not walk through a wall in his rush to see his girls. The door was repaired, but unlocked. He chastised himself for failing to keep his promise to Kate. He hadn't gotten a hammer to repair the damage he had done last time.

"Jenny? Kate? I'm here!" Nero closed the door behind him. He loved the idea of his ladies safe, even if the door was just a mirage as far as an angry minion was concerned.

"Here. I'm here." Her voice sounded strong and confident.

He followed her voice upstairs and found her smoking and drinking wine — his formerly blushing lover. She licked her lips when she saw him, and her sweet sundress looked out of place.

"Jenny?" Her demeanor was off. Something was wrong. "How's your arm? Where's Kate? How long has it been?"

She rolled her eyes and took a long sip. Finally she sighed. "It's been two weeks, Nero. Amazing. All those years raising Kate without you, and now I get two visits in one month. It's like I won the genital lotto. Are we going to have some hard, sweaty sex?" She shot him an aggressive look. "I hope so."

Her eyes were different. And she held her body as if there was no love left in her. Nero shook his head slowly. Of all his concerns, Jenny being healthy and angry hadn't been among them. She wasn't right.

"Where's Kate? Your aunt?" He moved closer to her.

"My aunt? She said Kate didn't need to see me like this. You know Katie — oh wait, you don't — well, she fought. She didn't want to leave. I'm proud of that little bitch." Jenny took a pull from the cigarette.

It was Brut. Somehow he'd contaminated Jenny. After all the eons next to that minion in Hell, Nero recognized the crazy in Jenny's eyes. He took the cigarette out of her hand and crushed it in his.

"That's sexy, you big fucker from Hell. Let's screw." Jenny poured her wine on the carpet of her bedroom, then tossed the glass, and it shattered.

Nero took her face, so dear to him, his very destination, and held it. She couldn't meet his eyes. Instead she squirmed and ran her hands over his chest.

"Stop looking at me. Take out your dick." Jenny reached up and untied her sundress, and it slithered to the floor.

Nero looked down at her body and fell to his knees. He traced the inflamed track Brut's knife had left. Her system was fighting demon blood. He looked up at her face and she tilted her head back, avoiding him yet again. She swiveled her hips, running her hands down his head and scratching his shoulders.

He could still see hints of her, the real her, but he had no idea how to fix her. At this moment he realized she was trapped with a bit of her worst fear inside her, so the only thing he could think to do was to love her, fill her, make her his.

Nero stood and grabbed a fistful of her hair, just enough to get her attention and turn her eyes his way. "Look at me."

She could only get as far as his mouth. He kissed her lips and pulled back. "Look at me."

She raised her eyes to his cheeks and stopped. Nero unbuttoned his pants, and they joined her sundress on the floor. Her let go of her hair and walked into her, knocking her backward, making her stagger. When she fell backward, he reacted, grabbing her hips and forcing her to sit on the bed.

She scooted to the center of the bed. Nero longed to see her smile. He loved her glow of health, but hated Brut's marks marring her beautiful skin. He followed her onto the bed and waited for her to respond with love, but she was grabby and greedy. He imprisoned her hands above her head and positioned himself between her legs. With one quick push he was in her.

Her silkiness surrounded him, and he had to stop before he lost control. His hand holding her wrists shook as he asked her, one last time. "Look at me."

And then she met his eyes. And she was there, home, here for him once again. Her eyes filled with tears, and the mania bled from them as she released her emotion.

"Nero."

It was Jenny, his Jenny. He covered her mouth with kisses, and neither of them closed their eyes. Nero didn't want to lose sight of her even for a minute. He let go of her hands, and she held his face, keeping him close. He let himself love her then. With every thrust, he let her know he'd fought to be here, he'd done those wrong things — let minions out of Hell and risked everything — so they could be like this, just Jenny and Nero.

She pushed him flat on his back and changed their position so she could straddle him. He watched her achieve her own bliss, amazed as her long scars of minion-induced pain healed. Like a reverse blood poisoning, he was somehow absorbing the venom that had been changing her.

She saw it too and ran her hands along her now-clean body. "How?" she said, still moving on top of him.

"Love," he answered simply. "I love you so much."

JENNY

Jenny felt like herself for the first time in two weeks. Lying in Nero's arms, in her own bed, without Brut's creepy stare, she was home. Actually, she felt the best she had in years. She couldn't burden Nero with her diagnosis now. As much as she wanted him to hold her and share her pain, she knew their time was limited. Jenny tried to force the conversations with her doctor out of her mind and away from this contented moment, but as always, they lay in wait for her. The doctor had been mystified by Jenny's decline after Kate's birth. He claimed it was as if she'd ingested toxins. Every blood test came back clean, but her pupils remained dilated, her balance off. Jenny wasn't sure if it was the demon DNA her body had nurtured or the fact that Nero had claimed her heart, but there was a price to pay for bearing his child. But none of it mattered. Any punishment was worth the gift of Kate. She looked at her lover and smiled sadly.

"I'm so sorry about the things I said to you, my sweet. How did you get here so soon?" She touched his cheek, letting her fingertips reassure her of his realness.

"It wasn't you," Nero assured her. "Somehow his blood infected you. And Kate is okay?" He grabbed Jenny's hand and kissed it.

"She is. I owe her an apology too. I kept saying the most inappropriate things. I felt stronger, but out of control." Jenny snuggled deeper into Nero's chest, smelling the scent of him, trying to bathe her hair in it, so she'd be able to prove he'd been here after he left.

"I consorted with other minions to be here. I promised them things. My first instinct was to kill Brut." He searched her eyes as he pronounced his murderous instincts.

She propped herself up a bit and looked at the whole length of him. "I would've killed him to keep him from Kate if I could've. I'll not judge you."

"Jenny, I'm not a good man. I wasn't a good man. I'm in Hell for a reason. But if I killed him, I'd have to do his sentence as well. I would have to shovel with two hands." He held them up.

"You're good to me. And you're Kate's father, so that makes you an angel. If she's safe, I'll bring her back. If I stay like this, back in my own head, I'll try to have her here so you might see her next time." She straddled him again. "I'd love you to stay, though. I dream of us here — in this bed, in this house, making breakfast, taking showers." She leaned down to cover him, hugging his chest. "Can you never stay?"

He stroked her hair gently. "Jenny, I have a sentence."

She sighed, expressing her disappointment eloquently without words.

CHAPTER 5

NERO

Nero replayed fixing Jenny with love in his head so many times. It made him stand a bit straighter on his breaks from shoveling. Brut, however, was furious that he'd missed his trip to the soil and had treated Nero to long, horrific descriptions of the plans he had for his love and his daughter. He repeated them over and over.

To take his mind off of killing Brut, Nero concentrated on making something for Kate. Every other stroke with the shovel, he grazed a lump of rock, carving it. He was trying to create a little puppy for Kate, like the one on her shirt. It took a million swipes to do it. Nero counted — out loud at times.

He took the puppy with him on his frantic runs to the waiting cave. Sin was still buzzed by her sunset, and she wanted to go again, rather than having Velvet or Ransom get their turn. More personalities made the situation even a bigger task.

When it was finally settled, Nero had to promise Sin he would try to smuggle a jack-in-the-box into Hell for her. And Brut was ready this time, tense and flinching at every sound. But Ransom handled the spastic, angry minion with ridiculous ease, pinning him face down in the dirt in moments. Sin took the position on the back of his legs as he seethed.

Velvet was athletic and poised, and she showed Nero faster, more efficient ways to get around the obstacles. When they lifted the rock together, breaking the seal between Hell and Earth, it was afternoon, judging by the sun. It took them both a little while to adjust their eyes. Then Nero wished Velvet well as she headed off to find a field to wait for the fireflies.

The trees seemed taller. Time had gotten away from Nero. But the hose was still where it was supposed to be, and he cranked on the flowing water, drinking and drinking until his tongue finally felt moist. Then he washed off the puppy rock sculpture. It had no color, just midnight black rock, but each hair was defined, the nose small and cute. He hoped Kate would like it.

But first, he needed to find Jenny. He had to break the door, again. There was no one home, but something was wrong. Out of place. Nero had no idea how to find Jenny if she wasn't home.

He heard the sound of a loud machine in the driveway and simply waited in the kitchen, holding his gift. After a moment a gorgeous young woman came around the door, pointing a gun at him.

"Get out. Get out of my house."

It took a breath, a moment before he saw it. Kate was no longer five years old. The long, black hair and clear, watchful eyes were the same, but time had lengthened his daughter, added bits of adulthood to her frame.

"Kate. I'm here." Nero looked behind her for some sign of Jenny.

She slid the safety on the gun and pointed it at the ground. "Father?"

He nodded and glanced at his puppy, so out of place for a young woman. Maybe a flower would have been a better choice.

"Your mother? Is she here?" He turned and set the puppy on the counter carefully. When he looked at her again, the pain in Kate's eyes made Nero's soul shake.

"Interesting question. Are you pretending to care? It's been twelve years, *Daddy*." Hate dripped from her voice. "What did you bring up with you this time? Vampires? Demons? Just bust open a door from Hell and let all that shit out so you can get laid." She stepped toward him, full of fire and anger.

Fear gripped him, because then he knew. The answer was easy to see in her eyes, her demeanor. *Jenny, Jenny. Please not Jenny.* "Twelve years? Where is Jenny?" Nero bit his lip.

For a moment he saw a tiny hint of compassion, but as she spoke, a door slid shut in her eyes. "My mother's dead."

Nero looked at the ground, swallowing his cry of anguish. Hope flowed out of him, love left him. Jenny could *not* be gone. She flashed before his eyes. For a moment, he saw her everywhere. And then the thought that she was nowhere turned his bitter soul to ash. He was left a husk of a being.

KATE

Kate watched the man in front of her lose his love, and as angry as she was at him, she could not stop her sympathy. He was so dirty, his nails caked with black. He looked as if he was created from darkness — that was surely how Kate thought of him. Her mother had lived in a dream world where lovely monsters came from the ground and said and did beautiful things. But Kate had watched as a second pregnancy had robbed her already weakened mother of something tangible.

When Jenny miscarried the baby, her health declined further. She'd been confined to her room, always with the window facing the shed open a crack as an invitation to the thing she claimed to love. It took nine years for her to die — long enough for Kate to learn to hate Nero. Long enough to hear the stories of their fairy tale love. Long enough to be warned to carry a gun, because the things that came out of the shed with her father might want to kill her.

Aunt Bess had wanted to move since the minion battle in the living room, but she'd stayed, despite her unease, saying she needed to help raise Kate. Eventually Jenny wasn't rational, and Bess had refused to leave her great niece to fend for herself.

Jenny's insistence on staying turned into resolve for Kate as well when her mother died. She'd been waiting for this day. Waiting to tell the man her mother had wasted her life on that she was gone. But the long lecture full of vehemence and violence that she'd planned died on her tongue when the huge minion buried his face in his dirty hands and quietly lost control.

His silent anguish was heartbreaking. He clenched his fists and bent at the middle, appearing to be in physical pain. Tears came to Kate's eyes, and she blinked them back. In her daydreams she'd yelled at him, listed off all the things she missed out on because her mother had died. She never imagined her heart softening, the edges growing touchable as her father took to his knees. She took a shaky breath. Her mother had told her all the time that her father was a good man. She couldn't explain why he was in Hell, but she would say, "Nero loves you, Kate. He does. You'll see. Someday you'll see."

And now she did. She watched as her father composed himself and settled his black eyes on her. "Kate, are you okay? Who's here with you?"

"Aunt Bess. She took the bus to the store." Kate rested the gun on the kitchen table. As her hate seeped out, it left only sadness and empty longing.

Nero stood, his hand beginning to shake. "Tell me what's hard here. What worries you?"

She shook her head. "What worries me? Mom didn't have any money. Aunt Bess is getting older, and she's stopped taking her blood pressure medicine because it's too expensive. You're not here, and Mom's gone." Kate paused while the knife that always followed the word *gone* slid into her heart. "And if I lose Aunt Bess? I've got nobody." She didn't mention that Aunt Bess also seemed to be losing time, forgetting small things and sometimes really big things like turning off the oven or which pedal on the car was the gas and which was the brake.

Nero listened solemnly. "What passes for currency now, in this time?"

Kate was confused for a moment, then answered, "Money? Dollars?"

Nero nodded once and left her standing next to a loaded gun. Her mouth dropped open, and she held up her hands in disbelief. She looked out the door to the open shed and shook her head. He was gone as quickly as he'd shown up.

Kate closed the door as best she could and returned to the kitchen. She opened the dishwasher and began slamming the dishes away. She cursed under her breath. Tears were trying to find a way out. As much as she hated her father, seeing him was her mother's dream come true. Kate could *feel* her smiling.

The noise of the door opening again startled her into grabbing her gun. Nero had reappeared in the living room with a large, red duffle bag. He pulled the zipper open and put it on the floor. "Are these dollars?"

Both of his hands were shaking now. Kate peeked into the deep bag. Her mouth went dry. She nodded.

"Is it enough for medicine? For a new door?" He was so earnest. His eyes were red and wet.

She found her voice. "Where did you get that? You can't just take money."

He bent and zipped the bag. "It won't be missed."

Chills ran down her back. Who was this man?

"Kate, I'll have to return in a moment. I wish..." He held out his hand to her and then dropped it.

There was silence. So much to be said, but there was no time. He was like a time bomb, exploding with emotion, changing the lives of the women in the little cabin with his detonation. She got it, though. She wished as well. She wished her mom were still here, thrilled to see her love. "Me too."

"I don't know what to do. I was expecting a little girl. I

wanted to be strong and have the tea. Do you remember the tea?" His eyes searched hers.

She nodded. She remembered the tea. She'd drawn pictures of the tea at school, at the counselor's, at night under her covers. Always Nero would hug her, and she had on her puppy shirt. But then, in the corner, she would draw the mean minion. The one who hurt her mother.

"I made it so Brut won't return. Should I tell you I'll be back, or is it better if you never have to think of me again? I'll do anything for you, Kate. Anything." Nero held his hand out again.

All he seemed to really want now was a hug. After all her opinions, declarations, and practicing, her father's hand was throwing her off. She was as weak as her own mother, wanting to love this broken, escaped demon.

"I miss Mom," she finally said. She'd been strong for a long time. Hate was the glue that held her together. Aunt Bess had become more of a burden than an adult, leaving Kate to make decisions, pay bills. She sighed and wiped her tears with the hand not holding the gun.

He nodded, his hand still extended. "I've just started to miss her, and it's the hardest thing I've ever done. I'm sorry you've been without her because of me. I never deserved either of you."

He believed it. She could tell. He wasn't some evil thing just looking for sex.

"Mom said everything happens for a reason. So there must be a reason you deserved it." She set her gun down again, this time on the duffle bag of money.

"The reason's not apparent to me. And now Jenny is…gone." He pursed his lips and was silent a moment. Then he seemed to will himself to speak. "Your existence is the only thing about coming to Jenny that I will *never* regret."

His arms were shaking, his extended hand barely visible now. "Tell me, Kate. What do you need from me?"

I need a real father. I need you to understand how this world works. I need someone every day here with me to miss Mom as much as I do. "You could come back. I guess. Yeah." She shrugged and contemplated his hand.

He nodded. "I love you, Kate."

He was gone. The room was empty. And then Kate began a wait she was already too familiar with. One she had mocked, dreaded, and raged about: waiting for Nero.

CHAPTER 6

NERO

Nero barely made it back to Hell in time. Brut had been twisting and twirling so effectively he'd almost escaped. He handed Sin her jack-in-the-box, which he'd swiped from a house on his way to get money for Kate.

The waiters tumbled back to Hell behind him, their entire beings shaking as well. As they disappeared back to their cave, Nero began shoveling to get some relief. Brut began to shovel as well, hissing and shouting about his evil plans for Kate and Jenny.

Jenny. Her name brought him such longing, and now there would be no more resolution. He was positive she was in Heaven. She was the exact opposite of Hell: light, laughter, compassion, beauty.

He wanted to cry, scream the anguish he'd denied himself in front of Kate so he wouldn't scare her. But then Brut would have yet another tool for his torture. It was better that the minion knew nothing of this — specifically that Kate was now all alone up there.

Nero's drive to return to her came from a different place, but was no less compelling than his longing for Jenny had been. He went to the waiting minions to arrange another visit to the soil as soon as he was able, and Nero couldn't believe the chaos he found. The waiting minions had been whipped into a frenzy by the jack-in-the-box. The toy provided a shocking, gratifying, nearly immediate resolution to their normally endless waiting. Each clamored for another turn, some while banging their heads against the wall, others while fighting with one another.

Giving them such a release was a huge mistake, Nero realized. He slipped away unnoticed. Soon after his discovery, the sounds of the waiters' punishment rang through Hell. Nero could hear their screams clearly despite their cave's distance from his and Brut's shoveling. Once their cries finally settled down and Nero could get another respite, he returned to the cave. What he saw there made him turn and gag. Their punishment would never be forgotten. They were still alive, but not a single one of them wanted to be.

It took much, much longer than Nero had hoped to get Sin, Ransom, and Velvet to talk again. They risked so very much to get him to his daughter. In the end, it wasn't any sort of compassion that brought them around, but Ransom's threat to turn them in if he didn't get his turn on the soil.

They made a plan, but Nero felt great trepidation about it. He had serious doubts that Sin and Velvet could hold Brut by themselves. Ransom promised he would hog-tie the minion to make it easier for the females, but still it was risky.

By the time Nero began the return trip to his daughter, he knew it had been a while. But he hoped he hadn't lost too much time. If he got to the surface and found that Kate no longer lived, Nero decided he would not come back to Hell. Instead he would see just what happened when a demon denies his compulsions.

KATE

Each day, Kate allowed herself a moment to wonder when her father would return. She could probably be considered a recluse by now. Aunt Bess was still alive, but her mind didn't retain things anymore, and the duffle bag of money had provided long-term care for her nearby. Kate figured her outings to the facility prevented her from being fully withdrawn from society, but they were hardly fun-filled adventures. Still, she was able to blog online and had a virtual store where she sold her knitting. Ironically, Bess had yet to lose her desire to knit socks, so Kate kept her supplied with pretty yarn. The two would knit together now, because talking got them nowhere.

The cabin seemed to lose her mother much more slowly than the rest of the world. Kate swore she could smell her mother's perfume every once in a while in certain rooms. And just when she felt she'd discovered everything, another memory-laden item from her mother's past would surface. She wished the things she found would soothe the ache in her chest, but they almost always made it worse. And sometimes she hugged her Hell-made puppy. She petted it like a real dog and told it secrets, which probably qualified her as crazy.

It had been three years since Nero's last visit when Kate watched as a light came on in the shed.

"Oh, crap." She ran to get her rifle and returned to watch some more. She prayed her father would not drag a busload of evil with him.

Two males exited. She listened through her kitchen window, and it seemed the taller one kept shouting, "Boobs, Boobs, Boobs!" over and over. The other one just shook his head. Nero was back.

In the harsh glow of the security light, Kate watched as her father took great guzzling gulps of water. She met him at the door, opening it before he could break it down.

"Kate." He stepped in and smiled as he shut the door behind

him. There was pain in his eyes.

Kate knew it well. The building didn't have Jenny anymore, and that took the home right out of the house.

"Father." She set her rifle against the door. It had been years, but his large presence in the room made it seem like they'd just parted.

He held out a pitch-black daisy, etched gorgeously. There were even what appeared to be tiny drops of water on the petals.

She nodded and took the flower. "Thanks."

"How have you been? How long has it been? Can we drink tea?" He shuffled farther into the room, glancing out the window toward the shed before turning his attention back to her.

She wanted to hug him. She wanted to hear that he loved her again. She wanted him to clean up and take her for ice cream, to intimidate a suitor who came knocking on the door. She knew she'd have to settle for turning on the teakettle.

"It's been three years. I'm fine, and let's go to the kitchen." She took the silver teapot from its resting place on the stove and filled it with fresh water. She glanced at Nero, who stood watching the free-flowing water while licking his lips.

Kate set the water on the fire and grabbed a tall glass. She added ice cubes and filtered water from the refrigerator, then popped in a slice of lemon she kept in the door. She offered it to her father.

His mouth dropped open a bit when she held it out to him. " For me?" He pointed to his chest.

She nodded, feeling shy.

"Thank you so very much." He almost bowed as he took the glass carefully. He seemed to fight with himself not to guzzle, not to be greedy, but soon enough the glass was empty. The ice cubes had melted at an alarming rate from the heat of his hands.

Kate took the glass and repeated the process. "Would you like to sit?"

Another grateful look crossed his face. "Not unless the lady in the room sits first."

He held her chair and she sat, setting the glass across from her for Nero. The spindly old kitchen chair creaked and complained as Nero sat and blew an exhausted breath before sipping his water.

Questions crowded Kate's tongue. She wanted to know so much. "Tell me why you're in Hell. What's it like there? Why was Mom worried that things might try and kill me?"

He nodded. "Such quick, important questions, Kate. You're so smart. This is how you wish to spend our time?"

She nodded and threaded her fingers together, needing information almost more than the hug she was hoping for.

"I'll answer your last question first, because that's the most important one. When I leave Hell, I must rely on other minions to help me get out. There is sort of a seal between Earth and Hell, and I cannot break it alone. The timing must be right — the precise sliver of moment must be seized. There are many obstacles put in our way, set there to protect humans from the likes of minions. I defeat them to be here with you."

Thank you should have been what tumbled from her mouth. Instead she asked, "Should you?"

His answer was quick. "No. Never. Not at all. I taint Earth with the presence of minions. So far our compulsions call us back, but if they didn't? There'd be horror here, far worse than mankind has ever known. And if more minions found a way out? Chaos and death. And your shed would be the doorway to it all. I should never come here."

"Wow. And I thought I had some pretty spectacular nightmares already. This information's going to kick them up a notch." She cleared her throat and stood as the steam from the kettle pierced the air.

Nero stood when she did. "Can I help? Where is your little basket with the small cups? Will Fuzz Bucket be joining us?"

Kate didn't tell her father the tea set had been smashed beyond repair in the brawl so many years ago. "We're going to use bigger cups this time. Fuzz Bucket's in my room on my shelf. Can you go get him?"

She was way too old for this. What was it about this man that inspired such adoration — first from her mother, now from her? She filled the cups as she listened to the floor protest Nero's heavy steps. When he returned, he had Fuzz Bucket and also her mother's white nightgown.

He set the bear down in a chair and had to readjust the stuffed animal's body a few times before it sat up straight. Kate set the cups down and then returned to pull one out for Fuzz Bucket, mentally chiding herself for the childish routine. Yet it seemed okay, for now. Her father gently placed her mother's nightgown on the remaining empty chair.

"It's too much to ask..." He trailed off before his question could be asked, and he waited behind Kate's chair while she sat. He tucked it in so she'd be comfortable and took his place at the table. "So, do we just pour tea on the bear?"

She smiled and shook her head. "No, I used to have him pretend to drink."

"Pretend?" He was perplexed.

Kate had no idea how old this man was, what time he came from, but the concept of pretending was clearly foreign to him. "It's a way of going through the motions in your head, but not really doing it."

He took a sip of the liquid. It was still way too hot, but he seemed not to notice. "So I'm a pretend father? I do the right things in my head while I'm shoveling, but I'm not actually doing it."

Kate blew on her cup and thought for a moment. "No, you do what you can. You're just not an *often* father." She reached over and made Fuzz Bucket take a noisy sip.

Nero's whole face lit up, and his smile made his black eyes sparkle. "That bear has no manners."

She found herself smiling back at him before she prompted, "What was too much to ask?" She glanced at her mother's nightgown.

Nero looked down. "I was wondering if I could have a small

piece of her gown. But it's too selfish to ask. I already took her from you. You should have all her relics."

Kate stood and opened a drawer, and Nero rose quickly to his feet. She got a pair of scissors and opened a cabinet to get some cookies. She placed the cookies in their package on the table and sat so her father would sit. He sighed again at the rest.

"So, you shovel? That's your sentence? Will it ever end?" She took her mother's favorite nightgown — it was the one Jenny had put on when she was missing Nero the most — and carefully began trimming the bottom.

"Kate, I'll shovel until the end of time."

She held up her hand. "No, stay sitting," she said as she rose and motioned for his arm. She tied the strip of white around his bicep.

He stood when she'd finished, ignoring her request. "I thank you. It means so much to me. My daughter, because my time constraints make me very bold, may I have a hug?" He opened his arms.

She waited a beat, remembering all the times she'd thought of this moment. In daydreams she would deny him, tell him to go without like she'd had to do without parents for so long.

But the five-year-old in her needed that hug. She stepped into his arms and was rewarded with his sigh of happiness. "My pride, my daughter. I love you."

He engulfed her with his large arms, patting her gently, careful not to pull her too close to his heat-emanating frame. She wanted to be tougher, but here, with this demon from Hell, was the peace she longed for. She hugged him back hard, too hard, and ignored the searing heat. Her wracking tears were years overdue. Sobbing, being strong for no one, felt like a release.

"Sweet girl, it's okay. It's okay. I'm here. I'm here."

He stroked her hair gently as she took shuddering sniffles. They must have stayed that way for a long time, because when Kate finally had the courage to end the hug, her father's hands were shaking.

He looked at them sheepishly. "I'm so sorry. I wish I could make them stop."

She took one of his big hands and held it tightly, concentrating intently. It stilled, but the other kept right on moving.

He used it to touch her face. "I'll be leaving soon, but I have help. I'll be back — but only if that makes sense to you."

She leaned into his hand. He was all she had anymore. "We're separate, but we're family."

He smiled. "Family is such a beautiful word. I'm so glad to be part of one. Part of yours."

She hugged him again, because he was here and soon he wouldn't be. Then an unearthly howl shredded the moment to ribbons.

Her father tensed. "Get your gun. That's Brut." He grabbed her shoulders and looked her in her eyes. "I might have to kill him now, which means I won't be back. Know that I love you. And I will be doing that forever."

He pushed her in the direction of her shotgun and strode toward the yard, looking exactly like a warrior from Hell. The white piece of cloth on his arm fluttered as he opened and closed her door.

It was such a change, such a shock. Kate steeled herself and pointed the gun at the door. If she saw the things from her nightmares, she would just shoot and keep shooting.

Cracks and screams filled the night. Explosions illuminated the windows. Kate wondered if she should go outside, though she could scarcely imagine stepping out and helping Nero. Would she just distract him? She was filled with doubt.

She never heard him, never even sensed him until he whispered something from behind her, against her neck. Her shotgun was wrenched from her hands before her brain could tell her to pull the trigger, and she found herself pinned painfully against a huge minion. She pictured Brut based on the glimpses she'd gotten of him before Aunt Bess had locked her in the basement all those years ago. But something was off. The minion holding her was not Brut. This one was taller than her father. And, despite the rage and anger outside like a natural disaster, this thing behind her was calm. Not even a hint of the shakes.

"As I was saying before you rudely interrupted me, I really love boobs." He waggled his eyebrows.

Kate could feel her own eyebrows climbing skyward.

"You have a set." He looked down over her shoulder at her chest.

She craned her neck to look him in the face. "Who the Hell are you? And if you say my worst nightmare, I'll pee on you."

He laughed, the rumble shaking her body as well. "I'm Ransom. Handsome Ransom. And you're one lucky little lady. I'm going to rate your boobs on a scale of one to ten — ten being the most firm and pointy."

Screeching from her backyard drew her attention. "Dad."

Ransom let her go, and she scrambled for her rifle. He ignored her and looked out the kitchen window.

"Nero's losing." Ransom bit his lip and seemed to contemplate his choices.

Kate aimed her rifle between his eyes. "Go help him."

He lifted his hands in half-hearted surrender. "Why do the girls protect the boobs so vigorously? Fine. I'll put Brut down."

The tall, lanky minion walked out the door, and this time Kate followed. Brut looked up from Nero's crumpled body and smiled at her. She fired. The shotgun blast hit Brut dead center, and Ransom stopped short, as if waiting to see if she was done. She wasn't. There were two shots in this double-barreled shotgun, and she planned to use them both.

Brut staggered a bit as he began to come for her. The second blast forced him back a few steps and set Kate's ears ringing, but to her absolute horror, Brut kept moving. He'd slowed a bit, but still coming. She tried her hardest to feel brave, but Brut was smiling and chanting, "Want. Want. Wantwantwantwant-wantwant!"

Ransom shook his head and advanced on the sick, freaky

minion. The restraining move he used on Brut seemed so simple, but it had to be complicated, because Brut ended up face down and almost completely immobilized.

Kate kept her shotgun and rushed to Nero's side. He was moving and seemed to be speaking, though Kate couldn't hear the words. They were swallowed by the fuzz in her ears. She was so grateful to see him moving. She bent, and Nero nodded. She could almost read his lips, catching a few words here and there. "Kate" and "okay" kept surfacing, so she spoke to assure him. "I'm fine, Father. I'm fine."

He nodded and seemed relieved. He rolled over and stood slowly. Turning his face silenced his words for Kate. She wanted to hear more, but all the minions were shaking now, their compulsions causing halting, jerky movements. She began to make out their conversation, her ears healing from the shock in little bits.

"If you're going to get rid of him, do it here," Ransom argued. "Maybe you won't have his sentence then. I'm not going to kill him. I could never be a shoveler. And I didn't even get to see boobs."

His eyes drifted back to her chest, and Nero slapped the taller minion across the face. "That's my daughter. Never look at her."

She almost laughed. The tea party, the hug, and now her dad was protecting her from a leering suitor. It was like all her dreams were coming true in a single nightmare.

"Do you want me to let Brut go? Don't disrespect me again." Ransom went from playful to serious in a heartbeat.

It was time. Even Kate could tell. Nero turned to face her.

"I'll never risk you again. Remember, the absence of me is my love for you." He hugged her quickly, his whole body shaking, and hers as well. "Never let anyone near the shed. Never show anyone this gateway."

Then together Ransom and Nero dragged Brut into the shed. There was a huge flash of light, and the backyard was empty.

It was just Kate. Again.

PART 2

Hell
2012

CHAPTER 7

EMMA

"Our Father, which art in Heaven, hallowed be thy name. Thy Kingdom come, thy will be done..." Emma's voice was just a whisper, and the sound of it echoing off the cement walls made her feel more alone. She tried to remember who she was, what she was. "What I still am," she said aloud. She held her arms and legs tightly to her body. The floor was alarmingly cold. It was cold for any floor, but this was particularly harsh since Emma was in Hell.

"I'm an angel in Hell. I have a purpose. I have people I love. I have a purpose." She took a breath to steady herself. Then she tried again. "Our Father, which art in Heaven, hallowed be thy name..."

If she hadn't been so dehydrated, she might have teared up. The prayer had been one of the first things she'd learned as a young girl. Soon after she knew her name, Emma knew how to say the Lord's Prayer. The lack of those words in her mind was a defeat.

Emma was in the middle of her worst nightmare: the Hell hallway designed specially for her by Jack, the previous Devil. As innocuous as the simple hallway looked, it was filled with terrorizing internal plagues, separated by slender respites from each of the exhausting, painful tortures. Right now she was between anger and confusion. Maybe it was her proximity to the air laced with dementia that stole the soothing words from her mind.

Her mind. Such a simple thing to take for granted. She never knew it could be attacked from within. She'd wanted to be a strong, fearless crusader for right, but since the Heavenly trial had come to an end, she'd been shackled with more than she'd imagined possible. She'd taken the punishment of Jack, the former Devil, and a good-intentioned angel, onto herself. So Jason, her handsome half-breed friend and sometime lover, had ripped her wings off, rendering her human. Sure, she'd asked for their sentences from the archangel judge, but her thoughts kept returning to all the other souls going about their regular existences again now. After being carried to Hell by Everett from the place she felt the safest, Emma's heart had yet to find its bearings. Her flouncy, ruffled panties had stayed in place when Everett had tried to force himself on her, which had infuriated him and confused Emma. Still, when he'd tossed her into the hallway, she'd panicked. She hadn't seen him since, and this was good...but probably bad in the long run.

Emma unfolded herself as carefully as she could, desperately wanting to avoid a bout with the traps so close on either side of her. She stretched her back, wishing she still had her angel wings. She imagined she could shield herself and her mind by tucking them tightly around her like a feather-covered shroud. But the only remnants of her heavenly decorations were two silver lightning bolt tattoos — or at least that's what she guessed. There was no mirror. And anyway Emma was glad not to see her reflection. She judged herself harshly enough as it was. No need to see her gray eyes staring their agony and loss back at her. Plus, if a reflective surface were available, she was sure Everett would make her watch next time. *Next time.*

Just the thought of Everett — on top of everything else — made Emma's heart pound. She needed more gumption to try to escape. She looked at the gaping exit, which seemed so close at the end of the hallway, though she knew there was nothing but pain between there and here. And, really, why? When an angel is sentenced to one thousand years in Hell, she has a certain desire to see her sentence to the end, follow the rules — even if the rules hurt every second.

Emma buried her hands in the short, flouncy skirt of her French maid's costume, trying to keep her elbows tucked close. The power in the air on either side of her was nearly tangible. What had stopped Everett that day? Did she have someone or something on her side here in Hell? She tried again. "Our Father, which art in..." The words scrambled from her grasp. "Damn it."

"Who arts in something? I always thought that was the most bullshitty of prayers they fed us." Everett's form followed his voice through the doorway, dripping with cocky arrogance. "Are you trying to remember the words? Still a believer after all you've been through, Emma?"

She hated that she shook when she saw him. She was scared of him, which was not only embarrassing, but she felt shamed by it.

Everett bit his bottom lip, trying for a moment to hold back a huge grin at her obvious fear. He was unsuccessful. "Not talking? That's okay. I don't need you to talk. As long as you can grab your ankles, we'll be fine." He began to unbutton his silk pajama shirt.

Emma wanted to look away, to deny him at least her attention if she could deny him nothing else, but she watched him the way she would a poisonous spider. His chest was sculpted with muscle, and he stepped forward with every button he unfastened.

Emma squirmed and closed one eye. This man was the Devil. He had everything, anything at his disposal in this damned place. Her flimsy panties would not shield her much longer.

Everett untied his pajama bottoms and inched the fabric down. The muscles below his hips were defined into a promise of horrible things. "You can't wait to see my goods, I know. Fantastic things will come in those who can't get away." Everett took another step closer. He was just inches from the Hell hallway entrance. With his next step, the first trap in the hallway assaulted him, and instantly he backed up. "What the fuck was that?" Everett pointed at the space in front of him.

Emma almost smiled. "That? That first one's hunger. It's the easiest because hunger moves you forward in search of prey. The second? That's depression. That one's a bitch."

He sputtered with anger. "But, but I'm the Devil. I can go anywhere!" "Try again, ass clown. It'll give me something to watch." Emma shrugged.

Rejection with a tinge of fear created a pattern of dismay on his face. He proceeded to try numerous things to get to Emma. He threw a rock, which bounced off the air in front of him like a wall and hit him in the head. Everett tried running with a large pole he'd dug up from somewhere. It cracked in half, and the pointy end stabbed him in the balls.

He paced back and forth like a caged tiger, snarling at Emma whenever they made eye contact. Finally, as if they'd been having a conversation instead of her observing his failures, he demanded, "Well, just come over here then."

Emma shook her head.

Everett tried pointing and snapping. He tried closing his eyes and concentrating.

Emma gave him the finger.

"I *will* get in there. You probably know better than anyone the crap I have access to in here. If I have to tear this place apart, I'll get to you." Everett pointed again.

Emma rubbed her forehead. It had been days, maybe weeks since she'd had a drink of water, a bite to eat. She'd have been dead if she were a human on Earth, but a human in Hell wasn't granted the freedom of death. She tried to pull her long, blond hair out of her face but gave up when her elbows came close to the traps. She let it tumble around her shoulders. "I hope your blue balls poison you." Emma looked at her feet, fairly confident she was out of his grasp, for now.

Everett crouched down to deliver his next promises. "When I

can finally lick your face, do you know what I'm going to do next?"

The sounds of Hell seeped in around his words. She looked over her shoulder, and he wiggled his tongue at her.

"Um, stick your Smurf nuts in some panties just like these and put heels on?" Emma tried to hold his gaze as she pointed to her underwear. His face crumbled into a very convincing mask of evil.

"You think you're sassy, but you'll pay for every word with screams. Every insult with blood. I'm going to chain you by the neck to my ankle for at least a hundred years. You'll lick my feet clean. I've so much time to play with. This hallway is just a speed bump. You should fear every moment."

He stood, and as instructed, her new best friend, fear, crowded into her heart again. Emma shut her eyes tightly, waiting for him to leave, and panic trickled down her back when Everett didn't walk away like he should have. His threats had provided him opportunity for the dramatic exit he preferred, and yet he remained standing there, just looking at her.

"Why do you hate me?" Emma finally gathered herself enough to say. Such a simple question. Why not ask?

He shook his head and turned his back on her. Emma tried to wet her mouth with her dry tongue.

Then Everett suddenly turned around. "You really want to know? Shit, how about I tell you? How about a little story time, whore?"

Emma was a captive audience, so she didn't respond as he disappeared toward Jack's old chambers just down the passage and returned with a chair.

He sat in it and crossed his legs. "Maybe you need to hear this, understand a bit about me. When we met all those years ago, I thought you were an angel on Earth. Funny, right? Isn't that ironic?" He waited for her to respond. She didn't.

"All that blond hair and those big ol' eyes. I thought you'd be the one who would love me forever. I did all the right things —

look at me! I look perfect, right?" He motioned to his body again. "I can even say all the right things. Listen: 'Emma, you have satin hair and the most beautiful smile. Touch me. Feel me.' Isn't that wonderful? But those things didn't make you quake. Tell me, why I wasn't enough, Emma? Why were you such a frigid whore?"

The chair squeaked with his agitation and the pressure of this impromptu heart-to-heart. Emma threaded her fingers together and looked at her dirty nails. She knew what he was talking about: when she'd been just sixteen and expected to marry Everett. He'd already been a man.

"Can a whore really be frigid? That's kind of a contradiction." Emma looked at the ceiling. It had crappy-looking drop tiles.

"I try to talk to you. I try to let you in, and you toss my words in my face," he shot back. "I shouldn't have expected any of your stupid angel talents to really exist. You've always been a fake, even a fake fiancée. No one sees you for what you are but me — well, and maybe God, 'cause He did let me leave Heaven with you." Everett stood and put his slipper-clad foot on the chair like an explorer claiming new land.

He had a knack. She had to give him that. He could cut right to the bone like a butcher. She'd doubted herself, her choices, but her one certainty had been God's love. Now, sitting in the cold hallway under the assault of Everett's words, it was hard to remember what had kept her so sure. She was having trouble remembering His prayer. What if soon enough she forgot Him?

"You're right, Everett. Maybe I belong here because I can't bring myself to forgive you. I can't find any bit in you that's worth heralding. You want to know why *I* hate *you*? Because the only true pleasure I've ever seen on your face is when you're delivering pain: hurting things, people, and animals. It brings you joy. How can I be asked to accept that?"

She looked at Everett, but really she was now focused on her challenge: this fear, this hallway. She wondered if God was letting her stay in Hell until she could forgive Everett for the pain he'd caused. She didn't think she could do it and mean it.

Everett put down his leg and sat again. He tilted his head inquisitively. "Wait a fucking minute. What game are you playing? Emma, I swear you'd better never say that to me again. How did you find out about that?"

He wasn't making any sense, or else her brain wasn't computing anymore. "You wanted answers," she said. "That's all I have."

"How did you know what my mother said to me? Were you there? Were you eavesdropping? I wouldn't put it past you." Everett stood and hurled the chair at her.

She flinched, but it exploded into wood splinters against the air, not touching her at all.

"That's almost exactly what my mother said when she left me!" He curled his fists and lip at the same time.

And then there was a blip in Emma's heart, just a smoke of a chance of sympathy for this evil bastard. "I'm sorry your mother left you." And she was. No child should be rejected.

"No, you're not. Fuck that, fuck her, and fuck you. She said I was broken. Because I liked to kill animals, because I hit her when I wanted something, that's why she was leaving." Everett spat his words.

Emma felt the ghost of sympathy give way to revulsion. "Did you do those things?"

Everett turned his back on her and shook out his long hair in an absolute rage. "I did. I killed the animals because they couldn't stop me. They followed the same patterns every time. Just one drop of kindness, and they were at my mercy. But she didn't get it. Every time I killed something, I *didn't* kill her... She didn't wait around to find out if I'd ever get brave enough for the real deal," he added softly.

Emma covered her mouth and nausea rolled in her stomach. He was the worst damn thing.

"So when I found you, I did the same thing. I followed the

rules, followed society's pattern. You said yes. You said you would marry me." He turned toward her again and stood close to the hunger trap, eyes wild. "But then you didn't!"

A horrible question forced its way from her lips. "What happened to your mother?"

"Don't ask about her! Don't you even open your lying mouth." Everett grew powerful in his rage. The whole room behind him glowed red, and heat came radiating out. He glanced over his shoulder and laughed. "Yes! Yes, this is what I needed. I needed to remember who I was to get to you. So simple."

Everett stepped into hunger, but his eyes never wavered. He didn't twitch with the need to eat like he'd done before. He took sure, confident steps toward her, and Emma's heart sank. Without the internal plagues, nothing would protect her now. She knew she should run...try...move...but she didn't have the coordination to rise anymore, so she just watched.

Three footsteps in, the floor around Everett began to vibrate. Both she and he looked around in surprise as a distinctly metal-on-metal noise clanked to life. Everett was yanked back as if on puppet strings, and a gate slammed down, sealing Emma in, away from the Devil.

The cement finally stilled, and Emma's mouth dropped open as Everett pulled himself to standing. Now, not only was Emma in the center of a Hellacious hallway, there was a jail-like door solidly separating her from an escape. Even if she were able to wade back through the perils, the gate would keep her inside.

"Did you do this?" Everett glared at her and grabbed the bars.

She rolled her eyes. "Yeah, I have a garage door opener stuffed in my armpit.

So glad I was able to keep that from you."

Then she saw a small square of cement begin to glow. When she squinted, she could tell it was a keyboard. Everett followed her line of vision and scrunched down a bit so he could get a glimpse of what she was seeing on her side.

"That's some sort of control panel," he announced. "Get over there and try it." He nodded like this was a brilliant plan, the obvious choice.

"Hey, dimwit. I'm not touching that keyboard — ever. Even if I knew what the Hell it did, I'd never do you a favor, especially one that'd make it easier for you to get to me." She slowly leaned back, hugging her body to make it more compact.

As she rested, she spared the fool a glance here and there to see if he was making progress. He wasn't. He tried a mirror on a stick to get a better look at the device, but the hallway prevented him from putting anything between the bars. Minion after minion — scary, hideous, and beautiful, in that order — was brought to stand in the hallway and offer advice, none of which worked. Emma got the distinct impression each minion was only interested in the Hallway as a spectacle, a story to tell the others. None appeared too fond of Everett and his ranting ways or showed the least bit of desire to help.

Emma twisted a bit so she could lie on her side. She focused on the control pad. Jack had installed it, she was sure. The keys were lettered in his messy handwriting. When used, the screen now visible above the keyboard would reveal...something, but clearly it was customized to keep Emma locked in. Jack had brought this whole nightmare into being while he was clearly on the side of evil, and she'd been a distinctly angelic enemy.

Now she knew they were more alike than either could've imagined. The last time she'd been in this hallway, she'd been searching for God. Jack had locked Him in the last cell, forcing the Lord to sit on a cot to protect an anonymous soul. But now there was nothing to try for, no one to save. Her job now, her court-mandated time here in Hell, required her simply to exist. So Emma closed her eyes and tried to focus on that, to make it her priority. Just breathe. In and out. Exist.

Exist without love, exist without her friends. Breathe knowing both Jack and Jason had forgotten her.

Emma's breath hitched, caught on her hopelessness.

CHAPTER 8

JACK

Jack exhaled as they finished interviewing yet another dead end. Violent, the escaped Minion of Sleep, seemed a bit touched in the damn head. Being on Earth's soil for so long seemed to have twisted her mind. She remembered hints and bits of things from hundreds of years ago and acted as if they'd just happened the day before.

Jack kept flexing and closing his hands, avoiding his last few cigarettes as best he could, while Jason and Dean did their damnedest to soothe the now- scared human who had no idea what Violent was talking about. They all stood in a dark, typical suburban backyard, complete with grill and blow-up pool.

Jack flexed and closed again. A clock was ticking, and with every moment the second hand slapped him in the head, heart, and mind. He couldn't go anywhere for her, or fight anyone, unless he could find an entrance to Hell. Considering he'd held the keys to the joint for over one thousand years, it should've been easier. But it didn't work that way. Although he was currently leaning toward stealing some explosives and blowing his way home action-hero style, he knew it wasn't just depth they needed. There was finesse involved with walking into the kingdom of the damned.

The stupid goddamn hallway — if he'd just built it a little carelessly, Emma might be able to get out on her own. She was clever enough. Of course even then she'd face the minions, beasts, and fucking Everett, the bastard keeping Jack's throne warm until he could figure out how to be the Devil again. He rubbed his forehead hard, trying to form a clear, convincing plan. The action did nothing but relay his frustration to Seriana.

"Listen, big guy, we'll get there. I promise we won't give up." She touched his arm, trying to be comforting although she was obviously still a little afraid of him. She moved as if she were touching open flame.

He put his endless brown eyes on her pretty face. "Tell me something about her. Tell me something I don't know." Jack wanted more of Emma, even if it was from someone else's memory.

As Seriana thought for a moment, Jack glanced over to Dean and Jason, who appeared to be listening intently as the human launched into a spiel about his latest gardening project. Jack didn't see a point in this line of conversation.

Pulling her hair back and twisting it easily into a soft bun, Seriana said, "She hummed all the time. I wondered if they were songs she heard in Heaven. You know 'Angels We Have Heard on High'? I always pictured them singing."

"I never heard her sing. We had such little time, and I spent most of it scaring the piss out of her." He snapped and unsnapped the leather cuff on his wrist anxiously.

"You know what? Ever since my brothers and I found out we were half- breeds, I couldn't see anything good about me. I just couldn't. I lost my mother and my normal. I love Dean and Jason, but they're guys. They aren't exactly sensitive to my feelings."

Seriana looked down for a moment. "We worked so hard to escape my grandfather — and to just exist — that moaning about the things in my head seemed worthless." She twirled her thumbs together and waved her hands like wings. "But when she lived with us, it was like I could be a girl again. I'd talk to her about anything. She refused to give up until I believed I was a gift, not a curse. I miss her." She shrugged, suddenly shy again.

"That sounds like her. Can you believe I hurt her? That I designed tortures to break her? And even knowing that, after living through that — she said she loved me. Me. Of all the damn things." Jack reached into his jacket, intent on his smokes.

Seriana stilled his hand. "Here comes Violent. Don't use those things."

The Sleep Minion hated Jack's habit. She claimed he was polluting her beloved plants' air, which he guessed he was. Violent had given up on humans and half-breeds, deciding instead to only love plants. She was tall, crazy, and gorgeous. Her long red hair and purple eyes made her seem like a superhero, though she was far from it. Though ridiculously strong, her lackadaisical attitude (and questionable mental state) prevented her from participating very effectively in good or evil deeds. She was only on this trip because she was all they had, she owed Jack a favor, and most importantly, because Dean evidently looked exactly like her dearly beloved and long-dead Italian lover, Giovanni.

"This isn't it. This is the wrong house. Be rid of the human. Best to kill him. Come, Dean, escort me to the car." She walked through the backyard and into the house, flinging doors open as she went.

The human looked in after her, stunned. "Um, sure, lady. Go right into my house." The man looked from face to face and seemed to sense that something wasn't right. "Why are you standing that way, like you're about to pounce?" he asked the half-breeds. "And why was that woman kissing my trees? And where did she *go?*"

Jack nodded toward the vehicles, sending the rest of them off. He'd make things right with the man. After all, he was the only human among the search party. As the backyard cleared, Jack shook his head. They'd visited fifteen houses like this, looking for the backyard Violent claimed was a portal to Hell. Each failure kept him from getting to Emma.

He clicked his tongue to get the man's attention. "Hey. That chick? She's married to a mob boss. If I were you I wouldn't mention this visit to anyone." Jack turned and walked through the man's house as well, grabbing a pack of cigarettes and lighter from an end table as he went. They weren't the hand- rolled perfection he preferred, but they'd keep his mouth busy.

Seriana was waiting just outside the front door. "Did you calm him down? Make it okay? You know my brothers and I have to stay hidden."

"Sure, pretty baby. He's calm as a cucumber's brother. Let's roll."

Jack insisted on driving Violent's ridiculous Ferrari. Unfortunately, the nice half-breed rode with Violent and Dean in his SUV. That left Jason as Jack's passenger. Things were awkward around that one, to say the very least. Jack avoided talking to him.

Jack started the beautiful car and closed his eyes briefly as the engine roared like a hungry tiger. He pulled out behind the SUV and followed, hoping the next scattered memory Violent produced would be more fruitful.

"We're not getting any closer to finding Emma." Jason gave Jack a hard stare.

Jack maneuvered the car with one hand and lit a cigarette with the other, cracking the window. "I think Violent's mind is shot. I just don't have a clue what else to do. I don't even know what she's looking for." He punched the steering wheel. "You remembering anything yet? Because that would be fucking helpful."

Jason looked out the passenger window. "You know I'm not. That part of my memory is just...gone."

"Well, you have to try harder. I don't know if anyone even understands how bad it is down there for her. It's just horrible."

"I don't see how you manage to blame everyone but yourself. If you hadn't screwed my girlfriend and broken stuff in Heaven, Emma would be fine. Even better? Don't flop around in Purgatory like a pussy so she has to go up there and *convince* you to make a choice." Jason turned fully in his seat to glare at Jack.

"I didn't want her to come to see me. I didn't even believe it was her at first." Jack was too good at lying not to know when he was doing it to himself.

"That's bullshit." Jason shook his head and sat back. "You whined up there until you got your way."

There was only the sound of the sports car's engine for a nice chunk of time until Jack answered. "If you remembered Emma, you wouldn't blame me for wanting to keep her." Jack blinked back his emotion, picturing her golden hair in waves holding the sunlight, her looking at him as if he was her every wish as well. "You should be thankful you don't."

Vittorio

Vittorio knew it was time. The three chosen descendants needed to procreate. He looked around the room. His half-minion army looked limp, to say the least. They had no fire in their bellies once they were satiated on blood. That's what his group lacked: vision. They had no appreciation of the fact that they were mythical beings with the very world at their fingertips.

But that would change with their twentieth generation. Twenty was Vittorio's favorite number. If everything he'd studied, hoped for, and lusted after came to fruition, the offspring of Dean, Jason, and Seriana would be full-blooded minions at last. They each just needed to lie with one of the half-minions among his ranks — he had some very choice partners picked out — and the product of those relationships would be unstoppable.

His great-grandchildren would find themselves under his command as soon as they opened their eyes. And they'd become the ultimate fighting machines. Vittorio smiled at his daughter, Rebecca. She did not smile back.

"Daughter, you know it's time to bring the children back to the herd."

Rebecca was chained to the wall in his living room as if she were some sort of decoration. "Father, you'll never find my children. This dream you have? It's going to die."

Vittorio felt determination burn within him. "Oh, but you see, I've the best bait for those children," he told her with a sneer. "Which one of your three wouldn't come back to visit their long-dead mother? It'll be touching — for a few seconds anyway." He stepped closer to her and various half-breeds scurried out of his way. Rebecca had been chained to the wall for so long, they scarcely acknowledged she was there.

"I'll never help you," she whispered. "You should kill me while you've all these assistants. Because make no mistake, I'll fight for my children's freedom until my last moment."

Rebecca barely existed any more, but the mention of her children started a fire in her that her father had to grudgingly respect. He didn't see that passion in any of his soldiers. "If only you'd be *with* me, Daughter. You're so misguided. You see, breeding vampires isn't easy. You've got to be strong enough to eliminate the ones that fail to thrive. You did continue the line, so there's some usefulness in you. You'll do this one more thing for me, then I'll put you out of your misery. No worries."

Vittorio didn't share the news that had stirred his interest. One of his sources had spotted three adults who resembled his grandchildren going house to house like vacuum cleaner salesmen. All this time they'd outrun him, bested him at this global game of hide and seek. But now they were slowing down, making mistakes. Tomorrow he'd pack up his army and his daughter. They'd surround the children and take them easily. It would be the sweetest victory.

CHAPTER 9

KATE

Kate had the evening mapped out: She was all set to finish the sweater she'd been knitting and cast on another online order for a glove and hat set. Her favorite chick flick was on cable tonight, and even though she had her own DVD copy of the movie, she still watched it whenever it came on. Why the commercials made it special, she didn't know. Maybe it was because if the movie was on the TV, being sent into thousands of homes, she could tell herself she wasn't watching it alone.

Loneliness was quite a battle. Sometimes the weapons were tears, sometimes loud music — Kate had a whole arsenal to choose from. She was an expert at filling empty holes with random things, but night was the worst. It always had been. For a long time now, the night sky that zipped tight around her little cabin had been laden with suspense. The wait for Nero. There'd been no more visits from her father, and when she was snug in her PJs she was the most restless. Unfinished.

It was like he was drowning in slow drying cement, and she'd no way to save him. And sometimes she doubted her sanity because she *did* want him free from Hell — if he was even still alive to hope for. He could very well be gone, punished for his crimes, for the very creation of her in the first place.

68

Kate put on her soft clothes and lit a candle. The sweater was so close to finished that her heart raced as she sat down with the intricately knotted yarn on her lap. Silly, because knitting was hardly an adrenaline-based sport, but this represented the culmination of a plan, a wait concluding. She bound off the project and sighed. After threading in the loose strings, it was finished.

The picture on the front was a puppy, similar to the one she'd worn for her first, ruined tea with Nero. Kate folded the garment and set it next to her recliner. She let herself feel the accomplishment for a few moments before grabbing the next set of needles. The movie's opening song began and the title flashed across the screen. A love story. Miscommunication and love at first sight: all the things a girl thinks she might want before she knows true heartache.

She began mouthing the words, putting herself in the lead role. Her attempts at love had been thwarted before she could even get attached to the hope for more. Her looks weren't the problem, but there was just something off-putting about her. Damned if she knew what it was. Kate set her head back. She *did* know what the problem was. She wanted something unreal: the fantasy love born of only the most unrealistic circumstances. And her baggage started with a capital B. The wash of exhaustion made her wonderings disappear, and she closed her eyes for just a moment, still listening to the movie.

She'd been dreaming of Nero's last night again when she sat up straight on the couch. Out of long-ingrained habit, she ran to the back window to check the shed. Nothing, of course. She grabbed her shotgun and closed her eyes, listening. A too-close car door slam and the murmuring of a group of people soon opened them again.

She glanced at the clock: two in the damn morning. No one should ever be here now. Aunt Bess had passed a few months before, so this wasn't a late- night courtesy visit from the nursing home. Kate had not one clue who might be coming to her door, but she planned to greet them with a trick, not a treat.

JACK

Jack leaned against the SUV, smoking one of his stolen cigarettes and trying to hear encouraging words from Violent. Dean had just finished asking her if this was finally the right place.

"I'm sure it's somewhere," she murmured. "Do you know any Italian at all? I can teach you." Violent reached a hand out and touched his face.

Dean patted her hand and gently pulled it away. "No, I'm sorry I don't."

"Okay! Let's get a move on," Seriana announced in a too-chipper voice.

"I'm curious to see whether Jason has killed Jack yet."

Jack smirked at the expressions of surprise on their faces when they turned and found him so close. The slamming of various vehicle doors sounded like a light smattering of explosions, and the lights in the cabin blazed as the group made their way to the front porch.

Jack stepped forward. They'd already determined that as a human, he'd look the least suspect under the harsh light of the lantern mounted next to the house number.

The woman who answered the door had a huge smile and placed herself exactly one rifle's length away from Jack's chest. "Go away," she said pleasantly. "I don't have time to go to court and explain why I killed five trespassers."

Jack lifted an eyebrow and looked pointedly at the weapon. "You won't be able to kill these four with that. And if you kill me, it'll just make them happy. Let's cut to the chase. You don't, by any chance, know where the fuck the doorway to Hell is? Because I seem to have misplaced it."

Seriana slapped him lightly on the back of his head, but he

just shrugged. He was pissed and sad, a horrible recipe for following rules.

"Pardon me? If you're looking for the crazy train, this isn't the station. Move on." The woman with her rifle pointed at his chest looked fierce, despite her hot pink pajamas.

Seriana stepped slowly to Jack's side and smiled. "Sorry about my friend here. He hasn't been taking his medication and gets confused. I'm Seriana. We're from the Department of Natural Resources to check the radon levels in your water."

The woman pursed her lips. "At two o'clock in the morning? Either I'm dreaming or you're trespassing. Whichever it is, I'm about to fire this gun."

Jack let one half of his smile show.

"Now you're grinning, crazy man? Why don't you tell me the name of your meds?" She held the rifle with a remarkable stillness.

"Rum. Got any? 'Cause I'm losing it here." He shrugged. "What's your name, Spunky the Kid?"

"My name's Kate. I'll write it neat and clear on the police report stating I blew your balls off. And now I'm counting to ten, just to give you guys a fair chance to leave, 'cause nobody's telling the truth." She adjusted her grip, and her tongue slipped between her lips as she concentrated.

"This is it. The gateway's here. This girl's part minion." Violent inspected Kate for a moment. "But she's kind of a dud. Every great once in a while a half-breed is born without anything extra — no real powers, no drive for blood. This one's weak."

With that, she pushed her way to the front of the group and in a smooth motion tossed the rifle into the yard. She'd moved so quickly, Kate's hands still cradled empty air.

Jack sighed. At least they were getting somewhere. And spicy little Kate was part Hell. Figures. She didn't seem like such a dud to him.

"Okay, now you're flat-out pissing me off. Leave now. All of you." Kate sounded scared, as well she should be, considering.

Jason stepped in and formally introduced himself like a suck up. "Ms. Kate, I'm Jason Parish. I'm sorry. We've been going about this in a horrible way... We wouldn't call so late, or early, but... well...we have an emergency. A friend of ours is in danger, and this kind lady led us to your door." He gestured to Violent who attempted to smile. "We intend you no harm, and I assure you we'll leave as soon as we can. Maybe even you might be allowed to leave?" Jason looked toward Violent again, who shook her head.

Then Dean stepped forward. "I apologize for the inconvenience. Is this your home? We're going to need to inspect your backyard briefly." He pulled a clipboard from behind his back and held it authoritatively.

Jack could see it held only a blank piece of paper, but the appearance of the banal object seemed to settle Kate down. Dean shrugged and lifted his eyebrows. It seemed the three sibling half-breeds were used to getting humans to cooperate.

Kate stepped back and nodded. "I knew this day would come. Well, night, I guess."

"Really?" Jack said. "You expected the Devil, a minion, and three half-breeds to come knocking on your door? I'm surprised."

Kate said nothing as they all crowded into the foyer of the comfortable cabin. Jack could hear a TV on in the living room as Violent closed the door behind them and ominously locked it.

Crossing her arms, Kate blew her hair off her forehead. "Well, I wasn't sure it'd be an entire conglomerate of weirdos, but I knew something was going to wreck my life eventually."

There was a long pause. The group waited.

"My father wasn't around much. He was a hard man to love."

Jack gave Violent a dirty look. "What was Big Poppa's name?"

"Nero." She answered as if this was her most guarded secret, covering her mouth after the word had escaped.

"Violent! Nero got to the surface? Please tell me you didn't know about this." Sure he was human now, but Jack took pride in having been in charge of Hell for a thousand years. No being was supposed to escape. Violent had been Jack's only known exception.

Violent picked up a pad of paper and pencil from the table in the next room. She ignored Jack and started working the Sudoku puzzles.

"V, answer me, goddammit." Jack moved in front of her. She was so much stronger than he was now, but she still cowered a bit as he took the book from her.

"Yes, Nero and few others would get out and come back. It was painful, and required precise timing, so they couldn't do it often." Violent clasped her hands behind her back like a solider.

"How many?" Jack demanded, back in his in-charge element. "Why didn't you come to me?"

"Five. Counting me it was six, as far as I know. You have to understand, sir, the Devil who came before you? We were all looking for a way out. The tunnels we built? We were trying to get out, get away. But as soon as you took charge, we knew we could stay. They were just visiting." She looked at the ground.

The hunting party was in various states of unease, like they'd stumbled into the most private of conversations. Seriana stood close to Kate.

"Five?! Five is more than zero. That's my job, Violent. Keeping the things damned to Hell *in* the fucking place. Do you know what this means?" Jack began pacing. "There might be a lot more half-breeds around than there should be. Nero procreated — did everyone?" He stilled again and waited.

"Some of the males tried to make young. Most times they failed — the host woman would perish. But there were successes. It's because of them I knew I could make it to Giovanni." Violent took a peek at Jack.

"Jack, why do you care if minions escaped?" Jason piped up. "Isn't the Devil and Hell all about horror and mutations?"

Kate's mouth dropped open, and she looked incredulously at Jason. Seriana whispered her apologies for her brother's remark, which tarnished Kate's father.

"I don't have time to talk job descriptions with you." Jack shot him a dirty look.

Violent interrupted. "The Devil before Jack didn't care, not really. But Jack did the job right. He wanted to keep the shitty things in Hell so the people on Earth could make their own choices: fall to Hell or rise to Heaven on their own merit."

Kate began clapping. "Can I just say something? Because now I'm positive I'm dreaming. This ridiculously handsome guy was a 'good Devil'? Isn't that ironic? And all of you, at one point or another, were part of Hell? I knew I shouldn't have had Taco Bell for dinner. It's either the shits or crazy nightmares."

Feeling a little panicked, Jack turned to Kate and put his hands on her shoulders. "Cutie, I don't have time to make this make sense for you. The girl I love? She's trapped in Hell. I believe I can get in there from here. Please, can you tell me where your father appeared when Hell barfed him up?"

He was asking her, but that was just a formality. He *would* find the entrance to Hell tonight. Now. Here.

CHAPTER 10

KATE

"I might tell you, but I need something in return." Kate stood taller. Even if this was a dream, she wanted to be brave enough to ask — to bargain for her father.

"Kate, understand this: I'll find this entry with or without your help. You have one more second to pretend you have leverage over me." Jack rubbed his forehead over and over as if willing himself to have patience.

"I want Nero to come here and stay here, with no compulsions. To be my father." She hoped she'd worded her request properly. If this dude really was Satan, loopholes and shoddy deals were his business.

"No way. I'd rather pop a whore's ass blister. Not exposing innocents to Hell. Now spill it."

He was just a guy, but the way he looked at her right then gave her chills. Somehow she stood her ground and shook her head.

"No." She bit the inside of her cheek. "You'd be surprised how much I can take. He's my price. You want your girl so bad? You're going to have make sacrifices."

Jack exhaled and inhaled with purpose. "Fine."

He withdrew a pistol from his waistband and had her pinned

before she could think of a counterattack. "Tell me, or I blow your brains out and find it anyway."

The feeling of a gun pointed at her head made Kate's whole body dry up. Her thought process began and ended with the barrel. She took in scared, half-empty breaths, and her swallow sounded loud in her ears. "No. I've waited for him for my whole life. I deserve a dad." A drip of sweat slid down her spine like the fingertip of a monster.

"Put down the gun, Jack. Scaring her with false threats isn't going to help." The politest of the group stepped forward, shaking his head.

"Shut up, Jason. I'm on my last fucking nerve. If you think I'm opposed to a little murder to get to her, then you don't know me." He pulled Kate closer. She could see her scared face reflected in his eyes.

The ridiculous Technicolor one — Violent? — picked up the Sudoku book again. "Jack would never kill that girl. But I'll do it if he tells me to, or if I get bored, which is starting to happen."

Jack pushed Kate away and stomped out of the room. Soon the house was filled with the sounds of his mad search. The remaining two strangers flanked Violent and seemed to be trying to keep her attention.

Kate shook off her relief to yell after him. "Bastard, don't you dare ransack my stuff! You'll never find the door without me."

Jason stepped closer. "Excuse me, Ms. Kate. I must apologize for all this callous behavior. Surely you have a life we've disrupted. Hell is a horrible place, especially when he's been in charge. As far as I can tell, Jack is a filthy beast."

Kate covered her mouth, as her inappropriate smile had no place, but Jason's eyes sparkled as she began to laugh.

"No, truly," he continued. "He's just the worst. All the ladies say he's charming, but I don't see it. He curses, lies, smokes..." Jason pretended to puff on a cigarette.

Maybe Kate was drunk on the absurdity of the scene or the adrenaline coursing through her, but she felt almost tipsy with her giggles. This was about as interested in her as any guy had ever seemed.

Jason bit his lip and stepped closer to speak in a stage whisper. "I swear he can smoke a cigarette with one inhale. Just a huge pile of ash when he's done." He smiled as she laughed out loud. "May I speak with you alone, Ms. Kate? You can bring your gun if you want to." He held out his hand as an invitation and gestured to her kitchen.

Jack must have dumped over the dresser upstairs. The ceiling reverberated, and he let out a string of expletives.

Kate shook her head. "My rifle's on the lawn somewhere." She shrugged and led Jason into the room.

He stayed a respectable distance from her as he began to speak. "My mom was from Hell too," he said as she turned to face him. "In a way, at least. She was a half-breed minion, like I am. She left us a long time ago to try to stop my grandfather from finding us. So I get the missing. I understand what it's like to want your parent. I'm sorry you know that same ache."

Kate leaned against her counter and tried to ignore the sounds of her house being trashed. "It's tough to find a greeting card with that on it," she said. This guy was earnest — or at least he pretended very well.

"I've seen a few at the dollar store, but you have to know where to look." He gave her a half smile.

"Do you think I'm being selfish asking for my dad?" She picked at her nail polish in between looking at Jason.

"No. I'd do almost anything to get my mother back." Jason shuffled his feet.

"Tell me about his girl. Why does he want her so badly?"

"She was my girl first before he got his hooks in her." Jason clenched his fist.

"Is hooks a euphemism for *penis?*" She raised an eyebrow.

He rolled his eyes. "I guess it is. She's an angel, so I didn't expect it."

"I think I'm sick of guys calling their girlfriends angels —

especially if she cheated on you." Kate had trouble picturing any girl walking away from this handsome guy.

"No, she's an actual angel. From actual Heaven. As there is a Devil with minions, there are angels." He sat in a kitchen chair.

Kate could judge Jack's progress by his loud footfalls. He was close to her room. "Really? Wow. I guess that makes sense. I've been so involved with what's in Hell, I never really gave a thought to the opposite end." She thought for a second. "And actually? That kind of pisses me off. If there are angels, there must be a God in charge of them. Why hasn't He helped me?"

She pushed her hair away from her face and hated the burning anger that suddenly consumed her. If there was a God, why did He have to take her mother? If there was a God, why did she have to spend so many years alone?

"I don't have any answers for you, Kate. My memory was taken from me so I don't remember my trip to Heaven or Emma at all." Jason shrugged sadly. "I just know I hate Jack."

"Her name's Emma?" Giving the damned angel a name made Kate feel guilty for holding her information ransom. At least the lady in question was sort of a slut...

There was a knock at the kitchen door. "Can I come in?" The other female poked her head around the door. "I was listening to your conversation, because I guess I kind of suck."

Kate waved her in. "Sure, let's see if we can make this any weirder."

"I asked Emma a lot of questions when she lived with us," the woman said. "I'm Jason's sister, Seriana, and Dean's our brother. I was mad that Mom was gone, that I had to face being what I am." Seriana sat in a chair and held Jason's hand. "And Emma was adamant that just because bad things were happening didn't mean God was mean or wasn't paying attention." Dean and Violent came to lean against the doorframe. "God gave us free will on this Earth. And with the blessing of being able to make our own choices, there are also down sides. Children die, wars are fought, all because we're allowed to live our lives. We make choices, and sometimes there are consequences. That's what she said, anyway. It made more sense coming from her. It made me feel more connected."

Jason patted his sister's hand. She smiled at him for a moment before she continued. "I know you just met us, Kate. But that angel? She doesn't have anyone else making the choice to help her. It's just us. God's not going to be her superhero. It has to be our free will that busts her out. At least that's my take on it."

The house was now quiet. Kate had just begun to process this when Jack pushed past Violent and Dean holding a pair of black sculptures, a puppy and a flower. Instead of angry, he looked sad.

"Nero loved you." He set her prized Hell rocks on the kitchen table.

Kate ran her hand over the shovel-etched art. "He loves me, wherever he's trapped. He keeps his promises, and he told me the lack of him here was his love for me." The dew on the flower gained a new, glistening addition as her tear fell and landed on a leaf. "Did you ever want something so badly that just wishing for it tired you out? I'm exhausted. If I don't do something, I'm not sure I can live this life anymore." Her words tumbled from a deep place, a place Kate often found in the earliest parts of the morning, before the sun met the horizon.

"I'm not taking you into Hell, Kate," Jack declared. "Not today, not tomorrow. *I'll* get him out. That's my word. After I defeat all the minions and the current Devil, and free Emma, on the way out I'll get Nero."

"How can I be sure you're not just using me?" she asked.

Violent spoke. "He'll do what he says. He always has."

"I guess that'll have to do." Kate left her gifts from her father on the table and headed for the back door.

She could hear the others filing out behind her. Kate stopped near her shed and was about to speak when Jason neatly tackled her and covered her mouth. Seriana pulled a matching maneuver on Jack a split second later, and Dean and Violent ran off into the woods.

CHAPTER 11

JASON

Jason shook his head with pleading eyes as Kate started to struggle. When she was still, he leaned close and whispered in her ear. "There's another half-breed close by. Not friendly. Shhh."

Kate nodded as much as she could with her head immobile. Jason checked on Seriana but Jack didn't seem to need convincing to keep still. The long car rides as they looked for Hell's entrance had provided ample opportunity for Jason, Dean, and Seriana to explain the circumstances they lived in: the constant fear, the burning feeling of being chased that kept them overly cautious.

Jason eased himself off Kate and removed his hand. He had to admit, he was impressed with her. This night must have been blowing her mind, and yet she was rolling with the punches like a champ. Her dark hair now had leaves tangled throughout, but her clear eyes assessed him. She bit her lip as she watched his eyes. He felt himself smile and realized his burning hatred for Jack and desperate need to remember Emma had almost eclipsed the way Kate's attention made him feel.

He tore his gaze from hers and mouthed to his sister, "Will they be okay?"

She shrugged. Then she pointed from her chest to the woods, obviously willing to trek after Dean and Violent.

He spoke quietly now. "Stay with Kate. Keep her safe."

He stood carefully, scanning the surrounding area until he could hear the gentle cracking of papery leaves on the forest floor.

He was interrupted by Jack arguing with Seriana. "What about me? He doesn't want you to protect me?"

Jason wanted to punch the Devil in the mouth. Instead he crept off toward the noises. In an instant, the woods went from peaceful cradle of the night to an explosion of curses and violence. Jason sprinted for the ruckus and found Violent and Dean straddling a spitting mad half-breed. He was covered in tattoos and piercings.

"Dean, get off of him so I can kill him." Violent crackled her knuckles.

"Wait, first we need to know who he is," Jason cried. He tried to get a better look at the prisoner's face while Dean slipped away to check for other unexpected visitors.

"I'm your worst nightmare, asshole!" the half-breed spat.

Violent stood and yanked him to his feet, easily restraining him. Jason shook his head. "You must be a friend of Jack's."

Dean came back, shaking his head. "Looks like he's alone."

Dean made sure the stranger's limbs stayed still, while Jason patted him down, producing a cell phone and three knives.

"I'm not telling you people nothin'." The man tried to swagger until Violent shifted his shoulders and cracked one of his arms out of its socket.

"Fuck you, bitch! That hurts."

Violent turned him so she could see his face. "Next time your balls will make that same noise."

Jason and Dean made eye contact and lifted their eyebrows. Dean smiled. "Damn, I'm glad V likes us."

Jason nodded as he switched his attention to the cell phone. After scanning the recent calls and sent media, he handed the evidence to Dean. "Looks like he was sending this stuff out. His first call was fifteen minutes ago." He scanned the area again. This was everything they'd been trying to avoid for years.

"Grandfather knows we're here." Dean dropped the phone and stomped on it. After picking through the wreckage and making sure none of the tracking devices were operational, Dean met Jason's eyes. "What are we going to do? I mean…"

Violent interrupted. "Just tell me what you need from this one and give me four minutes."

JACK

Jack sat up and hated that he had to stay with the ladies. Well, he loved the ladies, but being human was pissing him off. This damn close to the entrance, and most of the muscle had gotten up and bolted.

When the screaming started, Jack knew Violent was the cause. He comforted Seriana and Kate.

"What's she doing to that half-breed?" Seriana stood.

Jack joined her and held out a hand to Kate. She looked pale.

"You might want to cover your ears, princess. That's not going to get any prettier." Jack nodded in the direction of the inhuman wails.

After Kate put her fingers in her ears and started singing a horrible pop song, Jack shook his head and spoke to Seriana. "You don't want to know."

The sudden absence of the torture noises could only mean death. Soon after the silence, Violent strode back into the backyard with Dean and Jason.

"Killed him." She approached the largest tree and began petting it like a dog.

Dean and Jason looked spooked. Seriana hugged her brothers, and each returned her hug and kissed the top of her head. Jack hoped they could just avoid the inevitably ensuing discussion and just get the Hell to Hell.

Jason, of course, had other plans. "Jack, you need to take Kate and Seriana somewhere else. Dean, Violent, and I will get Emma. My grandfather has an army of half-breeds, and they could be here any minute. The thing we just killed said there were about twenty-five in the group. And their only goal? Finding us."

Seriana looked to the sky and exhaled, worry etching itself on her face.

"Anything about Mom?" She looked from one brother to another.

"Ah, he died before we could ask," Dean reported.

"She killed him before you could ask about Mom? I knew I should have gone. Damn it." Seriana clenched her fists.

Violent left her tree and approached. "They did try to ask, but the man stepped on a flower, and I lost my temper." The minion patted Seriana's shoulder awkwardly. "Don't be concerned. I'm sure your mother's long dead."

Seriana held her hands up in disbelief. "Thanks. That helps."

Violent pushed her long red hair out of her face and tried to smile, missing Seriana's sarcasm completely. "You're welcome."

Jack snapped his fingers until all present looked at him. "Okay, you... Kate, show me where the entrance is quickly before this place turns into a giant clusterfuck."

"You're leaving, Jack," Jason said, instantly angry. "Don't act like you can help."

Dean glanced at his watch. "Somebody better do something soon or we'll be handling an army, and we're far from prepared."

Kate clapped her hands as Jack and Jason circled each other menacingly. "Hey! There's a simple answer. We all go to Hell."

"I agree," said Violent. "The useless half-breed speaks the truth. You all need to go to Hell — except for Dean. He and I will go to Italy and grow grapes." She smoldered in Dean's direction.

"Useless?" Kate asked, offended.

Seriana stiffened. "Did you guys hear that?"

At first they didn't. But then the clamoring in the woods grew louder. Only a careless army would make that much noise.

Jack quietly threw a temper tantrum before rolling his eyes. "Fine. Kate, you can come. Violent, stop creeping Dean out and help us get to the gateway." He punctuated his words by pointing.

Kate jogged over to the shed with her companions right behind her. She twirled the dial on the combination lock, but whenever she yanked on it, the lock stayed closed. Her hands shook.

Calmly, Jason reached around her. "I'll get it," he said, then yanked the lock and hinge completely off the shed.

She pulled the door open and they quickly entered, shutting it behind them. The dirty window let in just enough moonlight to see shapes and silhouettes, but Kate seemed to have no trouble finding the spot. She moved yard equipment out of the way to reveal a large rock. "This is it. This boulder."

CHAPTER 12

VITTORIO

Vittorio knew he was closer to the chosen offspring than he'd ever been before. But the updates from Bick had ceased, which was curious. No matter. As he and the army of half-breeds headed for the cabin his spy had indicated, the old man smiled. He had the best grandchild-detector in the world. His own daughter. She hadn't shown life in years, but trailing the hunting party in chains she looked worried — nay, petrified — so he knew he must be close.

He indulged his fantasy again. In a few years, when he had his great-grand- children trained and raised, he could breed them as well. Once they'd created an army of full-blood minions, all minions — even the remaining half- breeds — would go from hiding in the shadows to living as kings and gods on Earth. Their nearly endless lives would be spent harvesting humans for food and pleasure. And he would be the king of the kings. Power fit him like a glove.

Through the forest, through the trees, came a scent. The wave of want hit them quickly, like a tornado, and every half-breed with him got a vaccine of power. Their veins pulsed with it, like a heartbeat of a mother. Without needing prompting, his army sprinted together toward what had to be the source of all power.

Jack

Jack set down his guns. He cracked his knuckles and looked at the rock.

"Hey, let's move it." Jason approached the proposed entryway.

Jack shook his head and went to his knees to lay his hands on the boulder's surface like a mason. He felt all around, finally closing his eyes.

"Devil guy?" Kate interrupted. "I can hear them right outside."

Jason pushed at Jack's shoulder to get him out of the way.

Jack wobbled a bit, losing his connection. "Bloodsucker, this rock is held down by more than *fucking* gravity. It takes finesse — not that I expect you to know what that is. It's kept in place by the sucking damnation of a million souls. If we don't time it right, we won't get shit done. Now shut up and let me think." Jack cradled the boulder again.

Jason stayed quiet but Jack could see him flailing around making elaborate hand gestures of frustration at his brother and sister. He was just about to tell him shutting up included movements as well, when he felt something shift. "Now! Pull it now," he yelled.

Jason shoved him over, and Dean grabbed the other side of the rock, but they could only wiggle it a bit. The shed door flew open and crazed vampire soldiers punched through the walls. Violent moved next to the men and joined them as they heaved. The rock began to turn. When it finally loosened — like an embedded tooth — everyone staggered backward. Brilliant blue light shot up through the sky in a shimmering pillar, and the invading half-breeds tumbled as if from a blow.

Once they sat up, instead of rushing for the safety they hoped

Hell would provide, Jason, Dean, and Seriana turned now-hungry eyes on Jack. He felt like a soon-to-be late-night snack. Violent pulled him off the ground and stood between him and the hungry vampires. The siblings seethed like beasts, their eyes glazed over.

"Hey, V?" Jack turned from the scene to face the open hole. "I'm leaving."

Kate, who surprisingly had her wits about her, pulled herself to her feet. "Not without me. I get my father. That was our deal."

Violent slapped Jason across the face as he lunged for Jack. He yelped and seemed to come to himself again. Jack held out his hand for Kate who grabbed it and wrapped her other arm around his leather-clad bicep. They watched as Violent whacked Seriana across the cheek as well. She seemed abashed and hung her head. But Violent just smiled at Dean as he looked her up and down with hungry eyes. She bit her lip.

Just then, Vittorio recovered enough to lift himself from the ground. "Children, I've found you!"

Violent was so fast that the others didn't register what was happening until she was almost done. She bulldozed her entire group into the hole and pulled the rock down behind them.

Jack landed unceremoniously on the ground, but at least they weren't trying to eat him now. One slap from Violent seemed to be all it took. Inside Hell, the rock had melded with the wall. The only evidence that it had ever been anything special, any sort of opening, was the ring of fingertips captured between the rock and the hard place.

"Ew." Kate took a deliberate step toward Jason. "You back to normal?" When he nodded and held out his hand, she took it.

Jack looked around Hell and shook his head. He tented his fingers and tapped them against his forehead. "Think. Think."

Jason looked at Kate and smirked. "Great. You have to tell yourself to do that? We're doomed."

She stifled a giggle.

Jack ignored the barb. "Did you grab my guns, V?"

She was busy petting Dean and holding him back. He now

looked like he was enjoying her attention, and still considering eating Jack.

"No, sir. I was busy saving our asses. Isn't he pretty?" She looked like she might kiss her great-great-great grandson.

Seriana slapped her brother in the back of the head, hard. Dean shook himself out of his stupor and regained his demeanor of disgust.

"Why did you do that? I hate you, spawn." Violent pulled Dean into a hug and snarled at the girl.

Jack rolled his eyes. *This* is what he had to work with? "No. No fighting. Violent, that's an order." He began to pace. The others seemed surprised when she let Dean go and looked at her feet. "And yes, Jason, we're most likely doomed. This is Hell, not a vacation. Ready for some honesty? Here's a fucking dose." Jack bit his lip. "I'm not here to *live*. For me, dying while trying to save Emma is better than living without her. I fully expect that most of us will die or stay in here forever. Now let's move." He started off confidently into the pitch dark.

Vittorio

Vittorio screamed and pounded on the boulder. Six of his half-breeds had their hands stuck in the crack and were howling in pain. He spun to face his daughter, and she knew she couldn't hide the relief that flowed through her. He, in turn, looked ready to spit nails.

"Why are you smiling? Are you proud of your children?" he raged. "They saw you and left you! Cowards. You raised cowards." He slapped her across the face and pounded into her midsection. The chain around her neck jingled as his rage manifested in his fists.

But Rebecca was beyond pain now. She'd been transformed

by the glimpse of her children. Vittorio was wrong. Not a single one of them had seen her, and for that she was grateful. Her children were too brave to protect themselves — Rebecca knew that — so she was thankful they were sealed, oblivious, behind the rock. Vittorio's fists and kicks brought her to the ground, and Rebecca retreated inside her mind, remembering love while she endured hate.

Chapter 13

Emma

Everett had decided to try to hole his way through the wall as opposed to getting at Emma through the bars of the gate. She could hear him pounding away. So far he seemed unsuccessful, but her senses were shot. Every breath she took was laden with a smoke-flavored humidity.

Enduring was her job now. She kept her eyes closed and tried to say the Lord's Prayer again. It would not come, and she couldn't pull forth God's face in her memory now either. She had no tears for that loss. Had she ever been more than this? An angel? Loved by God? It seemed so far away. There'd be no reason for her to linger. If God had even a modicum of decency, He would let her die here. Maybe this was the lowest low: doubting God so thoroughly.

She had taken to holding her own hand. She squeezed to try to comfort herself. This hallway had asked too much of her the first time she visited. Now it was taking her soul, filling her with evil by osmosis. A loud thump sent electricity through her nervous system. Emma closed her eyes and relived her last escape, cuddled in God's arms. She could still recall his healing effect. Exhaling, she tried not to want that feeling too much. She stretched her legs carefully. The floor was her bed, her captor, and her prison all at once.

As she extended, her big toe inched into a swath of warmth. Like sticking the tip of her toe in a bubble bath, there was the promise of relaxation. She pulled her foot back quickly, afraid of a trick, a hidden plague. But her whole consciousness centered on that small spot on the floor as she sat up.

It looked the same as every other square inch of the hallway. She regarded it, squinting — wondering how it might be different, tempted to find out more, knowing only her body could be the test.

She hugged her knees. The toe that had been warm was cleaner than the others now. A bit of glitter shone on the toenail. Emma tracked the path from God's past cell to the gate, once, twice, three times before it hit her. *God had walked here! God's feet had touched this very floor.* She put her other toe in the curious warmth. Greedily, her whole foot pushed its way into the spot. It could only be good. It could only be perfection. She scooted with as much control as she could muster, not wanting to slip into a plague now with a sliver of release in sight.

Her legs fit, then her body, and finally her back and head. The release was confession, a warm bath, and a new life to engulf her. Comfort. She was satiated and warm, and the floor felt soft and soothing. The air around her held her body effortlessly, like a hammock. No more hunger, no more pain, no more thirst. She tried again, knowing now:

"Our Father, which art in Heaven, hallowed be thy name."

Emma's tears finally came, and she pushed forward so she could kneel properly.

"Thy kingdom come. Thy will be done in Earth as it is in Heaven."

Her voice became louder, echoing in the hallway.

"Give us this day our daily bread. And forgive us our trespasses..." She stood then, proud, and spread her arms like wings.

"...as we forgive them that trespass against us. And lead us not into temptation, but deliver us from evil. For thine is the kingdom, the power, and the glory, for ever and ever."

For the first time in mind-altering weeks, Emma smiled. "Amen."

She smiled so wide it hurt her cheeks because God loved her. And He would never leave her. Even if she was still trapped. After a few soul-rejuvenating moments, Emma took careful steps, exploring God's path. Her muscles protested their use by cramping and twisting, but she pushed on. She found she could walk almost the entire length of the hallway — from just before God's cell to the gate and back.

Her horrible French maid's costume was now clean, and her hair smelled fresh. It had been so knotted it felt like tangled rope before. But now? Just silk. The best was her heart. Its true, healthy beat sounded like a promise. The air around her became fresh and clean, and the smoke cleared from her lungs. This incredible oasis in Hell gave Emma wings on the inside. Maybe it was ludicrous, but she felt she and God had a special relationship. He must know how devoted her heart was.

"Thank You. I really think I can endure forever, if need be, if I have You." Emma looked to the ceiling of the hallway, sending her words straight up.

"You can thank me after you've sucked my dick dry." Everett's voice broke her concentration. "What the Hell is going on here?"

Emma turned to face him, but she refused to give him an answer.

"If you can walk, move your ass over to the control panel. Open this gate. Now. Do it." Everett looked dirty. He'd been doing a lot of the digging to get to her himself.

"No, asshole." Emma strolled as far away from him as she could get. She reached out to touch God's door, the entrance to the cell where He'd spent a good chunk of time. Maybe she was greedy for more. Maybe she wanted to get even farther from Everett. Whatever her reason, she wasn't expecting the heat. The white-hot force that had protected God's door from her last time still remained. She yanked back her hand to the sound of Everett's chilling laughter. She might be within God's love, but she could still be hurt. She refused to turn around and see victory in the Devil's eyes while her tears flowed from the pain.

"When I get you — and have no fear, sweet Emma, I *will* have you — I've got all sorts of plans for you," Everett ranted once he'd composed himself. "Can you imagine your worst fear? Picture it. Taste it. Smell it. Tell me what it looks like. No lying, ex-angel. Give me the satisfaction I crave."

Emma rubbed her hand. There were no obvious burns, though it felt raw. She was stronger now. Angrier now. She whirled and took the hallway like a furious runway model. Just out of his arm's reach she snarled, "Fear? I have none. I'm not afraid of you." She smiled when she realized it was true.

Everett looked as if she'd punched him. His head reeled, and his eyes rolled. He growled, looking at her. "I'll make you eat every word you just said. And I'll build them out of barbed wire and cobra venom. I have power over you."

"Power is perceived. Power requires belief." She shook her head, and her now-clean hair tumbled around her shoulders. "I don't believe in you."

Everett's neck was red and throbbing. "You will." He crossed his filthy arms across his chest. "When I have you bent over — "

"Stop. You don't even know what you're doing. Like right now? You've been trying to bust in this cell for how long?" Emma folded her arms the same way he had his. "Isn't there anything else the ruler of Hell has to do with his day? I mean, surely the minions are laughing at you. Instead of taking care of business like a man, you're here slamming yourself into this wall like a bird against a window."

Everett took deep breaths through his nose, expanding his nostrils like an attacking bull. "I do what I want, *when* I want." His biceps tensed. "What do you expect? You think Jack's going to save you? You think God cares about you?" He paused and obviously had a thought. An evil smile spread over his face. "You know what? You're right. I should go check on things. Make sure and all that."

He spun on his heel and was gone, leaving Emma puzzled. Whatever he'd just drummed up had him excited, and that made her nervous, despite her newfound courage.

JACK

"You can't go in there without a plan." Violent's voice was quiet, but it echoed.

Jack stopped in his tracks. "You're right." He turned and faced his companions. Everyone waited while he stood, thinking.

"If this is going to take a while, maybe let someone else make the plan?" Jason suggested.

Jack noted the half-breed still holding pretty Kate's hand. It made his own feel more empty. "Hell? It's like a dog. Anybody can feed it, but it knows who its master is. I may hate it here, but this place knows me. There's no safe place for you. It's been built to confuse, trap, and ensnare you — by me and plenty of other Devils just like me." He kicked the ground with his motorcycle boot. "Violent, you stay here with Jason and fight the fucking army that comes through when that door opens. Dean, you — the half-breed with the sweet ass, and the new girl come with me." Jack made a wind-it-up motion with his hand and headed off.

"Wait, Jack." Violent spoke again. "You know I'll need more than one. And I'm keeping that." She pointed at Dean.

Kate cleared her throat. "Why do I have to go with you? I need to get to Nero."

"Truly?" Jack asked, incredulous. What was all this insubordination? Being human sucked. "I was going to lock you two ladies in a closet until I brought down Everett." He ran his hands through his hair.

"And if you failed?" Kate's eyes were huge as she waited for a response.

Jack stilled. "The closet? It'd be safe for a week. Then you'd succumb to the nerve gas. Seriana would lose her memory. She'd be alive, but she wouldn't remember who she was."

Kate and Seriana's mouths popped opened in surprise. Dean and Jason took threatening steps toward Jack.

"That's a good plan, boss," Violent offered. She didn't appear to be kidding.

"He's plotting to kill us, and you like that idea?" Kate gasped.

Jack was pretty sure her eyes couldn't open much wider.

Violent shook her head. "This is Hell. The choices you make here are not... how would you put it? Normal. That's Jack being one of the fairest Devils this place has ever seen. Because if you're caught? And he's dead or incapacitated?" She shook her head. "He'd be saving you both a millennium of pain and torture your tiny little brains can't even fathom. And because of his example, if things go wrong, I'll end Dean and Jason if I can."

Kate pointed from Jack to Violent. "So if we don't die, you people are going to murder us? And that's you being *nice*?"

Violent gave Jack a crooked smile of admiration. "Considerably so." There was an awkward pause.

"I'm not dying in a closet," Kate declared and walked right up to Jack. "You promised me my father."

"If I live, and I'm the Devil, I'll save you from the closet, and you and Papa can have a big, sloppy reunion. But there are a million steps between right now and that moment, and I don't have time to waste." He stepped closer to her — to intimidate her, of course.

Kate tilted her head and put her hands on her hips. "I'm not all that attached to you, so for what's it's worth, I'm going to try to get to Nero on my own. You can go screw your death closet." She stomped away into the darkness.

The others waited, silently.

Finally she returned, still mad. "Could you at least point me in the right direction?"

"I'm not sending you in there." Jack shook his head and folded his arms.

In an instant, Violent flew to Jack's side, apparently shocking everyone but him.

He listened for a moment as she murmured in his ear, then shrugged. "Fine. Don't say I didn't warn you all. Seriana, Dean, and Violent, you're to guard the fingery hole. Asshole and Kate, come with me, and I'll send you in the right direction to meet a crazy, horrible end where you might get a glimpse of Nero."

Dean and Seriana hugged their brother.

"Don't die. That's all I'm saying." Dean pounded Jason on the back. "Same to you guys." Jason kissed Seriana's cheek.

Jack walked into the dark, cursing under his breath. "Hard enough to save an angel, never mind all these damn hangers on..."

Chapter 14

Seriana

Watching the fingers was a horrible job. Violent kept trying to snap them off while Dean and Seriana worked to figure out how exactly they were to stave off more than twenty half-breeds.

"I guess we can just run deep into that place." He gestured to the dark cave behind them.

Seriana nodded but looked distant.

"What's up? I mean, besides being in Hell and all." Dean tried to get his sister to make eye contact.

"I think I saw something. After Violent grabbed us. I'm probably just crazy. There was a lot going on." Seriana looked up at the gateway.

"What? Spill it." Dean wrapped an arm around her and pretended to give her a noogie.

She didn't react, just stared at the macabre wall. Dean put his hands on her shoulders.

Seriana bit her lip before whispering, "I think I saw Mom. I mean, that's impossible, right? But I think I saw her...and she was chained up by her neck. What if we just ran from our own mother?"

Dean rubbed Seriana's arms. "No, sweetheart. Mom would never try to hurt us. She would have called out or something."

Violent continued beating on the fingers while she added to the conversation she wasn't supposed to hear. "Oh, there's a woman in chains out there. She's getting quite a beating right now. I can hear their fists." She turned toward the half-breeds. "So, good news: maybe your mom wasn't dead a few minutes ago. Bad news: now she's probably dead. Good news: half-breeds make excellent fertilizer, and the tree out there looked like it could use a boost."

"What?" Dean ran to Violent and stilled her hammering with his hands. The remaining fingers continued wiggling.

Violent smiled as Dean touched her. "Do you have a photo? I'll confirm it for you."

Dean pulled out his wallet and presented her with a very worn picture of Rebecca.

Violent nodded like she was agreeing about the weather. "Yes. That's her. My condolences. Sounds like her death is getting brutal out there. I think I can still hear because of all these fingers breaking the seal."

Seriana shoved past Dean and Violent and positioned her hands in the center of the ring of phalanges. She pushed with all her might to open the gateway.

"Looks like I have to kill your sister now, love." Violent headed for Seriana.

Dean stepped in front of her. "No. No, you don't. Listen, just for a minute. Seri? Do you want to do this? Right now?"

Seriana looked over her shoulder and snarled, "They're killing my mother."

Violent cocked her head and spoke to Dean. "She does know she'll never move it alone, doesn't she?"

There was the distinct sound of stone grating on stone.

"Well, even if she manages to open it, I'll take you far from here, and she'll die too. But then she's with her mother, which is nice. The more fertilizer the better." Violent seemed conflicted.

"But I have to follow Jack's orders. Hmm... This is a tough one."

Dean looked her up and down. "Violent? If you help us save my mother I'll kiss you with tongue and an ass grab."

"Done." Violent stepped next to Seriana and put her shoulder into it as Dean joined in. The stone continued grinding and creaking as the minion and half-breeds dared to open the gateway from Hell. After a few moments the gateway groaned again and there was a discernible shift. The fingers were now doing their part to facilitate the opening, curling and pulling. But it took more effort than it should have, and Seriana realized Jack had waited for an exact moment before opening the hole.

She put her ear against the stone and tried to listen, blocking out all other noise. She could almost hear screaming. It was part of the history of the stone. The screams of Hellish torture had been absorbed by this rock, and it hurt her soul to hear them, but still she listened. All at once it seemed the screaming souls took a breath.

"Push now!" Seriana hollered, and then the rock really started to move. Violent grunted with the effort, and Seriana put every bit of hope she'd ever had for her mother into her shoulder and focused. The rock slid into the earth's atmosphere, and its space was filled by flying fists and teeth and legs. Crunching bones and screams of agony punctuated the battle.

Violent stepped through like a monster, clearing a way for Seriana and Dean. There were just so many half-breeds, and the ones missing fingers seemed the angriest. Some slinked into the now-open hole to Hell.

Seriana got low and looked on the ground. She locked eyes with her mother who, sure enough, was enduring a beating. There was a flurry of fists and her mother's body vibrated with someone else's anger. Despite it all, when she saw Seriana, she smiled. Pure joy emanated from her as she saw her child after so many, many years.

Seriana smiled back and took off. She evaded three different half-breeds aiming to decapitate her, then forward-rolled and landed near her mother's head. Seriana saw her grandfather's eyes go greedy and victorious as she began beating the ever-living shit out of him. But after a few moments Vittorio's relentless laughter stilled her hands, and Seriana looked around. Violent had Dean pressed behind her and stood like a lioness as a good fifteen half-breeds surrounded her. Several other half-breeds were making for the hole to Hell, trying to move as stealthily as possible. Seriana moved to stand over her mother's prone body.

"Look at you! Such a spitfire," her grandfather said. "You honestly opened that doorway to come back to me, child? I knew we were meant to be." He laughed again, then whipped his head toward the escaping minions and stilled them with a low growl. "Halt."

"Where does that hole lead, my descendant?" He turned back to her and smiled.

"Hell. Where you belong. Where I will put you." She turned from him and helped her mother from the ground. She hugged her gently, afraid of hurting her wounds.

"My baby." Rebecca's arms were chained, as were her legs, and Seriana's efforts to break them were futile.

"I love you, Mom." She pointed at her brother. "Dean's here too."

Dean had to offer a blown kiss because Violent would not let him move out from behind her.

"Jason?" Rebecca's voice was so slight.

Vittorio started clapping before Seriana could answer. "This reunion is so touching. Of course, now I need you no longer, my weak daughter." He raised his hand over Rebecca, but Seriana caught his arm on its descent.

"No. If you hurt her again, I'll never help you." As soon as Seriana spoke, Rebecca and Dean began shouting their disapproval.

The old half-breed paid them no mind, his gaze flickering

with power. "Help me? After running from me for lifetimes? Why would you do that?"

"Why doesn't matter to you, does it? I'll come with you and bear the off- spring you so desperately want. My price is simple. My mother, Dean, Jason, and Kate are never sought again. For anything." Seriana took a moment to look in Violent's purple eyes, then made a decision. "And the minion is free from you as well."

She almost smiled at Violent's quizzical look, and her mother gripped her arm with surprising strength.

"Seriana Marie Parish, I have not endured all these years just to let him have you." She slumped with the effort of speaking.

Seriana caught her. "Mom, you've taken more than your share. I'm not afraid. I can do this. I want to go with...Grandfather." It was such an obvious lie.

"Seri, no. Please." Her mother tried to reach out again with her bound hands. The cuffs she wore had rubbed her wrists to the bone.

Seriana's impulsive decision seemed like divine intervention. They were outnumbered, and more half-breeds were traipsing through the woods. Even with Violent, they weren't getting out of here alive. She pulled her lips into a tight smile and turned to the man she'd been so frightened of. He was really rather small. He should have been a huge, looming troll for the fright he'd caused her.

"Unlock my mother, and let me watch her get away with Violent and Dean. Then I'm all yours." Seriana held her mother steady while her grandfather roughly removed her chains with his key. At times he pulled the metal away from skin where they'd melded as one.

Violent growled and dragged Dean like a teddy bear as she made her way through the half-breeds, scooping up Rebecca in a swift motion. The minion picked up speed, scarcely burdened by the two adults she carried. Dean struggled and finally looked right at Seriana who yelled, "Don't worry!" as they disappeared into the trees.

But she'd never felt as alone as she did watching them leave. Vittorio tucked her under his arm and began ordering his half-breeds around. If Violent hadn't been physically stronger than Dean, her brother would never have gone. It was a crazy idea, but at least her mother was alive, and now she would be safe. Seriana had one hope left: that her brother would save Emma, and Emma would save her. She started praying immediately.

CHAPTER 15

KATE

Kate watched Jack's back as he walked confidently through Hell in front of her and Jason. She felt less and less sure about her decision to come here. She wanted to save Nero, but the deeper they got, the more unimaginable the task became. There were steel doors, hallways, and caves that Jack navigated easily, but Kate had already lost track of how many turns they'd made.

Jason counted out loud as Jack made another hard left and parted a bit of moss to step into a secluded cave. "I'm trying to keep up," he explained. "I think I can get us out of here." He held the moss for Kate, and when it closed, they were in blackness.

She reached in the darkness until she found Jason's hand. He squeezed back gently. He pulled her close when they heard a huge crash and the sound of wood cracking.

"Jack?" Kate huddled into Jason. Without her sight she was useless.

"Just getting some fucking supplies. Hold on." Jack's voice sounded muffled.

The flashlight blinded Kate for a minute until the beam was turned toward her feet.

"Catch, asshole."

Jason snatched the end-over-end-flying beam and handed the flashlight to Kate. She instantly felt a bit more comfortable.

"Here." Another light launched through the air, and Jason had to let go of Kate to catch it like an overthrown football. It was a lantern, providing a halo of light. Kate could now make out the walls, dark and slimy, and the cracks on the floor.

Jack emerged from the closet he'd broken into carrying a rifle and a few handguns. He had a strap holding extra ammo across his bare chest, slicing his tattoos in half.

"You took off your shirt? Who makes time for that?" Jason sounded disgusted.

Jack made his way back out of the moss covering and into the bigger hallway. "I do, teeny balls. I need some of my minions to recognize me."

Jason held out a hand to Kate again, and she took it. With all the testosterone flowing between these two, she decided not to comment, though she did feel a little protective of Jason.

"Really? Do you identify people by nipples alone in this horrible place?" Jason glared at the back of Jack's head.

Kate swallowed a smile, and Jason slid her a glance and a wink.

Jack spun and faced him. "I could say all kinds of things about how I can identify your ex-girlfriend's nipples in a lineup, but I won't because I like to treat her like a lady, now that she's mine."

Jason clenched his jaw and was about to speak when Kate changed her mind about commenting. "Seriously? Ladies, I've somewhere to be. Can we stop the pissing contest and do some freaking work here?"

Jack gave her a once-over. Kate tried to ignore the chills his attention sent through her. "Fine. Though I bet I could pick your nipples out of a lineup as well." Jack turned to go when Jason dropped the lantern and jumped on him.

Kate flailed her hands and flashed the light on them as they punched each other. Jason was stronger, but Jack was a dirty fighter. "Stop! Oh, my God! Stop. Damn it. Stop!" She had no idea what to do until she looked down and noticed her boobs.

She lifted her pajamas and bared the tank top beneath. "Look! Tits!"

The men stopped fighting to stare at her. The thin material of her undergarment was more transparent than she'd hoped.

Jack smiled. "Yup. That's just what I thought they'd look like."

Jason slugged him in the face again.

Kate put down her shirt and waded in. She was about to hit them with the flashlight when its beam illuminated a person standing just past the shadows. "Holy shit!" Kate tried to voice what she was seeing, but she could only point and wave a hand in the direction of the new being. Jason and Jack followed the light and stilled their frenzied fists.

The woman smiled as she stepped out of the shadows. Her hair was a huge beehive of spun yellow, and she wore a Little Bo Peep dress. Relief washed over Kate at the sight of this cotton candy cacophony. She seemed harmless enough. Then just as Jack muttered, "Oh, fuck," the woman turned her hot pink eyes on Kate, and she felt a power and terror unlike anything she'd ever known — which was saying something since she'd been in the presence of minions off and on throughout her life. Her mouth filled with a sweet taste. Too sweet. Crazy sweet. She started to paw at her tongue, trying to eliminate it.

Jack scrambled up from the ground, pulling Jason behind him. "Tiffany, great to see you."

She looked Jack up and down and laughed. It was a terribly pleasing sound. Like bells coated in perfection. She bent at the waist as emotion took her over. Jack took the opportunity to step backward, and soon he and Jason were in front of Kate. She raised her rifle to aim at Tiffany, but Jack grabbed the barrel and eased it down, shaking his head.

"Save your ammo," he said, and not in a comforting way, more in a holy- crap-something-worse-is-coming kind of way.

"Jack! I feel so happy in my happy places to see you." Tiffany had finally stopped laughing. "You look so...how do I say it? Oh, that's right. Human." She took purposeful steps, swinging her hips.

Jack nodded. "You look sweet. As usual."

"This old thing? You were always quick with a flattering word. Still stunning them stupid and spread-eagled with your bad-boy act?" The closer Tiffany came, the more it smelled like the taste in Kate's mouth.

"Act? Do you think the Devil is a good man, Tiff?" Jack began unbuckling his belt.

"You're not getting in, just so you know. All those years ago? This is called payback. What you want you'll never get. I'm going to leash you like one of my poodles."

Jack continued to undress, tossing his weapons and clothes in a pile next to his feet. He spoke over his shoulder to Kate and Jason. "This pretty lady is full minion. She actually descended into Hell about four hundred years ago, give or take. After her damnation, she was so heinous that I promoted her to protecting the sludge behind her."

Tiffany clapped and gestured to a murky pond that was so still it looked like just another length of cave at first glance.

Jack unzipped his pants and spoke to Jason. "You might want to have Kate close her eyes if you ever want her to sleep with you, asshole. Because once I take off my pants, you'll always come in second."

Kate instantly put out a hand to stop Jason from returning to fisticuffs. Out of the shadows, three huge beasts appeared. The first thing she saw was teeth. After she took in the rest, and they sat at Tiffany's command, Kate realized the things were poodles. Giant, grotesque poodles.

Jack was naked now, but Kate didn't spare a glance for his taut buns. Okay, fine. She did. He spoke to Tiffany, but was obviously filling her and Jason in on the details they might need to know.

"Well, Tiffany, pond still disgusting? I'm guessing Everett doesn't know about the potential here?" Jack stepped forward.

Tiffany held up a ringed hand, and the poodles growled in

unison. "No closer. You know what the water does. The new Devil knows about everything. He's fantastic. Ten times better in bed than you."

Jack shook his head and took a few more steps toward the pond. The poodles went from sitting to standing. Their dark gray fur must've been white at some point, but it just hung in dirty clumps and knots now.

"Lady, you can spout whatever you need to if it makes you feel better about letting me fuck you and toss you into the Hellfires, but you and I both know that's a lie." Jack sauntered closer to her, and Kate watched Tiffany's hot pink eyes dilate with arousal. She wanted him. The dogs hunkered down and bared their teeth.

"You had me," Jack said, his voice intoxicating. "And I certainly had you. You remember it with every fiber of your being. If you could dream, I'd be all you saw. And of course, when you touch yourself, you picture me." Jack finally pulled her against his naked body.

Jason looked at Kate and mouthed, "Wanna go?"

And she did. She wanted to leave Jack to his horrible romancing and steroidal poodles, but the fact that the pond was so well guarded had her curious. And the fact that Jack wanted in it meant something. She shook her head. Jason didn't seem to like that, but he stood fast.

"I remember it only to make me angry. You meant nothing." The thinly veiled lust in Tiffany's eyes belied her words.

Jack lifted his hand and ran it down her cheek. "Liar."

The poodles stepped closer.

"Care for a swim, Tiffany? I can give you exactly what I gave you four hundred years ago. Interested?" He spoke the words against her lips.

The poodles were completely fixated on the couple and furious with the man who had their owner in an embrace. Kate had a clean line to the pond. She had no idea what it might do to her, but she ran as fast as possible. As she whizzed by the nearest poodle, it turned and snapped its jaws at her. Jason was shouting, and his words soon combined with Jack's. None of them wanted her to get in the water. A bit wary herself, she'd only planned to wade in, but with the poodle and everyone else now hot on her trail, Kate dove straight into a pitch black pond in the center of Hell.

Chapter 16

Everett

Everett tried to settle himself in Jack's lair. *My lair*, he amended. He hated how much he didn't fit this place. It was like putting on someone else's well-worn shoes. No matter how they looked, they just didn't adapt to the foot properly. They were always uncomfortable. Just like her. *Emma*. She was his worst obsession. He'd followed her from Earth to Heaven and now, to Hell. She was right. He had other things he should be doing, must be doing, but it all paled compared to getting to her. He kicked a stray bottle, and it landed far away, smashing into shards. He was the second-most powerful force in existence now, after God. Or at least he thought so. While he taunted Emma about the lack of her perfect Lord, Everett was starting to think she was protected after all.

It'd been too easy. He'd never tell her that, but his rise to Devil was a farce, a joke. All these minions should've fought him for the position, but instead they set their weapons down and kneeled. At first it fed right into his monster ego. Then it became obvious he was a joke to them. Only a few would follow his orders implicitly. Most took quite a bit of harassing and nagging. There was a backlog of damned people floating just beyond his chamber door. Supposedly Jack had dealt with and sorted them, but Everett just didn't have time. The only thing that made any sense at all was that his tenure here in Hell wasn't supposed to be very long.

There was a knock on his door. He deepened his voice and admitted the visitor with a grumble.

"Sir? There's been a breach. Somehow things from the surface are entering Hell."

She was a gorgeous woman — legs, tight ass, all the things Everett liked. Her eyes were like foggy crystal balls. In his first few hours as Devil he'd tried to force himself on her, and she'd smiled instead of protesting. He'd found out why when he dropped his pants. His ball sack had frozen solid, and it had stayed that way long after he'd dismissed her, having had no sex at all. His piss had come out like liquid nitrogen for what felt like a million years. When he finally had sensation back and his pee was a normal consistency — except for the occasional ice cube he had to painfully pass — he vowed never to touch her again. Her name was Snow, which might've given him a heads up if he'd bothered to learn it before exposing himself to her.

He touched his man parts now in her presence because he couldn't help himself. "So? Why do I give a shit?"

She looked annoyed. "Simple job requirement, sir. You need to keep Hell and Earth separate."

"Screw that. I'll run my Hell the way I want to. If things get in? Eat them, flame them, I don't care. Leave me to my thoughts." He waved a hand at her.

"Very well." Snow turned to leave. Her "very well" was easily interpreted as "Wrong choice, ass-packing dipshit."

"What? *What?* Can you just tell me what's going on?" Everett begged. "I hate trying to pay attention to the nuances." He sat in one of Jack's lounge chairs.

She faced him and looked at his nuts through his pants. They prickled painfully. "Okay. You let things into Hell, things get out of Hell. Earth becomes overwhelmed and decimated. That ends the trial period. Heaven wins. You better man up and quick."

Everett rolled his eyes. "None of what you said has moved me to do anything other than fart." He accompanied his words with his ass's soundtrack.

"You are sharp as a spoon, sir." She walked to the center of the room and snapped her fingers. "Smoke! Here, smoke. Come on, be a good pet."

Everett waited for a dog or something, but the pet she wanted was atmospheric. Actual smoke came to her call and surrounded her like a blanket. He could hear her whispering to it. Things just kept getting worse. He'd long wondered about the blob of smoke that had occasionally appeared out of nowhere to nip angrily at his heels. Now it was helping Snow.

Soon there was a screen, and Snow sat down in an adjacent chair. "Watch this."

The screen flickered to life, showing photographs of a time long ago. God and a shady-looking character walked together on what seemed to be Earth.

"Lucifer was an archangel. Eventually he moved against God and tried to have Heaven and the power it gives all to himself." She gave him a snide look. "Sound familiar?" The screen changed to show Heavenly Court, with God in His proper chair and Lucifer standing in front of him, awaiting judgment. "They'd been good friends, so God really tried to get Lucifer to understand that all the power of Heaven was not a gift, but more of a curse. He explained that the burdens on his soul from his children's cries were far more damning than any Hellfire could ever be."

She was lost in the tale now, and Everett leaned forward as she recited God and Lucifer's age-old conversation: "I created them. Don't you understand? Sweet Lucifer, I'd love to pass the burden to someone else — even for a moment, even to you. But what you create, you must represent. I offer you a world with tremendous responsibility. Take care of the damned, take care of my children who attempted the tasks of life and failed. By squandering the gift of free will, they cheated themselves, and yet I still love them. If you choose Hell, you must keep my children fairly and punish them with a righteous hand."

Snow held her hands together in what seemed like a prayer. "Lucifer said, 'What else? If I don't take this offer, what else is there?'" The picture shifted to show a being clearly defiant, but with a hint of sadness. Lucifer had seemed to love God as well.

"Two options, Lucifer. Go to Earth and start fresh, start as a babe. Or I can end you. I can put you out of your misery if you find that being yourself is too much to bear."

Snow stood and gently touched the screen. The smoke rippled a bit before solidifying again. "He couldn't do it. Lucifer didn't have the guts to try life again. Nor did he want to be ended. So Hell became his playground — or so he thought. The Dark Prince soon found that doing his job, taking care of God's damned children, was a burden. Every decision he made or didn't make had far-reaching consequences."

Everett was getting bored, and his balls were getting scared. They'd crawled into him like frightened woodland creatures. "So? So what. Lucifer isn't here. I'm the Devil. He must have blown his big, long-suffering motherload."

"He transferred most of powers to whomever was appointed Devil or fought their way to the top of the heap, like you," she said, looking him in the eyes.

"So where is he?" Everett stood and walked to the door, silently willing Snow to leave.

"He's at the bottom of a pond, protected by an evil shrew. He doesn't want to be bothered." Snow strolled to the door, and the smoke dissipated behind her.

Everett held out an arm to stop her. "So what do you think he'd have done? I mean, how does Heaven win? I don't get it."

"Lucifer? He would have had a few minions patrolling the perimeters. Jack would've as well. If we can't keep up our end of Lucifer's bargain, God's done giving Lucifer a chance to prove himself." Snow touched his arm, and he quickly moved it.

"So we're done too then? No more Hell? Just...gone?" Everett weighed the options. Being gone didn't seem frightening.

"No, that'd be too simple. You see, Lucifer was a bargaining man. He liked to bet God for souls, and eventually we wound up with a winner take all: If Hell fails, we become nothing, but we'll always be aware, awake — never gone, just never here. I'm pretty sure we'd be located at the ass end of snails, our awareness and existence spread with their slime. That could be just a rumor, though. You know, people talk and stuff." She waltzed past him mumbling about how Jack would've been shutting this place down as she turned a corner and was out of his sight.

Everett leaned against the doorjamb and wondered. If he was just a substitute Devil, and the real Lucifer was an ice cube in a pond somewhere, perhaps he could convince him to give him more power so he could get to Emma. Everett left Jack's lair in search of a knowledgeable minion that might be willing to take him to Lucifer's resting place.

EMMA

Emma was still rubbing her hand as the pretty minion passed by, coming from the direction of Jack's lair. The woman had cloudy white eyes, but they didn't seem to be sightless.

"You look cleaner." She paused and tilted her head.

"Uh. Thanks?" Emma stopped nursing her hand.

"It's a waste, though. We're all about to lose. Everett's running this place into the ground, and things are getting in. I'm glad *I'm* not in a cage." She shrugged and continued walking, her heels clacking on the stone.

Soon after, Emma heard the lair door slam and Everett reappeared, looking even more manic than usual. "Well, bitch, enjoy this reprieve. As soon as I get back, I'll have all the power I need to tear you apart. And then I'll put you back together and do it all over again. Can't wait." He ran backward down the passageway until he was out of sight, smiling the whole time.

Emma was scared, because her hope had jumped to an impossible conclusion: maybe in the chaos she could get free.

CHAPTER 17

KATE

Kate was a fairly strong swimmer, but the "pond" was a viscous, thick mucus that instantly slowed her down. She treaded water — or whatever this stuff was — and turned to see Tiffany laughing so hard she wasn't making any noise. Jason kept trying to walk into the water, but he was repelled by some sort of invisible wall. Naked Jack just shook his head slowly and scanned the water around her.

Kate waited for something to happen. Jack had seemed Hell-bent on getting in this pond, and Tiffany and her pooches had been here forever protecting it. She'd assumed swimming in the water would give her some sort of power. She was wrong.

"Um, Jack? What's going to happen next?" Treading was getting harder. Her pajamas were heavier and heavier as they saturated with whatever this pond was made of.

Jason was now cornered by two of the three giant poodles. He shot frantic glances in her direction. "Kate, get out!"

"Can't believe she jumped in," Tiffany said. "Wow. This is going to be quite a show. Bet it sucks her skin off first."

Jack was the closest to the edge, and she could see his jaw clenched. "Kate, it's one minion at a time in there," he told her. "You've got to get out. He's gonna get you."

Kate was not wild about the idea of her skin being removed, nor the concept that "he" was coming for her. "Why did you want in this, Jack?"

Her mouth was barely above water now. Her ears had filled with the liquid, making it impossible to hear his response. Judging from his lips, he was mostly cursing anyway. This had been a dumb idea. She'd hoped for a boost of the powers her half-breed body seemed to be missing — just something to give her an edge when saving Nero.

She was just starting to swim for land when a hand grabbed her ankle and yanked her underwater. There wasn't even time to suck in a breath of air. She was under and flailing. This was it. Whatever had her was crazy strong and super fast. She tried to open her eyes to see what the Hell it was, but the mucous pond was as black as her eyelids.

All at once she was pulled out of the liquid and into a cave. There was air, so she took care of her need for that first. As she choked and sputtered, the liquid seemed to come out of every hole she had. She rubbed her eyes again and again until she could finally see. The cave was well lit, and she sat on an oriental rug. TVs flickered in the distance, and classical music seasoned the air with a false sense of serenity. Over her shoulder she noticed one of the walls of the cave was not a wall at all, just a sheer, floor-to-ceiling rippling edge. It was the pond, being kept from filling the space in a way not apparent to Kate. And a man worked at hanging a portrait on the wiggling wall. How he was getting it to stick, Kate wasn't sure. Finally he stepped away.

He turned and regarded her as she tried to make sense of where she was. He was average height, average looks, save for his bright red hair. His outfit would easily have gained him access to a business meeting without pause: a nondescript, dark blue suit.

"And you are?" He waited for an answer as if Kate had arrived for an appointment rather than being dragged through a Hell pond.

"Kate." She stood. She was unsure why this painfully normal

man lived in a Hellhole, literally. He nodded and sat on a comfort-able-looking couch. Kate waited in the awkwardness. The man obviously lived here, and there was no exit except the watery wall behind her. She took another look. The picture he'd been futzing with was a simple landscape, and it was staying put, even though it shouldn't have. *How do you nail something to water?*

Kate cleared her throat a few times, but it was obvious the man wasn't going to explain anything. "Uh, sir? Can you tell me why I'm here?" Her voice sounded harsh mixed with his delicate music.

"You want me to tell you why you jumped in my house? That's interesting." He turned his attention to the wall.

"I, well, I knew there was something powerful in the pond, and I was hoping to get it...to help me find my dad. So I guess I know why I'm here, but I don't know what I need to do next." Kate twisted her fingers together in a complicated knot.

He looked bored. "So you want me to tell you what you need to steal from me? That's interesting too."

"You're not going to tell me squat, are you?" Kate exhaled loudly. She really didn't know if she could find her way to the top of the pond without his assistance. Could she just walk through the wall of water?

He stood and came closer to Kate, his voice soft and soothing. "Do you know what your appearance means for me, Ms. Kate?"

His eyes were so much older than the rest of him. She took a guess because the silence seemed to demand it. "Um, you need to clean this rug now?" She gestured to the puddle near her feet.

He looked tired. "It means that Hell has a breach in security. It means I have to *do* something. I don't like *doing* anything."

"That makes you different from the Devil — or at least the last Devil. Jack likes to *do* everything." Kate willed herself to stop talking. The whole room seemed to be losing air as the man in front of her grew angrier.

Before he could answer, the wall behind her exploded. Jack tumbled through the liquid and came to stop, panting and still naked, on the floor near her feet. She fell to her knees and pounded him on the back, trying to expel the thick, slippery water.

When he managed to get a breath, he hissed, "Quit slapping me!" Kate stopped. "I thought it was only one at a time in the pond?"

Jack pushed himself to sit on his knees. "One *minion* at a time. Or half-minion. I'm human, remember?" Jack began coughing again.

Kate tried not to look between his legs. She failed.

In one instant Jack glistened with the glop from the pond, and in the next he was dressed in a suit that matched the other man's. And he was dry.

Jack stood and held out a hand to Kate. "Thanks, Lucy. Can you clean her up too? Put her in something revealing."

In another blink, Kate felt hands all over her body, drying her, dressing her. "Whoa." As soon as she registered the sensations, they were gone. She now wore a suit that matched the boys', right down to the blasé tie.

"You've no fashion sense for a dude as old as you are." Jack tsked with a disapproving look at Kate's modest attire.

"Don't call me that, Jack. You being human just exacerbates your failings. Now what are we to do? Hell is compromised, and I have to *do* something." The red-haired man shook his head and sat back on the couch.

Jack continued to talk, but his eyes drifted to the many black-and-white TV screens at the back of the cave. "Condemning me for failures, Lucy? That's fucking ironic. Where's the hallway I created? Show me that feed."

"Call me Lucifer instead of Lucy or your genitals will be my head covering." Lucifer's head turned from side to side as if watching an invisible tennis match.

Jack found a remote and began clicking through the channels with amazing speed. "Your neck isn't strong enough to wear my giant dick as a hat." He stilled. "There it is."

He stepped forward and Kate joined him in looking at the screen. The hallway he wanted appeared to be empty. "Where is she? Where is she?" Jack muttered the question under his breath, but Lucifer answered anyway.

"The captive? I haven't been watching. Everett's let everything slide since that one's been here — a huge backlog of souls to be sorted. This is unacceptable, Jack." Lucifer's head moved faster from side to side, but his words were clear, as if his mouth wasn't moving at all.

"Where is she?" Jack clenched the remote, knuckles white. "Swing the camera to see the rest. Is the gate down?" He whirled and growled with furious emotion.

Lucifer's head stopped moving, and Kate was relieved. She'd been trying to prepare herself for when it spun all the way around.

"You *left*, Jack. You were the best I ever had, and you left. Now you know what's next. I'm not ready for that. I don't want to *do* anything."

"Lucifer, you giant taint punch. Really? What's the worst? You're forced to lose? Your huge punishment is awareness forever? What the shit do you think you're doing now? You've been in this hole for eons. *Eons!* He's not changing His mind. God's been here plenty, and not once has He decided to cancel this bet." Jack tossed the remote into the wiggly wall. It absorbed the device with an audible suck.

Kate cleared her throat, and both men focused angry eyes on her. "Listen, your catfight is adorable. No, really, it is. But I need to get my father out of here, so do I get out through that disgusting thing?" Kate pointed at the wall.

They refused to answer and turned back on each other.

"Lucy, God's done being your friend. You've got to let it go. Stand up and be the fucking Devil. That's what He wants from you." Jack loosened his tie and slid it off, only to begin wrapping and unwrapping it around his wrist.

The red-headed man showed a glimpse of sadness, a tensing of his jaw. "He might come around."

Jack exhaled loudly. "Not with the whole damn place coming down around your ears. You're not even trying. I'm here. I'll help. Make me Devil."

The redhead stood slowly. "I can't do that. You have to defeat Everett."

"I'm never going to win like this." He motioned to his human body as if it were disgraceful. "He's a big, slobbering asshole, but there's no way…"

Lucifer whipped his head toward Kate. "She's an example of your failure, Jack. Her mere existence marks a lapse in security. Which minion was responsible?"

Jack shook his head just a fraction as he met Kate's eyes, and she bit her tongue, which had already curled around who and how many, preparing to announce.

"If there's blame it's mine. I'll take the punishment that comes with the escape and procreation." Jack looked every inch a general as he refused to condemn his minion. "But with all due respect, I was doing *your* job. If there was something you didn't like, you needed to get your ass off this couch."

Lucifer changed then. Suddenly he was way too big for the small space. His red wingspan was three times his size, his crimson body laced with tense muscles and tendons. Kate fell to her knees as his wing slapped her on the back, and lust hit her like a tidal wave. If fear of Lucifer's immense wings wasn't keeping her down, she would've been air-humping him like unneutered dog. In the next heartbeat her soul filled with hate and rage. Kate hadn't realized her body was capable of harboring so many poisonous emotions. As the giant Devil turned to address Jack, her body was released from his spell and the turbulent feelings he'd caused. She went limp. She peered up from the floor to find Jack still standing his ground, unflinching.

Lucifer's voice could only be described as rocks grating on stone. "You will bow before me, insolent one."

Jack fought it, but soon his body collapsed under the words that fell like lava from Lucifer's mouth.

"You can make me bow, but understand this: killing me will never solve your problem. I'm the only one who can fix it, and you know it. Unless you found your balls recently and you want to man up and run Hell?" Jack tossed the words out while seething on his knees. "Then it's on me."

There was an edge to the room then. A moment of decision Lucifer had refused forever. As quickly as he'd inflated, he deflated. "Rise."

Jack stood and dusted off his knees. He helped Kate up, whispering, "Say nothing."

"I'll grant you as much power as I can, but you know it'll only be half of what Everett has at best." Lucifer sat on the couch again as if he'd never been a winged beast at all.

Jack nodded. "You should rethink this. Before everything gets out of hand, ask for a meeting with God."

Lucifer almost smiled. "He and I were friends once. Almost brothers. I wanted to make Him proud." There was such aching loss in his voice.

"Lucifer?" Kate ventured. "Um, God seems like a nice guy. I bet He doesn't like that you're hanging out in a Hellhole." Kate winced as Jack gently grabbed a fistful of her hair, a reminder, no doubt, that she was supposed to be quiet.

"Ms. Kate. No one leaves this cave. Ever. The trip down is a sentence. Are you ready to be my footstool for eternity?" Lucifer held his feet up as an invitation.

"No offense, but it doesn't sound like you have eternity to threaten me with. Give me power, and I can help Jack." The hand in her hair loosened a bit.

"Ms. Kate, you speak as if you have something to bargain for." The man's eyes were creepy and endless as he held her gaze.

"Unlike you, waiting isn't my style. I'll go down in flames before I stand by and do nothing." She lifted her chin a bit.

"Very well. Come forward. All that's required is a kiss. Jack, you first." Lucifer tapped his lips at his sexy servant and smirked.

CHAPTER 18

JASON

There were so many reasons Jason hated Jack. Big, horrible reasons. One of them was having to deal with the huge, disgusting poodles that now surrounded him. If their owner wasn't hating on Jack so much, she might not be Hell-bent on feeding Jason to her dogs.

"Why is Jack human? Where did you come from? Why are you not full minion?" Tiffany's dogs growled with her every question.

"Jack's a human because he's a jerk. I'm half minion because I was born that way. And I came from up there." He pointed.

One of the poodles gave a deafening bark at his movement. He tried not to be rattled, but he didn't have a lot of composure left. Kate could be dead. Jack too.

"So what's in the pond? Are they ever getting out?" Jason stayed as still as possible.

Tiffany licked her lips and looked him up and down. "Don't think so. Surprising her skin wasn't sucked off. The few times anything has gotten past me, that's the first thing that happens." She neared a poodle and petted its dingy fur. "I wonder if it's time."

"Time for what?"

"Well, everything comes to an end, right? Maybe this is the beginning of the end." Her maniacal eyes seemed to have a gloss of sadness. "Maybe it's time for it all to come to a head."

Jason longed to make a move, do something to help Kate. He hoped that by keeping Tiffany occupied he was helping a bit. As if in response to his thoughts, he watched Kate surface in the pond. He kept a poker face as she struggled against the thick liquid, wondering what to do. He didn't want the dogs to get to her. "Bark! Bark!" he yelled.

The poodles immediately fixated on him, cocking their heads and growling. But Tiffany whirled around, looking for a disturbance. Kate clambered to the edge, filthy and dripping. She glanced behind her, and Jack popped up next. Jason continued barking and growling, and the poodles edged closer, despite Tiffany's protests and demands that they turn around. When Kate and Jack were both finally standing, Jack clucked his tongue and the dogs sat and were silent.

"Attack! Gem, Fifi, Buster, attack!" Tiffany pointed at Jack with all the venom a woman scorned could muster.

Jason stood and waited. Tiffany waited. Jack smirked and turned to Kate. "So, anything yet?"

She shook her head. "I've been trying to get clean since I pulled myself out. No dice."

Jason held up his hands in a shrug and a question. Kate mouthed, "Tell you later." He couldn't help but feel incredibly grateful she was okay, even if Jack had to be the one who saved her. He felt at home when he stood next to her. Somehow it was his natural place.

Tiffany let out a growl similar to her poodles'. "Jack, get over here and die like a man!"

Kate ignored her. "Wish I had a picture of you kissing that dude, though."

Jack gave her a dangerous look. "What happens in the Hellhole stays there."

Kate laughed, and the poodles lay down as if it was a

command. "Absolutely not. I'm telling everyone who holds still about how you and I made out with the same guy." She walked past Tiffany with confidence and petted the chest of the nearest poodle. Its tongue lolled happily out the side of its giant mouth. Then Jason watched as she turned and headed for him.

"Jack and I sucked face with Lucifer," she explained as she approached. She wiped her mouth as if trying to get the slime away from it.

Tiffany dropped to her knees as Kate passed, holding her head low in subservience. Kate stopped and gave her a wide-eyed once-over.

Jack caught up to Kate. "I did not suck face with him. It was a very chaste pressing of skin, like a handshake."

Kate pointed at Tiffany. "What's she doing?"

"All women get on their knees when my dick is near." Jack smirked.

Kate rolled her eyes and focused on Jason. "Sorry I'm so slimy. And I'm pretty sure now I can find my father without Mr. Oops-I-forgot-and-stuck-my-tongue-in-a-guy's-mouth over there."

Jason looked from the minion on her knees to Jack shaking his head and taking off a very slimy suit jacket.

"It was either the bad lighting or your extremely active imagination," Jack protested.

"There's a guy in that sludge? What's going on?" Jason took Kate's slippery hand and squeezed it gently. She was beautiful, even sopping wet.

Kate pulled him forward. "Doesn't matter. We need to head this way." She looked over her shoulder. "Good luck, super sucker!"

Jack squeegeed the slime from his hair with his hands. "Fine. Leave. As soon as I get Emma, I'll find you two. Try to keep Kate out of trouble, asshole."

Jason stopped Kate one more time so he could retort, "I'm not done kicking your ass."

Jack gave him a dismissive flick of his hand. "Whatever."

Kate yanked on his arm, and he was stunned by her strength. He kept her hand tight in his. She seemed to know where she was going. He was so damn grateful she was out of the pond.

"So did you see a map down there?" His head spun with testosterone, concern, and confusion. She'd gone into the pond one way and seemed to have come out another.

She pulled him through the dark with no light to aid her. When they were in complete blackness and the noises of Tiffany's poodles and Jack's grumbling were absent, she stopped him with a hand on his chest.

Her voice sounded vibrant and fearless. "I met the real Lucifer down there. Turns out Jack and that Everett guy just run the joint while Lucifer hides in his hole. They're like the night managers or something. I was going to spend the rest of my existence as Lucifer's footstool, but Jack goaded him into giving us a chance to stop the end of Hell."

Jason's eyes adjusted. He could make out her profile.

"Eventually, Jack and I had to kiss Lucifer and swim out. I think I have some extra power. I'm guessing that's why Tiffany kneeled? A little diluted Lucifer? But I'm thinking... maybe...well..."

Jason tried to keep up. He had a million questions, but they didn't seem to have too much time left, so he asked just one. "Do you want me to kiss you?"

"Yeah...sort of. Maybe you could get a dose? I figure Lucifer's germs have to be worse than a cold sore. Maybe the power's contagious?" She shifted her weight and Jason heard a plop of slime hit the rock floor.

He'd been praying for an opportunity like this, and although his memory was shot, he knew Kate's lips would be perfection. He pulled her hard against his chest. He could only make out her shadow, so he pushed his face in her direction just as she leaned in as well. They bonked heads. Both reeled and held their foreheads. *Great job. Real smooth.*

Kate recovered quickly and felt up his chest to his face. "Don't move."

She found his cheeks and leaned in for a sweet peck. She missed his mouth and kissed his chin. Jason started a soft chuckle, inhaling just as Kate found his lips. The small, chaste kiss was over before it started, but the power hit like a lightning bolt. His whole spine quivered. A wave from his toes to his chest to the top of his head filled him with a hot-and-cold explosion. He moaned softly.

"Did it work?"

He could picture her trying to gauge his response in the dark. He turned his palms toward her, and they began to glow. He could see her now in a hazy blue light. As he ran them near her skin he warmed her. He mentally pictured her in jeans and a T-shirt. Dry. Her hair bounced and curled as the slime disappeared.

"It worked! Check it out, you're a flashlight. And a clothes dryer!" She ran her hands appreciatively down her body, snuggling in the warmth.

Jason got a little Lucifer, a little Kate, and, as he lowered his lids seductively he realized, a little bit of that bastard Jack. He reached for her and pressed her against him. He came in for a kiss with the carnal need of a predator. Kate was wide eyed with surprise and then willing, letting him gather her intimately. Jason bit her bottom lip, licking as he went. He kissed her deeply, an exchange of passion and power. Electric. They both began to glow.

Kate pushed away and wiped her brow. "Wow. That's a kiss for you."

Jason ran a hand behind his neck. "Seriously. I could do that all day. Thank you."

She smiled at him. "Always so polite?"

He held out a hand, knowing they were headed for Nero, understanding Kate's internal compass now. "Only with those who deserve it."

They smiled at each other in their self-created light, looking to save a minion from Hell before the place died around them.

Jack

Tiffany popped off of her knees to go ballistic on Jack. "How dare you? First, you were the one who told me no one gets in the pond. Then *you* go in? Lucifer? All this time I've been guarding the first-ever Devil? Why wouldn't you tell me?"

Jack unbuttoned his shirt and let it drop in a sopping heap. He proceeded to undress near his dry pile of clothes. "Tiff, if you knew what you were guarding, you'd have jumped in."

She hopped from one foot to another. Her dogs rose from their Kate-induced stupor. "You're damn right I would. And then maybe I'd get my dogs and I — "

"And then you'd still be down there if you made it at all. Who'd take care of the poodles? You know they'd have been eaten by the dragon."

She hemmed and hawed as Jack finished dressing and tied his hair back with a leather tie. "Listen. I've done the best I can. That new guy? He's trashing the place." While he spoke, Jack approached the giant poodles. They growled but didn't snap. When he placed his hand on the first, it was instantly white and groomed, smelling of shampoo. The next poodle shied away, but Jack calmed it like a nervous horse. Then he laid his hands on its chest. It was a girl, so its fur went from dingy gray to hot pink. Jack winked at Tiffany. "To match your eyes."

She went from one to the other. "They look amazing. It feels like forever since they've been clean. Ever since you left they've been so dirty."

The last poodle held out its massive paw for a shake. Jack braced himself and caught it. The final poodle blossomed into a ruby red color, studded with sparkling gems. He dodged its giant tongue trying to show him canine love.

"All right, Tiffany. Take the poodles and go somewhere else until I'm in charge again." Jack nodded toward the cave close by.

She didn't move. He took her reluctance as resistance.

"We're, like, hours at best from Hell changing," he told her. "You know the rumor? That we'll become awareness with no corporeal body? Well, it's not a myth. You'll be separated from the dogs. None of us will be anything other than a tortured presence, even more than you are now." Jack readied himself for her blows, not sure how much power he'd gleaned from Lucifer.

She didn't attack, she just stared. "It was you. All this time. You've kept my dogs groomed."

Jack shrugged. He'd made sure her dogs had the best life Hell could provide. It wasn't great, but it was as much as he could muster. "Forget it. It was nothing. Just get out of here." He pointed the direction he wanted her to go.

"No." Her hair wobbled in its tower over her head. "My job is to protect the pond. I'll be doing it. And my dogs will help me. Nothing'll get past us." She stood tall, eyes blazing. "It's the least I can do."

Jack couldn't waste any more time. He had at least a chance at saving Emma now. He nodded at this ridiculous minion and her fluffy dogs. Hopefully her loyalty was a premonition of more to come. Jack certainly couldn't defeat Everett alone, and he wouldn't have time to connect this way with all his minions.

With one last look at Tiffany, he trotted off on the most direct path to his old lair.

EVERETT

Everett had to torture four minions to find the way to the pond. Snow had been vague, and when he saw her again, she too would pay. His had been a meandering trip through countless side tunnels before he could finally see the pond, barely rippling behind another minion and her three giant poodles.

He scoffed as he approached. The poodles set to growling, and they were so large the ground beneath his feet rumbled. "Enough!" he yelled. He tossed pain in their direction, and each dog yelped and whimpered. The flouncy pink minion set her legs shoulder-width apart and rolled her head on her neck. She looked like a fighter.

"Step aside. I'm getting in." Everett strode toward her and tossed another wave of pain at the dogs. "Shut them up. Do you know who I am?"

She nodded but remained waiting, looking ready to fight.

"Where's the respect? Jack let this shithole fester into a cesspool. When I speak, you will kneel. Now!" Everett had finally reached her. He was taller and stood over her, but she held fast.

He tried again. "*Now!*" Her knees wobbled a bit, but instead of showing submission, she pulled a sword from behind her back.

He figured out what it was just as the cold metal slid through his stomach. He fell to his knees, pain his only emotion.

The crazy, pink-eyed minion screamed at him, furious. "You never groomed my poodles!"

Things began to get hazy as the poodles closed in, their hot breath searing his skin. The bitch's blade must have been infused with some sort of poison. He had a brief flashback to all the animals he'd tortured when he was human, and he wondered if being disemboweled by giant, stupid poodles was some kind of karma…Then everything went black.

Everett came to just as the first poodle attacked his leg with its viciously sharp teeth. He hated pain, not to mention weakness. What was the problem here? He was the Devil, for fuck's sake. He focused all his power into his foot and lashed out. The giant poodle tumbled backward in a horrible flurry of flailing limbs. That was more like it. Everett sat up as the pink minion rained blows on his head. He swatted her away like a fly. She'd seriously pissed him off. He pulled the blade from his stomach and pinned her foot to the ground with it. She screamed, her mouth so wide he stuck his fist in it to shut her up.

With his free hand he slapped at the two remaining poodles until they cowered. They still growled but seemed to understand Everett was the top of the pack. The third finally pulled itself to its feet and slunk over next to the others.

Everett turned his attention to the minion and removed his fist. "Name?"

She hissed at him, and he punched her in the face, her spittle mingling with her blood. She sprawled, but remained close because her foot was stapled to the floor.

Everett grabbed her by the yellow hair and dragged her to her knees. "Name?"

She spit on his pants.

Everett pulled the blade free and backhanded her. He grabbed the nearest poodle and slit its throat. The dog tried to fight, but its lifeblood poured from the wound, and soon it was gone.

The minion wailed in horror. "No! No!"

Everett gave her a half smile. His body had repaired itself. He could do this all day — with pleasure. He walked to the next dog.

"Tiffany! My name is Tiffany. No, please, no. My dogs are everything." She crawled on her knees in his direction. His dick started paying attention.

"See, Tiffster? Was that so goddamn hard? If you'd told me right off the bat, you'd still have this heap of shit-making fur." He waited as she dragged herself to him, her foot leaving a trail of blood that eventually mingled with her dog's. He took a deep breath. He loved the scent of fresh blood.

"Now, let's make this easier. You tell me how to get to Lucifer, and I'll let the rest of your flea bags live." He watched as wariness crept into her eyes. She was having second thoughts. He leaned down close to her face so they were eye to eye. "Do I need to make you cry some more, Tiffany? I will." He put the blade under her chin and lifted her face.

Her eyes were wild. "My mandate is to protect this pond. By doing so, I'm following the Devil's orders. No need to hurt the puppies." Her gaze darted to the dead dog.

"You want that one back? I'll bring it back for you. No worries. Whose orders? Jack's? Lucifer's?" Everett took to one knee like he might be proposing.

"Jack's. Please, my dogs did nothing wrong. They do Hell a service. You need them." Tiffany dared to reach out and touch his bended knee.

Jack's name lit Everett's fuse, and he was furious all over again, "Why do people listen to that fuck nugget? He's gone. He left. *I'm* here. Best to bow to the power in front of you, not the power that's long dead." Everett stood.

Tiffany said nothing.

"Show me how to get to Lucifer. He and I need a chat." Everett pulled her to her feet by her hair. The remaining dogs growled. "Shut them up, or I swear to evil I — "

"Shh." With a calm voice and a quick hand signal, the dogs

were quiet and remained crouched. "All you have to do is get in the pond."

She would suck at poker. The obvious lie was a ploy.

"You first." He waited.

She shook her head. "Only true power can enter the pond."

He liked that, but it still felt like a horrible lie. He pushed her toward the dark water. She began to fight, but he managed to get her injured foot in. Nothing spectacular happened. He pulled her to him. She would only look at his chin.

"You're not being truthful. You're the shittiest guardian I've ever seen. Your weakness is so obvious. Why would you and these mutts ever be in charge of Lucifer?" He grasped her jaw and forced her to look at him.

Pride filled her eyes as she answered him. "You're the Devil. Everything here is weaker than you. This is your world, and I'm just a minion in it. But I protect this pond from everything else."

"That's right. I run this joint. So tell me what the Hell is going on in that pond." Everett pointed with his pinkie.

She shook her head. "You can't get in there. He'll kill you and replace you. He's in a pissy mood." She shrugged, and her poodles whined.

"Everyone keeps keeping things from me. First Emma. Now this. I just want what I want when I want it." He shook Tiffany, enjoying the sound of her teeth rattling.

"Emma? The angel? She's still trapped in the cage?" Tiffany managed to ask questions despite the rough treatment.

Everett stilled. "Yeah. You know something about that?"

"I know Jack programmed the cage, and everyone was super impressed with it. Best trap ever, so they say." Tiffany winced and stood on one leg. Her foot had stopped bleeding.

"Do you know the code?" Everett was almost salivating.

"Well, they say the code is something a person can never do in Hell. So maybe see the sun? Or in your case, maintain an erection?"

Everett's inquisitiveness melted into his anger. "Is that all you know?"

She nodded. But he had to be sure. Everett could only think of one lie detector: pain.

He smiled an evil smile at Tiffany before he jabbed the sword into her other foot. Her screams made his soul bubble with happiness.

CHAPTER 20

SERIANA

Seriana hated everything about the half-breeds around her: the way they moved, the way they grunted, but most importantly, the way they hunted. In just the hour she'd been traveling with them, four people had lost their lives. They did it with such reckless abandon, treating the humans like free candy at Mardi Gras.

And Vittorio was within an arm's reach at all times. When he wasn't shouting orders to the members of his army he was able to pry away from the gaping hole to Hell, he was whispering, encouraging evil. "So long I've waited," he rambled. "I wanted your brothers as well. I'll get them, though. I'd love to breed Violent too. The pure blood would work wonders on some of these diluted descendants. I bet if she mates with Dean, that offspring would be perfection. I must find them. First things first. I need to get you to the pen and notify them to ready the stud I've chosen now that you've been found." Vittorio gave her a look that felt like a complete genetic assessment.

"Clearly this is meant to be," he added, practically dancing with delight. "You're already in heat! Soon I'll lock him in with you. His temperament is fantastic," he continued like some sort of perverse matchmaker. "There was a bit of inbreeding so his manhood is overlarge, and he enjoys killing so much — not one care for society's perceived restrictions. I've kept him from any sexual conquests. He's not even allowed to pleasure himself. When he comes at you, I think his sperm will be carrying spears." Vittorio chuckled at his joke and grabbed Seriana's chin, stopping her in her tracks. "Your breeding will be the best ticket in town! I've already got a website up. Thousands'll watch you mate and whelp. Your screams of pain will be the cries that rally my armies!"

Seriana pulled her face from his hands. *It was worth it. It was worth it. Mother is alive. Mother is alive.* Despite her internal pep talk, tears rolled down her face. In all these years, she'd never been with a man. Now she'd be with one no better than a beast in front of countless strangers.

DEAN

When Violent finally set Dean and Rebecca down, they were miles from Hell's gaping, open mouth. Dean had struggled the whole way while Rebecca wept softly. Now he gathered his mother in his arms. She clutched his shirt with a weak hand. "Son."

He pulled her to the ground, cradling her. Violent paced, agitated.

"Mother." She looked awful. Being alive all these years at the mercy of Vittorio was obviously worse than dying.

"Where's Jason? Seriana — we've got to get to her." She began crying again.

Violent pulled Dean's hair until he looked at her. "My kiss? With tongue?" She puckered up.

Anger coursed through him. He pried his mother's hands from his and stood. Dean stepped into Violent's space, and her lips parted.

He grabbed her hair and pulled her mouth to his. He filled her demonic mouth with all his hopeless anger. He grabbed her ass and forced his tongue into her, blocking out the horror that in a remote way, he was related to this dreadful thing.

She melted in his arms, almost boneless. He reflexively held her weight until he felt his kiss was thoroughly done. Then he released her, and she fell unceremoniously on the ground. He turned back to his mother, who appeared to be drifting away in her weakness.

Violent hugged her knees with one arm and touched her lips. "It wasn't the same. It wasn't the same. It wasn't the same."

Dean was too angry to mince words. "Of course not. He's dead, Violent. There's no substitute for that."

She petted the grass next to her. "What else is there? If there's not this?"

Dean shrugged and tried to figure out where he'd get his mother some blood, short of killing someone. So much was unknown. Would he ever see Jason again? With a whole army around Seriana, how would he save her?

Violent stood. "I think I'll kill all the humans. That'll fix it."

Dean had been letting Violent's craziness roll off of him, but her words seemed louder now that he was so despondent. He whirled on her. "*You* did this. You ruined the world. How dare you think a minion could play house on Earth? You shouldn't be here. I shouldn't be here. You know your long-lost love? He would've married a nice girl, painted *her* pictures. They would've had babies that didn't *eat* people. Your solution is pillaging the world you've already shit on? How about you do us all a favor and go back to Hell where you belong?"

He shook his head. It was harsh, but it was how he felt. Maybe he could steal some blood from a hospital for his mother. He leaned down and lifted her into his arms. "Don't forget, Seriana included you in her demands to Vittorio," he told Violent. "Some thanks killing everyone would be. She'll be real happy she made sure you were protected. Do you even feel anything anymore,

Violent? Selfish bitch. If you really loved him, you would've let him be."

He started toward the lights he could see in the distance. Her footfalls were scarcely audible, but she followed him. When Violent finally walked next to him, stride for stride, Dean's explosive anger had subsided, replaced by planning in his head. As long as he was alive, he'd work to save Jason and Seriana. That's what big brothers did.

"I don't think he would've found another woman." Her voice was quiet. For a being so freaking old, she was as single-minded as a toddler. Maybe love had returned her to factory settings. "I ruined him in his dreams," she continued. "No human would compare."

She stared at him, even though they walked at a good clip. He ignored her.

"My love destroyed this whole world — will destroy this whole world. I don't know why I thought love would make things better. I should never have believed."

He was silent for a long while before he spoke. Violent's words made him think of Emma. She was so set on reassuring them that God loved them. She said love should make them see that their lives were tough, but worth living. This, in turn, meant that Violent was loved too. "Love never leaves," he told her. "So what will you do with the love you still have for him?" He finally looked into her crazy purple eyes.

She gasped. "I don't understand."

"As long as you love him, he's still here. That's what an angel said once." Dean pictured the scene he'd stumbled on when Emma had comforted Seriana late one night. Violent stepped in front of him, and he stopped.

"I'll take direction from you. Instead of killing everyone. For now." She bowed low.

"Really? Why the change of heart?" Dean stepped around her and kept walking, cuddling his mother's frail body to his chest.

"Because you care for your whelp mates and this bitch that

birthed you. I think Giovanni would want that." She seemed as resolute as she ever got. "Your mother needs blood, yet we're passing the humans by. Shall I get a few for her to feast on?" Violent asked the question like she was offering hors d'oeuvres to a guest.

"My mother never wanted to hurt humans. I won't force that on her while she has no control." He stepped up his pace as his mother moaned.

"Well, what's your plan?" Violent went from desolate to interested so quickly.

"I'm going to steal blood from the hospital. Then find my family."

Violent made a face. "That'll keep her alive, but fresh from the body is much better for her." She'd raised Lord knows how many half-breeds, and about this she was possibly the only expert. "How about a newly dead? The blood is still warm and fragrant, but no moral consequences." She smiled broadly.

"We don't have time to wait for that exact circumstance." He watched her carefully, not knowing how long Violent might remain affable.

"People are dying all the time! They're helpless little morsels," she assured him. "I'll be right back." Violent took off running.

Dean shook his head and yelled after her. "Don't kill anyone!"

CHAPTER 21

JACK

Jack followed the familiar path to his lair, scouting for minions where he knew they should be stationed. Soon enough he found that most had left their positions. Unchallenged, his mind wandered to wondering exactly what he'd been granted in Lucy's lip-lock bag of tricks. He shivered as he thought of the power kiss. Awkward, but effective. He just wasn't sure *how* effective. Regardless, Kate would never let him live it down. He wished her luck in his head. Her spunk reminded him of Emma.

Emma.

He'd never expected to make it this far. But to actually lay eyes on her, to hold her and save her from Everett, that would be a gift. He exhaled as he passed the entryway where the souls come down to be judged. There were tons of them, just hanging in midair. A few were huddled in corners of the hallways, confused. Jack scoffed. It was just flat-out cruel to make them wait to understand. The souls deserved to be sorted, to know what was coming and how their life had ended.

Some called out to him as he passed, but he ignored them. He had no time. Everett had to be close, and he assumed Emma would be in his chambers. He closed his eyes as anger and worry washed over him. It'd been weeks. His angel would be so broken now. Even a half-wit like Everett could use the Devil's most basic skills to render a soul useless, empty.

He broke into a light, quiet jog until he reached his own front door. There should've been a better plan, but he just wanted to bust it down and fight. He kicked the doorknob, but the door wouldn't budge. As he trotted back a ways to give his old boot a running start for another blow, he heard her voice behind him.

"You bastard. How dare you? Of all the things…"

Jack whipped his head around so fast he made himself dizzy. There was the hallway he'd created, and there was Emma, staring at him with tremendous hate. Emma was here, alive, coherent, and feisty. He dropped his weapons. He put a hand against the wall to steady himself. Emma was alive.

"Forget it. You might as well go back in there and whack off — preferably with a cactus, wankero." She crossed her arms and leveled a venomous look at him.

He staggered toward her. The gate was engaged, and he started to piece it together. Everett had tossed Emma in the hallway, and somehow the gate had dropped. She was in the trap he'd designed to keep her in the hallway on the off, off, off chance she escaped his lair, but she was also protected from Everett. He had her all tarted up in a cheesy French maid costume, but she looked healthy and clean. Relief flooded him. If he could just get her out, she could make it. If she was angry, she was thinking and feeling. She wasn't empty.

Holy fuck she was beautiful — *is* beautiful, he amended. All this time he'd remembered her scent, her smile, the way his insides hummed when she said his name, when she said she loved him, but he'd forgotten how stunning she was. Long blond hair, stormy gray eyes, soft skin. The slope of her nose was perfect, her rose-tinted lips were the exact color of a kiss.

"Hey, pretty child. You're a sight for sore fucking eyes." Jack approached the cage, afraid she might disappear.

"Don't call me that. And don't think you could ever pretend to be him." She took a step back as he got closer.

She should be in a plague, hunched over and dying from the inside out. Instead she lifted her chin in defiance, even if she was confused.

"Listen, most sexy angel, I don't have a lot of time right now. I just want to get you out of here. You can tear me a new one when we get up top." Jack tried not to feel the crushing disappointment of this bittersweet moment. He wanted to kiss her hard, sweep her behind him, and growl at the world. Instead it was all business, and she didn't even believe he was himself. "Just go over to the panel. I'll give you the code, and we'll make tracks."

She shut her eyes like his words were knives. "Screw you. I'll *never* open that gate. Everett, you crazy bastard, Jack doesn't even remember me. So take off his face. You don't fool me, and you sure as shit aren't fit to wear it." She opened her eyes and very deliberately looked above his head in abject disinterest.

"I love when you curse. Don't ever stop." He stepped as close as he could and reached his hand through the bars, fingers brushing against the first plague. Softly he added, "I'm not him. He's not this clever. What can I say to convince you?"

She looked wary. "Nothing. I set it up so Jack was free to be a good man."

"You tried. I remember you taking the punishment. It plays on a loop in my head. It's all I have." He tried using their last promises to each other to win her over.

"Everett heard that." She took a step closer to him.

"Yes, he did. But would he know that when you pictured me in the pause you put me in sunshine? Did he know you tossed your sundress above your head, and it caught in the trees? Does he know you're the most stubborn, beautiful, selfless girl that I love?" His voice broke with emotion. He swallowed it. "Does he know that?"

With every question she stepped closer. He watched her body for evidence of plagues, but nothing made her twitch, and he was grateful. Jack tossed his weapon on the ground and pushed his other arm into the cage. Both arms opened for her.

"If this is a trick, it's the worst one." She had hope in her eyes.

"I wouldn't trick you. What can I do to ease your mind?" He wanted to feel her in his arms. He needed her free to keep her safe.

"The smoke. It hates him."

She was almost in his reach. He could smell her clean hair when she flicked it off her shoulder in a nervous gesture.

Jack clicked his tongue once. The smoke seeped through the cracks in the chamber door and flooded toward him. He staggered a bit as it hit him in the back, surrounding him. It made happy little hurricanes around him.

She started to smile, but she was hazy through his translucent pet.

"Show her how I feel," he snapped, and his smoke created a flashing, always-changing show for her. There was a heart shape, a rose, the intertwined symbol of eternity. Then it shifted into a giant, realistic penis, followed by breasts. "A little too much," he snapped again.

"It's you!" She took the few short steps at a run. They struggled to get a hold on each other through the bars.

Jack gathered her against him, metal pressing into his skin. "Emma."

He kissed her cheek and dug his hands into her hair, then skimmed his fingers down her back to give her a proper hug.

They sighed together. Such contentment, Jack had never known. Here, in this damned place, he cradled the most fragile thing. "My love."

She pulled her face away from his and threaded her hands under where his hair was bound from his face. Hungrily she looked at every inch of him, then found his eyes. "Jack, you were supposed to forget. You've got to get out of here."

She was trying to chastise him, but her smile made her words a welcome.

"I told you I'd find you. I'd fight dragons for you — forsake everyone, trick the world, anything." Jack leaned toward Emma, and she looked back now with no fear in her eyes.

"Kiss me," she said.

Emma watched the victory in his deep brown eyes. Him. Jack. He was here to save her, and damn it, she was totally ready to be saved. She put her face next to the bars and pushed her lips forward, but they managed only to flutter against Jack's. She pulled away, laughing, and laughed harder when she saw Jack with his lips also extended — looking more like a camel or fish than the rush of lusty endorphins he usually was.

"Stupidest kiss ever," she declared.

His eyes popped open, and he chuckled. "I owe you a good, wet one. What's up with this? Why are you okay? Get over to the panel, and I'll give you the code."

She shook her head. "Where God walked? That's safe. The panel's in a plague. Hunger."

Jack left her reluctantly and made his way down to get a better look. "Well, I can't reach it. Smoke?"

His smoke seeped through the bars but could not make itself corporeal enough to press any buttons.

"I'll get there," Emma said. "Just...encourage me and stuff." She shook her hands to get the nerves out. It didn't work.

"Walk close to the edge here, and I'll push you along if I can. I'm so sorry, Emma."

"Don't be. Your little prison has kept him out. He hasn't had a chance to do anything to me." She smiled at him, then faced her goal.

"I'm glad." He murmured, poking a finger through to caress her cheek.

She inhaled the scent of him and tears came to her eyes. "You're really here. I thought I was alone forever."

"Never. You're never alone. I'm here."

She could tell he was worried. He kept glancing over his shoulder. She stepped out of God's path and instantly the hunger crippled her. She wanted to eat so badly, and her stomach turned inside itself in a fury of need. Jack's hand stood guard at her lower back. He pulled it out when the bars blocked him, only to touch her again in her next step. Her focus on his hand became her guiding force, for despite her time on God's path, the plague tore her apart. Her human body was so weak. Finally, finally she was able to see the control panel.

He couldn't reach her anymore, but all she needed to do was press the right letters, and then they could be together. She could do it. She focused and pulled her hand to the panel.

"Okay. Great. You okay?" Jack asked. "Never mind. First, type 'I love dick.'"

With more spare energy, Emma would have rolled her eyes, but instead, she pressed the buttons.

"Now, press twelve, then: Satan rocks."

The panel beeped, and its screen blinked: *Final step, to lift gate, enter code.*

Emma looked toward Jack to make sure she'd understand his next, all-important words. She screamed as Everett slammed his face against the bars, and her handsome knight in leather armor slid to the ground.

CHAPTER 22

JACK

Jack felt his legs give out and cursed his own stupidity. He should've been watching his back. Instead he'd been enraptured by an angel. Everett kicked him hard, and Jack knew before the impact with the wall that it was going to hurt. As the pain hit, so did a blinding white flash that stole his consciousness.

He woke when his smoke invaded his body and opened his eyes for him. He reflexively breathed his pet out. He took a quick assessment and closed his eyes again, using his eyelashes as a shield. Everett was against the cage yelling at Emma. She'd propped herself up against the panel, enduring hunger still.

"You bitch. Open the door! Punch the buttons, slutbag."

Emma sounded weak in voice, but strong in conviction. "You bet your sorry ass I'll open this gate. Then I'm going to kill you."

Jack almost smiled. He knew she'd never figure out the code, and that was good. She was safe in the cage. As soon as he had Everett where he wanted him, he'd test his Lucifer-given powers.

"The dog whore told me the code was something no one could do in Hell. That give you any hints?"

Jack stifled a smile again. Under other circumstances, it

might've been comical, Everett and Emma both wanting the same thing, yet denied.

"Well, smell your horrible balls isn't the answer, then."

Jack had a feeling Emma was using precious energy to give Everett the finger.

"You know what? I'll just beat it out of your girlfriend," he announced.

Jack watched as Everett stomped in his direction and managed to catch his leg as he came in for a kick. Everett flipped backward, and Jack felt his broken ribs knit back together. Okay. At least he was strong enough to push Everett around and to heal.

Emma began punching buttons on the control pad.

Everett rebounded quickly and gathered the darkness. He bound Jack tightly within it like a straitjacket. This pissed Jack off for numerous reasons, but the worst was that if Everett had figured out how to use the dark as a weapon, Jack might have more of a battle on his hands than he could fight.

Emma

Emma could barely see past the hunger. Everett's stupid hint had whittled the code's options to, oh, only a few million choices. She tried to focus despite the fact that Jack was now fighting Everett mere feet away. *What couldn't be done in Hell? Pray?* No, she'd done that.

Everett recovered from Jack's last blow. She tried again to tune them out and focus, but tears filled her eyes as Jack grunted in pain. She was so damn close. He was here. He was here. She typed in a word: D-I-E.

Jack hollered, "Don't you dare press buttons!"

She shook his words out of her ears. The panel beeped:

Denied. Two MORE tries, sucker.

Emma wasted energy looking for Jack. He was on the floor, face red, with Everett's muddy foot on his neck.

"*Stop!* Everett, stop! I'm pressing buttons. I know the answer. I know the code." Hunger made her words sound raw.

Everett lifted his foot and came close. "Really? What the fuck is it?"

Jack rolled onto his stomach and scrambled toward the guns he'd dropped when he first locked eyes with Emma.

*Something that can't be done in Hell...*She wanted to try "happiness," but she'd felt that when Jack arrived. "Shit." Hunger threatened to drag her to her knees. She locked them.

"She can't tell you, cooch waffle," Jack taunted. "She doesn't know and will never figure it out. You're gonna have to beat it out of me." Jack pointed a huge rifle at Everett's middle.

Everett turned like an angry bear in a cage. "You know what? That's a great idea."

Jack fired the gun, and the walls rattled with the explosion. Emma tried to think. *What can't I do?*

Everett didn't slip to the ground like a dead man should. Instead he faced Emma briefly to show her the bullet he'd caught in his teeth. He was laughing around it. Jack kept firing until his gun was empty. Everett let the bullets he'd caught fall from his hand to the floor.

"Come to papa, you weak-nutted boner," Everett announced. "I'm going to screw you in the ass."

"You have no idea how taunting works, do you?" Jack caught Emma's eye and mouthed, "No, you don't."

She figured out what she couldn't do: F-I-G-H-T.

She waited. The panel beeped encouragingly:

Success! Stand back!

There were even some grinding noises that sounded promising. Jack used the distraction to run at Everett and start swinging. The panel beeped again:

Not really, loser. One try left.

Emma would've punched the panel if she could've. Instead she collapsed to the floor and dragged herself back to God's path. She needed some clarity. Her blood pounded in her ears, her stomach distending with the hunger. By the time she pulled herself into His comforting reprieve, Jack was taking a horrible beating from Everett.

His sick smile was familiar by now. He was having a good time as he flung Jack from one edge of the room to the other. Emma barely noticed that her hunger was satiated now that she was in God's path. All she could do was flinch and yell, begging Everett to stop hurting Jack. In all her time in Hell, she had never felt so helpless. *Think, think.* She needed the code.

Everett had somehow beckoned a handful of minions. They seemed reluctant when he demanded they haul Jack to his feet.

Jack spit out a blob of blood and looked in Emma's eyes. "You stay there." He ignored Everett's threats and orders to the guards, and tried to smile at her.

"This isn't how it ends. I didn't do all this to see you hurt here." Emma stood and ran to the bars, trying to get closer to Jack. He was swelling up, bruising. His long hair covered part of his face.

"Keep praying. God won't forget you," he said.

With that, the guards dragged Jack away. His smoke followed, looking droopy, and the door to his lair opened and closed. Emma stepped back just before Everett could get his hands on her.

He grunted in frustration. "Whatever. I'm going to get you. Do you know what I've planned for that asshole?"

Emma shook her head. She was sure he was going to tell her.

"Humans can't die in Hell. Amazing, right? But you already

knew that. So I'm going to skin him. Then I'm going to remove each of his organs, one at a time, and burn them in the fires. But the best? I'll leave his head intact, so he can watch as it happens. And how soon do you think he'll give you up? Pretty damn soon." Everett stepped back and grabbed his genitals. "Say hello to your new king: my penis. You'll be worshiping it until the end of time."

Emma shook her head. As soon as Everett closed the lair door, Jack's screams permeated the air. She sound of his terror etched itself into her soul as she scrambled for a way to save him. Seeing him here was ridiculous. Jack was supposed to be safe. That's the whole reason she'd come here. It was getting so very hard to make one thought connect to another. Jack's hollering was obviously involuntary. Emma's tears covered her cheeks. She knelt and tried to pray, but all she could do was cry and clutch at her heart. She had to try one last time. The code — but if she got it wrong, she was stuck listening to her love die a thousand deaths.

"Stop it. Stop it. Stop it." She knew Everett couldn't hear her, nor would he care. But she had to put her wishes into the world. If she were still an angel, she could protect Jack. Her gaze trained immediately on God's door. The memory of ripping off her own wings was metallic in her mouth, like blood.

But they might still be weighing down the scale God had been sitting on when she rescued Him. They must be. The one thing that mattered to God was that one of his children's souls would be lost if he stood. And He'd refused to tell Emma whose soul was in jeopardy. All she could think about now was her wings. It was a chance. Perhaps the wings were still there, perhaps they could do something on their own.

She looked at her hands. Her punishment was to be here, in this place, at Everett's mercy. But screw it. Jack's screaming had no words, only intense agony. Emma stood. She would stop at nothing. Jack had fought dragons for her. She could walk through fire for him.

She strode with purpose and hardly flinched as she reached

for the door handle. It had not been locked last time. Her body began to shake, and the primal part of her brain bucked. Her human body knew to stop itself, so her brain had to be willing to override.

It seemed to be willing until the first licks of invisible fire ate her skin like fuel. Then she could feel her brain crumpling like burned paper, turning black and ashy. Only her heart could move her now. *Jack.* He was so close, yet being tortured. *No.* Not her Jack. Not while she still lived. Emma pushed herself through the flames. Her air became tainted with the dying. There was no smoke, just the hottest, melting flames. It took all her life, courage, and love to touch the door.

Her skin cooled, and Emma cried the tears of a young girl, where pain was liquid. But she opened the door. She realized, as she shuffled, that she'd remained on her feet. She was stronger than last time. She staggered into God's old cell like she was on a boat in a cyclone.

All of her senses were jumbled, but once her eyes adjusted to the dark, she found hope. Her wings were still on the weighted scale. She turned to the meter on the wall. The soul was still in balance. *Now what?* She was a human. Those were angel wings. But unless she could use them as a weapon somehow, she was still stuck. Emma realized her ears were no longer filled with the dull roar of the flames when Jack's anguish announced itself again. So very loud. Then she heard Everett's voice. "You think you're tough, asshole? How about I make you cry in front of her? She can see what kind of man you are."

Emma closed the door quietly, hoping the movement would go unnoticed. *Let Everett think I've escaped.* She could hear Everett's anger and frustration despite the closed door. She exhaled. Her decision was made: defy God's wishes for the soul in jeopardy and steal back her wings...somehow.

"I'm sorry, Father. I have to try everything." Emma climbed up on the bed and lay carefully on top of her wings. She closed her eyes to the sounds of more grunts of pain from Jack and anger from Everett. She needed to think like an angel.

She waited and thought. Just having her wings under her cleared her thoughts. The feathers. The feathers have power. She reached underneath her arm and pulled a feather out. She examined it briefly and then thought, *Knife*. She tossed the feather, and it solidified in the air, glinting with silver, and embedded itself in the wall. The bit of stone surrounding it turned gold, as if being poisoned with goodness.

I'll just take handfuls of feathers, and maybe I can hit some of the minions through the bars. Or disable the keypad. She sat up to get some handfuls when it started. It was a familiar feeling. She'd lost and gained her wings a total of three times. This version was diluted a bit, but the joy made her gasp and smile. God's love turning tangible cannot be denied. It was a wedding day, a birth, and a death all at once.

Emma peeked over her shoulder. Her wings were attached. Her flouncy French maid's costume lengthened into a long satin gown. She hugged herself. "Thank you. Thank you. Thank you." Emma hoped it wasn't a glitch. Just taking feathers was no longer an option. Her wings had attached. She looked at the meter. She had to get up. And the anonymous soul in jeopardy would slip away. Jack's screaming grew even louder.

She made her choice. She stood, and the little flickering light, so much like a candle, faded away. It was a simple, emotionless action, but Emma wanted to mourn the soul God had been so devoted to. She sent up a quick prayer for the departed, then shook her head and went for the door. She yanked it open and flew through the fire as fast as her wings would take her. The plagues were speed bumps, but she weathered them quickly.

She returned to the bars and craned her neck to see Everett standing with a stupid look on his face. He sensed her and stood aside so she could see the small, huddled man at his feet in the doorway of the lair. Jack was still breathing, but the skin was gone completely from his chest and arms. He was only tendons and muscle. His face twisted in mind-melting pain. She yanked on the bars. They didn't budge.

Everett laughed. "Look at that. You have wings but still can't get out? Isn't that precious? Look, boys! We can pin her wings to the walls like a freaking butterfly. Love it!" He had to hold his knees with the hilarity.

"Jack, tell me the code. Please." Emma got on her knees by the bars.

He was too far away to touch, but his eyes locked on hers as he shook his head. "Never."

Everett bent down as well. "Awww...You wuv him. Take his face off, boys."

Jack began to struggle as two of the minions reluctantly positioned themselves. And then she knew. Emma knew the code. There was one thing that seemed impossible in Hell, especially for her Jack. But with her wings firmly secured, Emma knew it could be done. She rushed to the panel and typed the letters: B-E-L-I-E-V-E. The second she hit the E, she flew to the gate and waited. She smiled a victorious smile as the gate began to creak and groan, slowly lifting.

Everett and the minions stopped tormenting Jack as he swore loudly. "Damn you, Emma."

The gate opened painfully slowly, but she had their attention, so that's all she needed. She stepped back a bit and Everett made a greedy, come-here gesture with his hands. Before the gate was open enough to allow him through, Emma reached over her shoulders and pulled two handfuls of feathers from her wings. When she threw them, they whistled through the air, sounding like angry harps. They stuck true in every target, and the gold began to spread. Concentrated goodness poisoned the evil each feather had embedded in.

She'd made sure two feathers would lodge in Everett's chest and another three in his groin. His screams were much louder than Jack's. And the minions were pinned to the floor or walls. They looked desperately for a way to dislodge themselves as the feathers began to smoke with glitter and light. Emma took a running start as soon as the gate was open enough to fit under. She wasn't sure where to go next, but far from Everett felt right. She swooped low and gathered Jack in her arms, grateful that she was angel again and strong enough to lift him.

His arms hung limply, and he whimpered as she touched his bare, bloody muscles. Her tears formed again. She was grateful to have him but overwhelmed by his sacrifice for her, and so very sorry for his pain. She took the caves of Hell at high speed, making random lefts and rights until Jack whispered for her to stop.

She landed as gently as possible and set him down. He collapsed to the floor. The thought of his bare muscles touching rock made her cry again. She knelt next to him and one of her tears, glistening with gold, slipped from her chin and landed on his chest. A small dot of skin appeared.

"I can heal you!" Emma sat back and focused. She held her hands over his body and pictured the golden energy of a seraph. His skin regenerated, fresh and new, flowing over his muscles until he was whole again. She evaporated his pain, replacing it with the intense love she felt for him.

She covered her mouth with her hands when he was whole and whispered, "Thank you, thank you, thank you." She knew God had allowed this to happen. He'd let her have her power back in Hell. She pulled Jack off the floor and into her arms, cuddling him. She wrapped her wings around his body and hers, forming a feather-filled cocoon.

He opened his eyes. "Is this a dream? Did I pass out?"

Emma leaned down and touched his face. "No." She kissed him over and over.

"Are you sure?" He stretched out his arms and touched his chest, sitting up as he did so.

Emma kept him in the cocoon, but sat back and let him assess the situation. He must've been out of his mind with pain, and yet he never gave her up. "Do I normally wear clothes in your dreams?" she asked him.

"Pretty child, it's real?" He laughed then, a sound filled with relief. "You're real?"

She nodded and touched his chest.

He scrambled to his knees and pulled her into a welcoming kiss, full of all his talent — and victory.

Chapter 23

Seriana

Vittorio smiled a deranged smile as he paraded his granddaughter into the chamber. His old, bony hand squeezed way too tight, but Seriana refused to complain. Or cry. Emma had sacrificed so much. She could too.

The cage was in the center of a small arena, surrounded by old theatre seats arranged in the round. Vittorio nodded as a half minion with dark, greasy, long hair followed her into the cage, and it was locked behind them. Seriana held her head high as the room filled with other rowdy half minions. After a few minutes Vittorio silenced them with one long finger in the air. He didn't need a microphone. His voice was plenty loud now that he had the floor.

"I've removed the other cages. There'll be only one mating." He took a sly look at Seriana. "For now."

The crowd rumbled their disapproval, and Vittorio snapped his fingers. "Have you forgotten, young ones?" He walked to a huge covered box. He pulled the black velvet from it with a flourish. Inside, a beast jumped at Vittorio. The old man stepped back just in time.

After closer inspection, Seriana realized the beast was a man: a dirty, huge, powerful man. His eyes were crazed, and his growls shook all of her courage.

"We have this." Vittorio was more a circus ringmaster than anything else. "This being is the closest we've come to a full-blooded minion. His bars are comprised of the bones of our fallen, the only thing strong enough to hold him in."

Seriana watched as some of the half-breeds mouthed the words along with Vittorio. They'd heard this speech plenty in the past.

"He's not eaten in at least a year, but as you can see, he is adequately prepared." The beast growled again.

"Fiaon, disrobe the bitch." The half-breed in the cage with Seriana approached.

She whirled and stepped into a fighting stance. "The Hell you will."

Vittorio drew close to the cage, clucking. "We had a deal, Seriana."

She responded to her grandfather without taking her eyes off the other half-breed. "You just told everyone here that my brothers were in danger again. You don't keep your promise, I won't keep mine."

He lowered his voice. "This is a volatile crowd, darling. I've got to give them hope. You're my blood, but they're my vestals to power. Just disrobe and prepare to be mated. That's not too hard, is it?"

Seriana looked around the hostile room and swallowed. She could fight the half-breed in her cage, but not the entire army. She shook her head and dropped her fists. She never imagined she'd be doing a striptease in a crowded room, but that's just what she had to do. When she was completely naked, she refused to cover herself, instead pushing her shoulders back with pride.

The beast in the next cage began to howl and claw, his arousal poking through the bars in his desperation to get to her. Fiaon slipped a simple white sheet with a hole for her head over Seriana.

After loud boos at the covering of her nudity, Vittorio tsked at the crowd. "Would you have him kill her before he puts the seed of our world domination in her belly? Are all of you that stupid?"

Chastised, the crowd quieted. Fiaon stepped out of the white cage and locked the door again. Seriana didn't know what to expect, but a hush came over the crowd. The experience she was about to endure seemed to hold a religious wonderment for them. A dozen half-breeds approached, all wearing white. They began to push the cages together. The beast in the other cage stopped all movement and stood, just breathing the deep inhalations of a warrior, his eyes intent on his prize: Seriana.

When the cages were flush against one another, a brave half-breed scaled to the top. The beast didn't even try to swipe at him as he slid up the two dividers between them. His growl came from deep within his chest. Seriana could see his eyes now that he was close. They were crystal blue and flashed with pent-up desire. He was covered in battle scars and teeth marks, and he circled her slowly, with every pass coming closer.

Fear dripped into Seriana's veins until he was all she saw. The crowded room was haze behind him. The noise of the crowd faded until all she could hear was his breathing as he stalked her.

"Wet them!" Vittorio's voice commanded.

Warm water began pouring from somewhere above her, but Seriana paid it no attention. They were so close now. If she lifted a hand she could touch him. The water came pounding now, a waterfall washing over them, and the beast in front of her became a man as he became clean. His skin emerged and his hair dripped in front of his face. The crowd gasped as she moved slowly and pushed the hair out of his eyes. He was handsome, this man in a cage. His eyes didn't contain blind fury, as his noises had led her to believe, but pain.

He parted his lips and licked the water from them. He was terribly thirsty. Seriana made a cup with her hand and caught the water. She brought her hands to his lips and tilted them while he drank. She did it again and again, until he was finally holding her hands in place, his tongue occasionally touching her fingertips.

She could hear little snippets of her grandfather over the pounding of the water. "See! She tames him! No, this isn't failure! Only a true bitch can be with him. Watch and see. Watch and see." The simple kindness of offering water to the beast/man was obviously not what the crowd had been anticipating.

"Do you have a name?" Seriana whispered.

He shook his head gently.

"I'm sorry they keep you here."

He stopped drinking but continued holding her hands. "I'm sorry too." His voice was deep, but soft, and his eyes added depth to his apology.

"For what?" Seriana was confused.

He let go of her hands and pulled her wet body against his hard one. "For this."

He began to kiss Seriana like he could change the world with her.

DEAN

Violent returned with a just-dead body. Dean was not pleased.

"What the Hell did I say? No killing!"

Violent defended herself. "This old thing breathed his last natural breath, then expired. He's still warm. It took more patience than I've ever used before not to cork him off early. I thought you'd be thankful." She pouted. Maybe letting him make decisions was a hasty choice.

"Fine. Thanks."

Violent set the old man down, and Dean laid his mother next to the body's neck. Her desperate suck-slurping noises made Violent smile.

"Look. She likes it. I did the right thing." She tried to make eye contact with Giovianni — no, Dean — it was so confusing.

The resemblance was still startling. Just the sight of this man made her happy, even if he barely tolerated her existence. Dean ran his hands through his hair. Giovanni had made that same movement when he was frustrated.

He looked up at her. "So now what do I do?"

Violent sat across from him in a bed of dried pine needles. The noises of his mother draining the body mixed with the night's natural symphony.

"Well, you want to save two people. Either decide who you like better or who's likely to die first." She loved to watch Dean's hands move. She just wanted him to hold her hand in one and a paintbrush in the other.

"I'm not deciding between my brother and my sister." He punched his fists together.

"Well, I can navigate Hell, so that's in the plus column. Jason's most likely damned or dead by now. So that's a negative." She tossed her head back to look at the stars. She really didn't want to go back to Hell.

The slurping noises stopped, and Rebecca tried to stand. Dean rushed to her side and aided her. "Please tell me I didn't kill that man," she said.

Dean shook his head. "No, he'd passed of natural causes — recently." He turned to Violent. "Please bury him."

The minion finished the task just as Dean finished explaining to his mother the dire situation of his two siblings.

"We go for Seriana first," she said. Rebecca was far from better, but she seemed determined. "I know where Vittorio has taken her."

Dean nodded. "Okay, I agree. At least Jason has others to rely on. Seri's all alone."

Violent cocked her head to the side. "Well, let's get on this."

They headed in the direction Rebecca's shaky finger pointed.

CHAPTER 24

KATE

Kate and Jason held their glowing hands together as they traversed the caves. Kate could feel her sense of time and the urgency of her task ebb as they made their way into what had to be a lower level of Hell. She continued trying to gear herself up so she'd get angry when she was scared crapless, as it was sure to happen at some point. Hell wasn't a day in the park. Having Jason hold her hand gave her courage, but she wished she didn't have the nagging suspicion that maybe Lucifer had sent her to her doom — he was the ultimate Devil and all.

She closed her eyes and thought of her father, and suddenly she just knew where to go. She had to move. The knowledge was compelling, almost a compulsion. And at that thought, she stopped. Compulsion had kept Nero from staying on Earth. It hadn't been a good thing. He couldn't stop it when it took over.

"What?" Jason looked both handsome and concerned in the hazy blue light of their hands. "You okay?"

She looked at her feet. "It's just...my mom was waiting all the time, then I was. It feels wonderful to be *doing* something finally. But what if it's a trick?"

Jason grabbed her other hand. "I hate Jack. So much. But he'd never let you leave if he thought this was a long-term punishment for you — I don't think so anyway."

Kate nodded and bit her lip. "I want to save Nero so much. I — "

Jason kissed her again, silencing her fears. She smiled against his lips.

"Sorry. You're just so pretty." He traced her face with the tip of his finger.

"I...it's okay. I like it." Kate wrinkled her nose at this new, stupid attraction at the worst possible time. "Let's go."

As they turned a corner, the narrow passage they followed opened up into a much larger cave. Jason and Kate stopped abruptly when a crowd of minions turned to watch them enter the space.

They whispered the same word at the exact same time: "Crap."

Kate gave Jason an alarmed look. He'd plastered a tight smile on his face. She tried to think quickly. The minions seemed content to wait for her to speak, but they were a scary lot of monsters. Kate cleared her throat. "We're from Lucifer."

The minions shuffled their feet.

"Tell us where Nero is. He's served his sentence." Kate raised an eyebrow and met Jason's eyes again.

"Or else your punishment will be extended!" Jason let go of her hand and held up his glowing palms.

The minions took a step back. Kate held her palms up as well. The minions looked at one another. They seemed to be waiting for a more spectacular show.

"Good to know," a voice finally rumbled from the crowd. A huge minion stepped forward.

Kate recognized him immediately. Handsome Ransom had been holding down Brut the last time Nero came to the surface. The jig was up. He mouthed the word "boobs" to her, and Kate felt her eyes widen. At least he was still obsessed with the same thing.

"I'll be glad to take you to Nero. I know right where he is." Ransom walked casually over to Kate and Jason. The minions behind him began twittering like a pack of nervous birds. "This way, Lucifer's messengers." He bowed at the waist and pointed to the back of the cave.

Jason held her hand again as they made their way through the center of the room. It was like swimming with sharks, except a million times worse. They were sniffed and assessed until they finally reached the passage.

Ransom put his hands on their shoulders, which caused them both to jump. He pushed them faster until they were clear of the pack and around a bend. Kate exhaled with relief at the lack of the scrutiny, but Ransom's voice brought the unease back.

"Well, fancy meeting you here, little lady. You recently admitted?"

Jason pulled Kate slightly behind him. "You know him?" he asked her.

Kate sighed. "Yeah, a little. He helped my dad once upon a time. I doubt he's doing this out of the kindness of his heart."

"I am not. Seems I have something you need." Ransom opened his lips around his teeth in a semblance of a smile.

"Actually, I'm pretty sure I can find Nero on my own now." Her inner compass seemed to be calling her forward.

"You need me not to go back and rile up all those waiters," Ransom clarified. "We wait. That's our sentence. If I give them something to do? They'll lose their minds and their cool. So you totally need me." Ransom snapped his fingers like he was listening to music.

Jason shook his head. "What do you want, then?"

Ransom's gaze stopped on Kate's chest. "Well, I want a few things...but I'll take a passage out. 'Cause some creepy shit's happening. You guys aren't supposed to be here, and I want out of this joint."

Kate shrugged. "Fine, come with us, but I can't promise you anything."

They continued through the caves, Kate fighting Ransom for the lead, until they heard the clang of metal on rock. Kate let go of Jason's hand and took off running. She rounded the last curve, and there he was. Sweat pouring over his skin as he shoveled with two old, rusty shovels. One in each hand.

"Dad?" She wanted to cry and cry. This work he'd been doing for who knows how long looked so desolate, so lonely.

He kept shoveling, even though he clearly did not want to. "Kate?" He kept working through his scream. "Not my daughter! No!" Nero's shoveled desperately, his eyes manic. "Tell me you're not here. You are not here!"

Kate tried not to take her father's immediate rejection personally, but as she wiped fresh tears from her cheeks, she knew she was failing. "I'm here to get you out of Hell. I made a deal with the Devil — well, the old Devil — and he said I could have you. On Earth. As my dad. If you still want to be, that is."

Jason put his hand on her shoulder. Through her distress, she could still feel the pull of their shared power.

Ransom approached Nero. "Hey, care to take a break?"

Nero nodded and closed his eyes. Ransom neatly restrained him on his back on the ground. Kate's father began vibrating, instantly blurry under Ransom.

"Let go of the shovels, Dad." Kate dropped to her knees and inched closer.

Ransom quickly gave her his version of the situation. "Nero's doing his work and Brut's because he killed that bastard. So he doesn't get any reprieves anymore, no chance to rest."

Kate couldn't even make eye contact with him, Nero was too out of focus. The piece of her mother's nightgown still on his bicep made an arc, flying like a flag in a hurricane. She turned to Jason. "We've got no way to help him. Only the Devil can remove a compulsion, or at least that's what Jack said. How're we going to get him out?"

Jason wiggled his glowing fingertips. "Well, we've got a little bit to work with, right?"

Kate inhaled sharply as hope rose within her. "Let's try."

They approached Nero, getting as close as they could while staying clear of the shovels, still trying in vain to gather coal. The only stationary part of him was his middle, where Ransom had him pinned. Jason grabbed her hand and motioned with his other. They would touch Nero at the same moment. Kate tried to focus the power coursing through her and laid her hand on her father's flailing forearm. The skin there glowed blue, but it continued to move with a mind of its own. Jason and Kate waited. And waited.

Finally Ransom exhaled with exasperation. "Aren't you going to say something?"

Kate met Jason's eyes. He seemed to take a wild guess. "Release Nero!" he proclaimed.

The power poured from Kate's fingers. It took everything she had to keep her hand steady. It was as if her blood had solidified and was being pulled out like splinters.

Nero's buzzing slowed to a stop. His grip on the shovels released. His hands were bloody messes.

Nero stood then, knocking Ransom off unceremoniously. "Kate. My Kate. How? Why?"

He enveloped her in a moist hug. She closed her eyes. This was it. The reason she'd found her courage and balls. Jumped into ponds and followed weird things into Hell. Her father's hug.

She wanted to cry and laugh, but instead she answered him. "The presence of me is my love for you." She patted his chest.

"My pride, my sweet, I never wanted you here. We must get you out immediately." He turned and scanned the area, grabbing her hand to lead her. "They collapsed my escape tunnel after I killed Brut." He moved back toward the waiter's cave, collecting a shovel as he went and thoroughly ignoring the men Kate had with her.

She dug her heels in and pulled on her father's hand. "No, seriously. Father, give us a second." She hugged his massive arm until he stopped and turned to her. "We need a better plan. Things are crazy right now."

He raised his hand as if to place it on her cheek, but stopped when he saw all the blood. "You look like Jenny. It's amazing and hurts so much at the same time."

"She loved you. She never gave up hoping you would be together."

Ransom made violin noises. "This is so freaking lovely. But we've to get out of this place before it collapses."

Kate looked at Jason and hoped it wasn't too soon. "Dad, this is Jason. He's a good friend." Jason met her eyes and smiled in a way that made her skin prickle. She felt pure joy when he stepped forward and held out his hand to her father.

"Sir, your daughter is truly amazing."

Nero wiped his hand on his pants and reached in for a manly shake. "I agree. She's the only reason this world shouldn't curse my existence."

The walls of the cave began shaking, pieces of rock coming loose. Nero pulled Kate to him and covered her body with his. "Where did you get in?" he asked her. "That's where I will get you out."

Kate stepped in front, still holding her father's hand, and smiled in spite of their uncertain situation. "Where *I'll* be getting us *all* out. Let's go this way."

She winked at Jason, who smiled back. Ransom gave them all the finger, but he followed the way Kate led.

CHAPTER 25

DEAN

Dean and Violent had carjacked a vehicle so they'd make better time.

Now Violent drove, and Dean tried not to watch. She was ridiculous behind the wheel. Road signs, paint markings, and lights didn't even register as suggestions to her. He focused on his mother in the backseat. She was looking a bit better. Dean patted her hand gently and leaned closer to hear her words.

"He's going to try to breed her. He's fixated on it. Your grandfather's a zealot. The thing they have in a cage as a stud? Dean, we have to find her." Rebecca squeezed his hand.

He nodded and told her what he knew could very well be a lie. "We'll find her before that happens, Mom. That's all I want now: our family together."

Violent whipped her head around and watched his mouth. He never knew what to expect with her, but she seemed to be saying a little prayer.

In no time they were over the bridge Rebecca had described. She propped herself up. "It'll look like an old warehouse, but inside he has a little city set up. The cages were in the middle of the compound, and there were always a ton of guards."

Violent pulled the stolen car into an empty parking lot. She

166

hopped out like a woman headed to a manicure appointment, not a war. Dean tried to convince his mother to stay put. "You're too weak. We need you out of the way so we can focus on Seri."

Rebecca crawled out from the back of the car, now able to walk on her own. "No. I've been protecting you kids your whole lives. That doesn't stop now."

Violent walked right up to a broken-down door and put her foot through it. The loud crack echoed through the seemingly empty expanse of rooms. "There are no guards. Are you sure of this place?" Violent turned to stare at Rebecca.

She nodded slowly. "The only reason they'd be gone is if there's an event to watch. The mating. We have to hurry."

Rebecca shuffle-ran until she encountered an empty vending machine. She struggled to move it aside. Dean reached around his mother and pulled, sliding the machine. A long, dark tunnel behind it led to a descending staircase. Violent strode past them like they'd opened it for her personally, but Dean grabbed her arm. She lifted one eyebrow in question.

"You sure you're with us?" He didn't trust her confidence.

She almost smiled. "Family was important to Giovanni. Shall we go?"

He had no choice but to believe her. He held out an arm for his mother, and she grasped it.

When they reached the first landing, they could hear the eerie chanting — a tuneless song that sounded like prayer. They began to run at the second landing when the crowd burst into cheers.

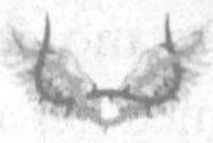

SERIANA

Seriana was drunk with him, this beast/man. The crowd began chanting and lighting incense. It took her few seconds to realize the man was whispering to her in between kisses.

"You must act in lust with me." He lifted her hair and licked her neck.

She moaned. It was actually hard to remember she wasn't. "Okay." She pushed his hair out of his face and held it with one hand. The warm water continued to pour down on them. He twirled her through it over and over, using the rushing sound to drown out his words for everyone but her.

"If I get out of this cage, I can get free. I would like that. I can kill them all." His hands explored her with a primal greediness.

She had to try twice to get the words out. "Me too."

"You'll kill everyone?" He sounded amused.

She shook her head. His hair was heavy now that it was wet. He tilted his head back and swallowed more water. Seriana watched his throat move. She took a moment to look around her. The audience of half-breeds was in various states of undress, obviously aroused by the show. Four spotlights came on with an audible pop. Closest to the cage were the elders, some with notepads, others with video cameras. She shivered. This had to be the most surreal experience of her life.

The man was looking at her when she refocused on him. "You have no name. Really?"

"I'm simply yours." He twirled her, and she was forced to let go of his hair. He pulled her back against his chest. "They think they know how this ends. I mount you, we copulate, and then they part us until you produce a live birth." His hands were everywhere on her, pressing the wet sheet to her body.

She tried to concentrate on his words, on the horror of being watched during this intimate moment. Instead her veins filled with true lust for him. It shamed her and made her gasp.

"But when they separate us? That's when we fight back. Are you with me, Seriana?"

"You know my name?" She turned her head to watch his lips.

"I know everything about you. We are destined, Seriana." His mouth was so mesmerizing.

He leaned down to kiss her, turning her again so they were

chest to chest. He was taller than she, so he simply lifted her so they could be eye to eye. The female half-breeds sighed like he was a movie heartthrob.

"Do you know I don't want to get screwed in front of a crowd?" Hearing the words come from her own lips crystallized the situation, and she swallowed a sob.

He looked concerned. "I did not know that." He hugged her harder, covering her as best as he could with his arms.

She nodded and looked again at the audience.

He nudged her with his nose until she looked at him again. "Don't see them. Only me. Only feel."

Seriana just needed a second to process. Was this man seducing her? Was she part of his escape plan? Would she really have to do this?

He began kissing her face again, and she nuzzled into him. At least he wasn't hurting her. Then she saw it out of the corner of her eye, heard her grandfather's words carrying across the room. "He needs to be angry. Electrocute him."

She was hooked around the middle at the same moment her beast man was. They were pulled apart as the water pouring over them turned painfully cold.

Like mating dogs.

He began growling at the sight of the stick poked into the cage. Seriana put it together too slowly, not that she could've done anything but watch.

Her "mate" was hit in the back and stunned silent, the electric current turning him colors, stiffening him rigid. Seriana screamed, begging her grandfather to stop. He gave her a half smile and touched the stick to the water she stood in. She felt lightning throughout her body, turning her senses white, just before she passed out.

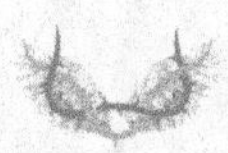

Dean

Dean pushed Violent forward and ran past her when he heard his sister scream. His mother ran after him, but Violent eventually caught up so she could be in front. The screaming was unreal and distractingly horrifying. Dean couldn't even get his bearings before he was restrained by a group of half-breeds.

Their scuffle was stupid and brief. Soon enough, he was locked in a cage with his sister, a naked man, his mother, and Violent. Seriana and the man both lay unconscious.

Dean and his mother arrived at Seri's side at the same time. Violent attacked the cage bars with a primitive anger. Seriana began to stir, and Dean pulled his shirt off and covered his sister. He hated to think the man might have already raped her.

"They've not mated," Violent said, transfixed by Dean's bare chest. "I would smell it."

Seriana's eyes fluttered open. "Mom? Dean?"

Vittorio informed the crowd and the prisoners of his plans at the same time. "Tonight is a victory! Look, friends, we have a full-blooded minion and another one of my grandchildren for the mating!" He spun to look at the cages, tapping a finger on his wrinkled forehead. "Yes. This couldn't be more perfect. The beast mates with the girl, and the boy can mate with the minion."

A heckler shouted from one of the seats in the back. "And your daughter?"

A slow smile leaked onto Vittorio's face. "We'll kill her if her children don't play nice."

Dean swallowed and looked into Violent's hungry eyes. She was doing her best to roust the naked man. When she was successful, he immediately planted the same famished gaze on Seriana — as if she were food on a plate, water in a desert.

CHAPTER 26

JACK

There were other pressing things to handle. The world was coming apart around them. Promises had been made, people needed protecting — but damn it if Jack could stop feeling her, being with her. Her smile, her skin.

He'd wrapped her in his arms, and she buffered them from Hell's evil with her angel wings. He wanted to dominate her, submit to her, everything. He had two handfuls of her hair, and she purred his name over and over between kisses and groping. She'd figured out the code. The hardest thing in Hell — well, besides his dick — was to believe in anything. "You would believe," he breathed. "Of all the damn things. You would."

She put a finger on his lips. "I believe in love, which means I believe in you. I've missed you so much. I just knew we'd never be together — "

He stopped her with a hug, burying her beautiful face in his chest, kissing her sweet-scented hair. "I was never gonna stop. Until someone killed me. I was never gonna stop."

They embraced for too long. Far too long. He knew better than to stay still. But it was her. She was an angel again. She could fly free — and in a second he would demand it — but right now her arms wrapped around his middle, and that made his whole body happy. They kept kissing, almost as often as they took a breath, tracing each other's faces. Just tender, just together.

She began to trace his chest, and he stopped staring at her long enough to watch her repaint his tattoos. Emma took her time recreating the clean lines on his forearm. The cross, music clef, and knife were perfect when she was done.

He rumbled with a laugh. "Angels give tattoos now? What's next? Are we doing shots?"

"This one does. You need to look like you again." She traced her name back onto his chest. "I'm sorry you had so much pain. I'm sorry I didn't think of the wings sooner."

She was tearing herself up about the torture. He'd never tell her it had been agonizing in the kind of way that made pain a god. He was just glad he'd had enough Lucifer in him to withstand it and not reveal the code. Because if Everett had done that to her... He kissed her again, pulling her into his lap. Her lips tasted like angel cake. He breathed deep, stopped, and touched his forehead to hers. "You've got to leave. Please."

She pulled back. "Yes, we have to leave. Let's go." She got to her feet and tried to pull him with her. When he did not stand, her cocoon of Heaven loosened a bit, her face grew wary.

"No, I have to stay, pretty child. I have a job here now." He pulled himself up and gathered her to him.

"Are you kidding me? No. No way. What the Hell is going on? You saved me, now I save you. We're getting out of here." She was angry now, and her wings had tinted pink in places. They'd be going red soon enough.

"I have to help a few more people. Then I'll follow you out." He couldn't meet her eyes.

"What's going on here? You're scaring me. We have forever now, Jack. Forever." She put her soft hands on his cheeks.

"Any chance you'll just go and trust me?" He leaned in for another kiss. She obliged him.

"No. Because you're not looking at me, and I feel like I'm

missing something. Tell me. Everett might find us soon." Emma bit her lip, her eyes brimming with gold-tinted tears.

"You're so beautiful. Why do you give me the time of day?" He touched her nose.

"Because you're great in bed. Tell me." She was joking, but not smiling.

"The soul in jeopardy? I only had one to use as bait." Jack couldn't look at her as she pieced together this information.

"No. No, no. Do not tell me I just damned you. Do not tell me that." She moved his chin up, trying to look in his face so he could deny the terrible truth.

"Baby, you didn't damn me. I did that a long time ago. It's just that I can't leave now. So if I'm going to be here, I'm going to fight to run the joint." Jack wanted to run with her, so fast and far — have her angel wings take them to the clouds and just make love until time ground to a halt. But the wings that set her free had chained him to the ground.

She dropped her hands and unfurled her wings. They were scarlet as she fumed and paced. The loss of her touch was painful.

"So what happens if I just scoop you up and run?" She headed at him, and he smiled. She was so determined to be with him. God, he loved her so much. It wasn't a figment of his deranged imagination. Everything he ever was wanted to be near her forever.

"In the past? Let's just say the body never gets to leave. And the whole skin thing? That will have been a picnic compared to what I'd go through in your arms." He held a hand out to her. Even angry he needed this time.

She stormed over to him and curled into his chest. "No. I love you. I'll stay."

And now it was time to lie. He'd passed time with the best liars who ever existed, but no one had topped him yet. But he still had to prepare his heart when he lied to her.

"When you get out? You can appeal to God," he began. "That's the only thing that can save me."

She turned her hopeful gray eyes on him.

"If He believes I'm worth saving..." It would be enough. He could tell. "God loves you," she answered immediately.

Her knee-jerk response made him love her more.

"So there's no way your soul's doomed. I say we try it. Let's go to Him."

Jack shook his head. He didn't want to tell her she'd be as doomed as he was if she tried to take him out of Hell. He'd never let her experience the stripping of her soul. It was easy to lie this time, picturing her in pain made his words flow like silk.

"No one's ever been able to vouch for a doomed soul. There was no love. So the more quickly you get out, the more likely God will save me." He looked her in the eyes and refused to blink. He would show no tells as a liar.

"I don't want to leave you. If Everett finds you? No. I'll stay here and protect you." She turned her back on him and spread her wings like a wall, shielding him.

"Emma, please. You have to go. I was here to see you, but that's not the only reason." This lie would be harder.

She looked over her shoulder but kept her wings out.

"I made a deal with Lucifer. He's going to let me run Hell again." She scanned him, confusion cluttering her pretty face.

"Being a human sucks. I need to be in control. Hell is falling to pieces, and I can save it. You have to leave. No angels allowed." Jack put on his most vicious façade.

She whipped her wings out of the way and twirled. He was expecting a fight, but instead she came close and touched his chest, his neck, his lips. She smiled at him, and he smiled back.

"I'm not leaving you. Right here, right now is the happiest I've ever been. I love you. That means I don't leave. Sorry." She went to her tiptoes and kissed his forehead, her wings humming happily. "Whatever you fight, we do it together."

She spun back around as he exhaled a sigh of defeat. She wasn't going to leave, and his lies wouldn't scare her away. She spread her wings again: his beautiful barrier against the terrors of Hell.

He stepped to her and moved her hair out of the way to kiss the nape of her neck. "You're thick-headed and stubborn."

She snaked her hand out from under her wings and grabbed a handful of him. "Lucky you."

The whole cave corridor began to shake around them. Emma shifted positions and curled her wings like an umbrella around him. "What do you think that is?"

"I think that's the dragon." The dragon would sniff out angel Emma like a truffle pig.

"Hmmm...I tamed him last time. What're the chances I can do it again?" She kissed his lips, in the middle of chaos.

"You keep kissing me, and I'll take you right here." He pulled her to him and traced her lips with his tongue. She made a happy moan that tantalized his dick. But he had to stop because the rumbling became an all-out earthquake. The dragon's fire flashed before his face. Emma used her wings to shield them both.

"Ow!" She flinched as the heat made her wings luminescent.

"You all right, gorgeous?" Jack touched her lower back and imagined her in white leather armor. He smiled when her silk disappeared and his hand touched her bare skin. She rolled her eyes when she noted the change. He gave her low-heeled boots so she could run. They both flinched when they heard the way-too-close sniffing of the dragon.

"He's not ripping us up," she noted in a whisper.

"Not yet." He took to his toes to look over her huge wings. The dragon was indeed there, and the last time they'd faced off, he'd tried to kill him a lot of different ways. And failed. Eventually, Emma had loved the dragon to death, or some shit like that.

"Does he have a name?" She'd joined Jack in peering now.

"Death Mobile? Fire Burp? No, he doesn't have a name. He's a weapon." Jack tried to remember the special combination of words that might distract the dragon momentarily.

Emma tilted her head. "I think he's kind of cute."

The spiky, scary dragon was not cute. Emma's ass in those white leather pants was another story.

"I'm naming him Smoosh." She lowered her wing a bit and held her hand out as if the dragon was a friendly dog.

"Don't!" Jack whispered harshly.

She did it anyway. The dragon twisted his head to examine her outstretched hand with one big, green eye. After what felt like forever, the dragon sniffed, his giant nostrils letting out an acrid smoke. Emma and Jack coughed. The dragon tensed.

Emma recovered quickly. "Shhh, Smoosh. That's a good dragon. Look how sweet you are. You're a good dragon." The beast snarled, and Emma and Jack took a half-step back.

"You need to say something nice to him." Emma nodded encouragingly.

Jack put all his doubt in the one word. "Really?"

"For me." She batted her eyelashes.

Damn it. He'd do a back flip if she asked right now. "There's a good killer." He held his hands up in frustration as Emma tsked at his words.

She took his hand and held it out with hers. The dragon sniffed again. The whole cave rumbled as it thumped its tail.

"Smoosh likes you."

Jack kissed Emma's cheek. "I'm betting he likes a lady in leather, not me." The dragon thumped its gigantic tail again. "See?"

Emma put her finger to her lips. The dragon stilled as if it understood the command, and Jack listened too.

Voices. Everett was shouting orders, and someone or something responded.

"Where are we, Jack? What's next?" Emma turned her back on the deadly beast and looked for answers he didn't have.

CHAPTER 27

EMMA

Jack ran a hand through his hair, and Emma blessed it in her head. She was praying all over him. For however long she was granted the gift of being an angel, she would cover him in goodness. It seemed the least she could do since she'd damned his soul by stealing her wings back. But the damned could be changed, she was sure. What Jack hadn't said, but Emma hadn't missed, was that God had known Jack's soul was in the meter. God Himself was willing to let the world die so Jack's soul could be saved. So she was sure God would see to it that the damnation be reversed.

At first, Jack's soul being the one that must be negotiated for seemed horrible, but now she felt better. She knew what she was dealing with, or rather who, and this man she could love. This man she *did* love. And love made the impossible a reality. Now she just had to get Jack to safety while she figured out how to save him. Again. And again. Whatever it took. He was willing to be skinned alive to keep her safe. She could only return the favor. He kept touching her. And it was perfection. His eyes were so welcoming, despite his poor attempts to chase her away.

"Well, we should make our way to the new exit," he said. "Maybe we can run into Jason that way."

"Jason?! What the Hell is he doing here?" She could feel fury blazing through her. Another man she'd tried her damnedest to protect, and he was here too?

"He's trying to save you, baby. He doesn't remember you, but I guess he's not a complete asshole. And he's with a girl I made a few promises to."

Jealousy made the dragon behind her fire up a bit. She could feel the sparks deflecting off her wings.

"You made promises to a girl?"

He bit his lip as he watched her flare. "I'd do anything to get to you... and I did."

Their voices combined with running footsteps in the distance.

As sounds of approaching feet grew closer, and Jack reached out and yanked on her hand. "Fly me to the moon?"

She snarled at him, the dragon mimicking her.

"I'll send you to the moon if you screwed her." Emma held out her arms for an angry hug. He took advantage of the closeness to nuzzle her neck.

"There's only you now. And I already had thousands of women, so you can't be jealous."

She whacked him hard on the butt and motioned for the dragon to follow. It slithered and scrambled behind them, trying to keep up.

"Did you just pimp slap my ass with your angel hand?" He was flat-out laughing at her.

She rolled her eyes. "You better beware, hot stuff."

He snuggled into her breasts and occasionally shouted directions. When he finally told her to slow down and stop, his playfulness had evaporated. Emma set him down at the shores of a disgusting pond.

"That stupid fucker." Jack ran to the side of a woman dressed in red.

As Emma came closer, she realized the woman wasn't wearing red, she was covered in it.

She rushed to Jack's side as he pushed yellow fuzzy hair out of the woman's face. Her eyes were endlessly open and hot pink, her mouth cemented in a horrified circle.

Emma centered all her energy, but she could feel her reserves were diminished. Jack had required so much healing and this woman was clearly...

"Dead. He killed her. I didn't even know it was possible. Holy crap, what has he gotten into? Can you...?" He trailed off as she answered his question with a sad shake of her head. She couldn't fix this. There was no soul to claim, or so it appeared.

He stood and went to the nearest huge, furry lump.

"He killed the dogs? He killed Tiffany? Emma, I don't know what this means."

Emma went to another furry lump. It appeared to be a huge, dead poodle. She went to the last, just to make sure.

It was panting, gently. The dragon came closer, and Emma watched as it nosed the poodle.

Jack hollered, "Don't let it eat the fucking dog!"

The dragon snarled and resumed nosing the poodle.

Emma shook her hands and laid them on the dog. It wasn't dead, though it was close.

She found her last little pool of healing energy and hoped it was enough. Light flowed through her fingertips. She gently laid her wings on the dog. It was a bit before the dragon's happy snarfing snapped her out of her reverie. The poodle stirred. Jack clenched and unclenched his fists. Emma patted the dog and left the dragon to its nudging.

Jack looked ready to do battle. "These are my minions. He's killing *my* minions. Sure, they're in Hell, but they do what they're told. They deserve at least a chance. I've no idea what he's into, how he killed her and her dogs. I can't leave them at his deranged mercy. How can I do that to them? They trusted me."

Emma admired him, but mostly she wanted to shake him. These things he wanted to keep safe were the worst in the universe.

The poodle she'd managed to save staggered to its feet, only to ignore everyone except Tiffany.

It lay down, put its huge head on its paws, and began to mourn her death with loud howls.

"Crap. Make it stop! Jack, it's going to tell Everett where we are!"

She watched as Jack looked over her right wing. "No worries, baby. He's already here."

She turned and found Everett smirking. Behind him was row after row of minions, poised for battle. The corridor was wall to wall with muscle. Emma stepped in front of Jack and spread her wings. She would fight them all.

Everett had a different plan. He wanted to chat. "So, you two wasted your chance to get out of this place. What were you going for, Jack? Wanted to suck Lucifer's dick one more time?"

"I could never after he'd had you. I'm sure your experienced blow jobs are far superior." Jack pulled Emma's belt loop until she was next to him, tucking himself in front of her wing. "Let me be a man, Emma."

She wanted to suggest that talking about who gives better oral sex might not be the most testosterone-filled conversation, but she let him have his moment.

The minions behind Everett whispered to each other. Emma tried to hear what they were saying to no avail. The poodle had started growling, and the dragon copied her. Emma crossed her arms and grabbed a handful of feathers. She was armed for at least the first blows.

"Did you tell the minions you killed Tiffany? How'd they like that?" Jack stepped forward.

She didn't like it, but Jack had the demeanor of a general.

"No one cares about that hot pink piece of trash. She gave me what I needed. And you were too stupid to at least screw Emma while you had a chance. Better for me, though. I hate a messy hole." Everett leered at her.

It took tremendous restraint to not fly at him like an angry eagle. Emma tightened her hold on her feathers. She liked the way his eyes twitched when he looked at her hands. She bet the feathers had been painful. Emma glanced at Jack's angry face. His jaw was tight, but the rest of him showed no fear.

Jack addressed the minions. "He's gotten into something that can not only hurt you, but kill you — "

Everett interrupted. "Oh, sure, listen to him. He left you. And now he stands with the enemy? He came here to get her. Her pussy is like the Holy Grail for him. But with me? We can return to the Earth. How'd you like that?" Everett stopped and smiled like a generous father offering his children an expensive vacation.

The minions buzzed and began to come out of the tunnel, filling the room. The poodle and dragon's presence prevented them from completely surrounding Emma and Jack, but it wasn't looking good. Jack shook his head, not at all alarmed as the room filled with hundreds of Hell's minions.

"If he gets us — Emma and me — hear me now: You have to take him down. He's able to kill you. It shouldn't be that way. Tiffany's dead. His promises are false." Jack pointed at Everett.

Everett laughed. "If you care so much about them, Jack, challenge me. Challenge me for the Devil's position. It's that simple."

It was obviously what Everett desperately wanted, though it wasn't clear why. Emma was about to tell Jack not to do it, but he answered quickly.

"No, I'm not a match for you. Yet." Jack seemed to be meeting the eyes of all the minions, one at a time. The conversation with Everett was secondary.

"Well, how about this? They die one by one until you do try to claim the title again." Everett grinned and slashed the air with his hand. The nearest minion fell dead, his skin erupting with blood.

"No!" Jack's protest was harsh and loud.

Emma reacted because her wings gave her no choice. She flew to the fallen minion's side and tried her best to bring him around.

She had no healing energy to pull from. Jack and the poodle had drained her. It'd take time she didn't have for it to replenish.

Everett's snickering was close to her ear and sent a shiver through her spine. "On your knees. Just how I like it. Hello, Emma. No bars now."

She reacted before she could think of the consequences. She gave him a quick uppercut to the balls. He screamed in pain. She stood quickly and went for a handful of feathers, but Everett grabbed her wrists, stilling her movement. He was still writhing from the waist down, but he forced a smile.

"You know, touching you is all I want."

Emma hissed at him like a cat. The dragon lit them up, and she covered herself quickly with her wings. Everett stumbled back and let go of her hands, singed and burning. Jack caught her as she ran to the ragtag group. He was busy trying to update his minions.

"Just leave us here," Jack urged them. "You guys have to go. Go to the pond and see if you can get Lucifer out of his Hellhole. Everett's going to kill you, and I can't stop him." He pointed toward the exit. His minions looked perplexed.

Everett coughed and brushed off charred skin like it was dirt, revealing unmarred flesh beneath. "No one moves. Forget not who rules you. Jack's nothing now. *Nothing.* Of course I know Hell is dying. That's why we're going up." He pointed at the ceiling, which started to rumble.

Emma wasn't sure if Everett had caused it or if the place was really compromised. An air of confusion filled the room as the minions wrestled with the awkward task of trying to make a decision. Jack put his arm around her shoulder.

"They can't think for themselves. Most of them are used to being ordered around." He shook his head.

Emma turned with everyone else as Jason, a woman, and two minions appeared on the scene as if they'd been called. Emma immediately shushed the dragon, who looked ready to fire up again, and the poodle, which growled menacingly.

Jason froze when he saw Emma. She shrugged and smiled, thrilled to see him despite the ridiculous circumstances. She left the comfort of Jack's arm and flew straight at him, giving him a huge hug. He dropped the woman's glowing hand to embrace her, looking bewildered at the sudden affection.

"Emma?" It was more a question than a greeting.

She landed and touched his face. "Jason. Thank God you're okay." She hugged him again, and he came away slowly, shaking his head. He truly didn't remember. "You can leave my wings on this time," Emma continued, needing to speak, even if he didn't understand. "I never said thank you when you stood up for me in Heaven." She touched his lips. "Thank you so much. It meant everything."

Everett's furious voice bellowed throughout Hell. "Hey, Slutacular! Can you put away your wanton ways for a fucking second?"

Emma turned to see where Everett was, but her gaze got stuck on a desperately angry Jack.

CHAPTER 28

JACK

Jack watched as Emma pulled away from Jason, suddenly seeming to remember the rest of them were here. He wanted to be understanding, but he was so goddamn furious. The last thing he ever wanted to see again was Emma entwined with Jason. He had fucking Everett, his minions not knowing what to do, and now his angel was flying the coop. Figures.

He tried to command the dragon to eat his frigging enemy, but the giant lizard just squirmed and watched over Emma like she was the dragon whisperer. Great thing to see before he died.

Emma turned to look at him. "He's safe!" She seemed surprised he hadn't cut up a wad of confetti to throw.

Everett grew tired of waiting. He commanded his army stupidly but efficiently. "Go get 'em."

Jack turned and made sure his body was between the minions and Emma. His former employees walked slowly and shrugged. They didn't seem to know how much was required of them.

Nero spoke up from behind him.

"Fellow minions, this day we make a choice. Follow Everett or Jack. I choose Jack, and you know what my sentence has been."

Nero's deep voice stilled the minions. He spoke clearly, and he looked better than he had in years, to say the least. Jack nodded at Kate. At least she'd freed her father.

Wait. She released her father? It was impossible. Unless...Jack looked at her hands. She glowed around the edges, and a quick scan told him Jason was glowing as well. He looked at his own hands. Lucifer's power. It was the only way Nero could ever be released of his compulsion.

Jack used the stillness to his advantage. He approached the little group, pushed past Emma's wing, and drew her close to him.

She touched his lips. Her hands were so soft. His whole body instantly wanted to lie on top of hers and feel the satin she was.

"Don't be mad," she said. "You know I love you." Her eyes were limitless. He wished they were anywhere but here, about to be crushed.

"Back at you, pretty child." Jack held out a hand to Kate and grudgingly let go of Emma to hold a hand out to Jason. Jason sucker punched him instead of grabbing hold. The half-breed was still a fighting dick shaft, apparently. "You stupid bastard. You think I want to play ring around the rosy with you in Hell? I'm going to tear you apart." Jack cursed under his breath and composed himself. "Fuck nugget, seriously. I'm trying to meld our Lucifer powers to make a goddamn wall."

Emma begged Jason. "Please, we need help." She touched his forearm.

Jack missed nothing and saw Kate's eyes fill with tears, yet she grabbed Jason and Jack's hands. Jason growled the whole time, but he took Jack's hand and squeezed it almost to the point of breaking. Connected with the two, Jack let the power course a bit and infuse his heart and mind before he spoke. "Simple wall."

The minions were almost within arm's reach when they were repelled by a clear divider. Jack had used the same power to block intruders from Emma's Hell hallway. It was harder to form it now. Kate and Jason had to maintain the circle to keep the protection stable.

"Hey, ass pillow, could you stop squeezing my hand like it's your dick? I'm working here."

Jason leaned forward and head butted Jack. He saw stars for a moment but was able to keep his grasp.

"If you two don't knock it off, I'm going to spend all my time left alive kicking you both in the balls," Kate hissed. "I just found my father, and we're getting him out of here. *No matter what.*"

Jack shook his head, sure he'd be unconscious if he hadn't been chock full of Lucy's power.

Emma came close to Kate and touched her, beckoning the half-breed to look at her. Kate resisted, and Jack knew she was pissed. He looked over his shoulder and saw Everett pacing the perimeter, seething. This protection wasn't permanent.

"Your name is Kate." Emma either missed the fury in the woman's eyes or ignored it. "And you're good. So good. You are a being created from singular, pristine love. Such a beautiful creation, a testament to God."

Kate's mouth dropped open, and she inhaled. Emma's words had been such a surprise.

"You have doubt, but that's part of everyone's burden. With my wings I can feel your past and your future, and you're here for a reason, sweet girl."

Emma pulled Kate's hair off her shoulders and kissed her cheek. The angel then walked close to Nero, whose nose flared at her wings. He flinched a few times when she reached for his hands.

"Hmm. An old one. You've seen so much time. May I, please?"

It was like she was anesthetizing them with kindness. Nero lifted one hand. She placed it between two of hers and hummed. "I hope I have enough energy for this," Emma murmured as she began to work. From their contact point, she healed his wounds, cleansing him. His skin glowed, his bloody hands became unmarred, and his dark hair took on a glossy sheen. It was mesmerizing. Jack shook his head and looked at Kate. She smiled, and Jason pulled her closer to kiss her lips gently.

Oh! So it was like that? No wonder Ms. Kate was so distressed by Emma. The angel's head whipped around like the kiss was an alarm.

"Love?" Emma fluttered just above the surface, bypassing Ransom, who reached for her wings. She moved before he could clasp a fist on her feathers. Jack caught his eye and shook his head. It was getting tiring holding the wall, and the minions were starting to attack it.

Emma flew to the center of their circle, tucking her wings close to fit in the small space. She touched Jason and Kate's joined hands. "How perfect. You're worthy of him and he of you." Emma lifted their hands to her lips and kissed them. Jason and Kate looked like newlyweds.

She stepped back into Jack's chest. He couldn't embrace her because his hands were busy, but she leaned against him like he was a wall. Jack kissed her shoulder and nosed her hair out of the way so he could kiss her neck as well. Emma turned and hugged him around the neck.

"They're going to break down that wall. How long?" She smiled, despite her question.

"Soon. I can't hurt my minions. They'll have us cornered." He exhaled. "One of us has to challenge him for the Devil's position."

The dragon showed its teeth and the poodle growled. Jack turned to see Nero had stepped closer to the circle.

"It will be me," he said, coming farther forward. "My daughter receives safe passage — "

Emma moved so quickly, it was as if she were made of mercury. She obviously stole Nero's voice, as his lips continued moving with no sound. Her hand had clasped in a fist. Jack knew Nero was pissed. Jack had hated it when Emma did that to him in Heaven. He shook his head and went to make the proclamation himself, but speaking of pissed, he found his voice captured as well. A quick glance told him Jason had the same affliction.

Emma put a single finger on Jack's lips. "If Everett wasn't here, would the minions listen to you?"

Jack tried a million curses, but none came. He didn't like the look on her face. He'd seen it before. He just shrugged and mouthed, "Maybe."

"Try hard. I love you."

She kissed him so thoroughly — he was lucky Jason and Kate had such firm grips on him or he would have forgotten himself and pulled her to him. She flew out of the circle and approached the divider. Everett approached as well, the minions' attacks now dwindling. The whole room seemed to center their attention on Emma and Everett.

Jack felt rising panic, but he held tight and focused his energy on maintaining the wall. He'd be shouting, cursing if he could. Her wings were iridescent, and she didn't look back. She seemed so slight compared to the army she faced, like a perfect white rose in the center of a garbage dump. Jack screamed anyway, his voice useless.

"Everett. It's me. I'm what you want," she told him. "The minions? Running Hell into the ground? It's all to get to me." She sounded so sure, but Jack watched her clenched fist shake behind her, the feathers on her wing quaking.

Everett smiled a crocodile's smile.

"So how about you get what you want?" She scanned the crowd, and Jack saw her in profile. So pretty. He tried to drum up some sort of weapon from Lucifer, tried to call him telepathically. The dragon whined.

"I'll hold you down by your wings." Everett licked his lips.

"Fine. Bitch, I formally challenge you to a battle to the death. This is a winner's crusade to become the Devil." Emma peeked over her shoulder, missing Everett's victorious dance.

It was done. She'd uttered the words — the correct ones,

goddamn it. He had nothing to offer. He had no way to stop her. She gave him a sad smile. Then she turned away.

"Come get me," she called.

Emma shot straight up, spinning like a drill, and she pierced a hole in the cave ceiling, neat and clean. Jack's voice was restored the moment she was out of sight. He immediately tried to rescind the challenge.

"As former Devil and future Devil, with the power of Lucifer coursing through my veins, I challenge your position, right now."

Everett just laughed and spread a pair of flame wings. He mimicked Emma's maneuver and created his own escape hole, debris flying and landing on the minions.

Jack's heart crumbled because he realized he couldn't leave Hell to save her. His soul was trapped in Hell. He fell to his knees as the wall collapsed between his little group and the hundreds of minions on the other side.

Chapter 29

Dean

Dean wanted to fight someone, something, anything to help his sister and mother, but he was bound by chains and threats. Violent had also been restrained in the same cage. His evil grandfather had Seriana and the naked guy in another cage and his mother in a separate one. The group of surrounding minions was full-on partying, and Vittorio accepted their praise like a preening peacock.

A persistent grinding noise caught Dean's attention. The naked man was almost out of his bindings. How the Hell he'd managed to get out of the thick chains was a mystery. But as Dean watched, he used sheer strength to break free from the last bit. Seriana, clad only in her indecently wet sheet — his shirt was gone now — watched with wide eyes as well.

Obviously, keeping them wet allowed Vittorio to control them. The threat of electricity was a huge motivator, and Vittorio was nothing if not efficient at moving unwilling prisoners. Dean noticed he, Rebecca, and Violent were surrounded by puddles.

The man prowled toward Seriana with tremendous focus. And Seri didn't look scared, which made no sense. Had she been drugged? Instead of touching her, the man stopped and stared at

Vittorio until he turned around. When the old half-breed did so, the naked man pointed at the floor.

Vittorio looked at him curiously for a moment, then finally seemed to understand. "Ah! Our specimen would like to mount in private. See how evolved he is? Lower the cover, and bury the cage."

Dean watched a half-breed press a few buttons, and the sound of ancient machinery filled the room. Slowly, the cage holding Seriana and her attacker disappeared from view. The man was strung tight, every muscle ready to pounce. Vittorio smiled indulgently when his crowd began to boo. He fumbled with a remote until a large screen on the wall lit up. "That's a heat-sensor camera!" he announced proudly. "We can still watch. The most important thing is that Seriana gets a seed inside her." Vittorio motioned to the screen.

Dean's hands shook with fury, and he yanked on his chains. If the naked man could get out, he could too. He pulled and pulled, then paused to check on Seriana. The man was removing her chains. He made it look so easy, but Dean was rubbing his skin raw. He tried his feet, kicking and tugging. He realized he was bellowing with the effort now, but as the man lowered his sister to the floor of their cage, his brain saw red. He didn't even see Vittorio approach, but as the electricity coursed through his system, he knew he was getting a reprimand. The last thing he saw was the man appearing to thrust into his sister.

SERIANA

Seriana could hardly draw a breath. He was on top of her, whispering.

"I need them to think this is done," he explained. "Are you okay?"

Everything was in the right spot for them to mate, except her sheet still covered her. She shivered as her body responded to his primal movements. She wanted to tilt her pelvis up to meet his. She didn't.

"There are cameras on us. Tell me, Seriana. How did you avoid your grandfather all this time?"

He was calm as he caressed her. Anyone watching would assume they were doing anything but having a conversation.

"We ran. My brothers and I. My mother — "

"I know her. She's very brave. I'm sorry to see her back. I hoped she had escaped."

Seriana's eyes began to adjust to the dim light. She put her hands on his face. "Surely you have a name?"

"I'm sure I did, but I don't remember it. I want to escape, and I would like to keep you. All these years, the only steady diet I've had is you. Facts about you, sometimes clothing with your scent, a fuzzy picture. I've not had blood in...a long time." He pulled her hands from his cheeks and kissed her palms, inhaling deeply.

"I want to name you." She leaned forward and kissed his forehead. It was a crazy place to fall for someone, but as much as he'd been conditioned for her, she felt her heart had somehow been conditioned for him.

He growled. "And I want to claim you."

He thrust deeper, her sheet working its way up her thighs. She twisted her hips until there was nothing between them but want.

He paused before entering her, tension rippling through his body at the effort. She hooked her legs around his back and tilted her pelvis up. With one strong motion he was in.

Seriana gasped. It was in every sense a mating. Her permission had unlocked something in him he'd been holding back. He went at her relentlessly, religiously. She could not hope to keep up and instead just hung on for the ride. He began biting her and moaning in a way that sounded like he was gearing up for a fight.

"Come with me," he growled around his words, daring her to

lose control. Seriana forgot the camera, forgot the fear. His scent and his presence pressing into her released the vampire. She pushed when he pushed and met him in the middle. He'd been fast before; he was incredible now. She increased her tempo until she just had to bite his shoulder. His blood poured into her mouth as his release poured between her legs. Ecstasy blinded her, and he grabbed a fistful of her hair and a handful of her ass as he left his DNA embedded deep inside her.

"Your name is Mine," she whispered as he collapsed on top of her.

DEAN

Dean came to as Violent stroked his head. She was blurry at first, but then he could see the concern in her face.

"You live. That brought back some horrible memories." She wasn't smiling. She helped him sit up.

"Seri?"

"She lives as well." Violent pointed to the screen.

The two figures lay in a heap on the floor, caressing each other.

"No." He bit his lip as he saw his sister locked in an embrace with the beast man.

"Do not overreact or they'll shock you again." Violent seemed less interested in making a pass at Dean. Her eyes scanned the large room outside their cage.

He punched his own hand a few times. "Where's my mother?"

"He took her. She fought and was shocked as well." Violent pulled him to his feet like he was a ragdoll.

"Grandfather?" Dean looked at the audience and was

surprised to see just a few half-breeds lingering. They looked distracted.

He was about to ask what had happened when he felt it. Something deep in his body recognized the hum in the air. Hell. It pulled at him, offering power as easy as breathing.

"You feel it? Yes. Things will change. We do not want to be trapped when the minions come." Violent made sure he was stable before she went to the cage's bars.

"The minions are getting out?" Dean felt fuzzy. He massaged his head.

"Oh, yes. Like rats from a sinking ship. They will likely hate the half-breeds being drawn to the place right now."

Dean walked as close as he could get to the screen, unable to look away, though he desperately wanted to avoid seeing anything indecent. He needed to protect his sister, even just by watching over her, but he couldn't make sense of this. The man seemed to be gentle with her, as best as he could tell from the streaky heat images.

"Why would they hate them?" Dean asked as an afterthought.

"Well, handsome, they'll realize that some minions have escaped and procreated. Jealousy is one of Hell's driving forces. They'll want what others have had. It will be a frenzy of death, and the humans will be involved — eventually if not immediately." Violent motioned to a skinny half-breed left in the audience.

Dean touched the bars of the cage, sickened that they were the bones of beings just like him. His grandfather was a single-minded asshole. He glanced over his shoulder to watch Violent turn on her version of charm.

"You're a small, worthless half-breed. What name do you think I should call you?" Violent was gorgeous enough to get away with the way she talked.

"Lunge." The young half-breed's Adam's apple bobbed up and down.

"You are able to resist the call of Hell?" Violent leaned closer to the bars, inviting him with her vivid eyes.

"Um, Vittorio has me collared for shock. So I, um, can't." Lunge shifted from one foot to the other.

"How barbaric. You deserve the freedom of a plant." Violent bit her index finger gently. She was shameless.

"Okay." The half-breed was transfixed by Violent, totally missing her weird words.

"So let me and my lover out of this cage. I'll introduce you to some lovely trees."

Dean tossed up his hands. It was the worst bribe in the history of bribes.

"Can't let you out. Don't even know how." The tree talk had obviously set off alarms for Lunge.

Dean sprinted to Violent's side and tried to grab the half-breed. He scurried away.

Violent turned on him. "Now you scared him off!" Her gaze drifted past his face to Seri's screen behind him, and her eyes widened a bit. She pulled Dean into a hug and whispered in his ear. "Your sister and the nude one are not on the screen anymore. Don't look."

Dean hid his alarm with a fake smile. Had his sister escaped? Did the man take her somewhere? Then he had a chilling feeling. What if she was too dead to register with the heat sensors?

SERIANA

Seriana followed Mine as he snaked through a passage in the basement. He found them both coveralls hanging in a closet. She shrugged off her wet sheet after she'd pulled them on.

"Where are we going?" She quickly plaited her hair to get it out of her eyes.

"Away. We will live in the forest." He held out his hand, serious.

"I have to get my mother and brother. I won't leave without them." She tugged on his hand.

"We are family now. Just you and me." He picked her up and strode toward a long hallway.

She touched his lips and he stopped, eyes flashing with lust.

"They make me happy. I can be with you if I'm happy." She watched as he considered her words.

Mine looked from her mouth to her eyes. "We have little time."

Leaving her mother and brother behind wasn't going to work. Ever. She put that determination in her eyes and simply said, "Please."

Exhaling loudly, he set her down. "I've been in a cage for longer than you've been alive. But I'll go with you."

She touched his shoulder and smiled. "How is it you're so kind? When you've had nothing of the sort."

"An angel visited me in my dreams. Many times." Mine took her hand and pulled her toward an old heating vent, not witnessing her shock.

Seri knew only one angel, of course, but she felt certain it was her Emma that somehow gave this man his kindness. A wave of peace washed over her. Things might just be playing out exactly as they were supposed to.

Mine pulled himself into the old vent and held out a thick, strong arm for her. She climbed up the wall and into his arms. He kissed her again. As they inched through the heating vent, Mine revealed his plan.

"The tops of the cages have a weakness. The builder was hungry and sloppy when he built the lids. That is how I was able to get us out of the mating cage. You will stay here, and I will decimate the half-breeds and free your family." He put his fingers to his lips and motioned for her to stay. Mine scanned the open room through the vent. He whispered to himself, "Two, four, nine altogether."

He removed the grate slowly and dropped to the floor at least twenty feet below. He landed in a crouch. He looked once at her, probably to make sure she was staying in place. But as soon as he'd begun battling the half-breeds, Seriana dropped down into the room as well. Mine was ferocious, a swirl of punches and kicks, and he paused only to jab or readjust his fighting stance. A look passed between them as Seriana pulled a male half-breed out of the circle that had formed around Mine. She could see he was angry with her.

She turned her attention to the male and neatly crippled him by busting his kneecaps in quick succession. When she turned back to Mine, the rest of the half-breeds were scattered on the floor. She smiled at him, pleased that she'd been able to help. He shook his head but waved her over.

"Well done. Get to the top of your brother's cage. Don't touch the water. Will the minion help?" Mine hopped up carefully, looking for Rebecca.

Seriana approached Dean's cage. He lay still and Violent cuddled him. As Seri approached, she hissed.

"Is Dean okay?" Seriana carefully pulled herself up to the top of the cage.

Violent addressed Mine instead. "The old man's daughter was taken."

"Is Dean all right?" Seriana was getting worried.

"They shocked him too much. He's still alive. I'm trying to get him to feed." Violent sat back a bit on her heels, and Seri could see the red staining her neck and chest.

Mine landed softly next to Seriana. "We need to move fast. The reminder shock is coming."

Confused, she shook her head. Mine pointed to a large antique clock. "Every hour the shock is released. It reminds anyone in a watery cage who's in charge."

The clock was just seconds from the hour.

"He won't make it through another one," Mine observed. "I've seen a lot of healthier looking half-breeds die from it." He went to work on the top of the cage, trying to locate the weak spot.

"If you open that, I might leave Dean. I will go to heed the call of my master." Violent cuddled him closer.

Seriana joined Mine, frantically tugging on the bone bars while he methodically checked each one. "You have to help us, Violent. That's my brother."

The clock tolled an unnervingly loud strike. It was midnight, so at least they had twelve bells.

Mine seemed unaffected by the noise, and Seriana began beating on the cage. "Why will you go?" she asked. Violent made no sense, as usual.

"Lucifer calls. I'll have no choice. I don't want to leave him. I don't want him to die." Violent hugged Dean even closer.

Seriana lost count of the strikes, but there had been so many. She couldn't watch as her brother was shocked to death. "Be strong, Violent. You can do this."

With the last strike, Mine ripped open the cage, and Violent tossed Dean to them as if he were made of paper, seeming to fight her own legs' will to jump. She took the shock that would have killed him by herself.

Seriana and Mine dragged Dean through the hole in the cage while Violent convulsed. It was awful. She began to froth at the mouth, her purple eyes rolling in her head.

Mine had already jumped from the cage with Dean on his back. "Come, lover. They wake."

The shock had roused some of the half-breeds, who were now pulling themselves to sitting. Seriana watched Violent collapse, even as she growled at her.

"Go. Take Dean," she demanded. And then Violent slumped to the ground.

But Seriana couldn't leave her. It was stupid, and Violent probably deserved to be stuck in a cage, but she was proud of her momentary selflessness — even if she was delusional. Seri dropped into the watery cage as soon as the shock seemed to dissipate, and pulled the minion onto her back. She jumped, almost touching the top bar. Mine fought his way back through the groggy half-breeds and climbed to the top of the cage. He offered his hand awkwardly as he shuffled Dean on his back.

Seriana didn't have time to smile, but she jumped with all her might, and Mine pulled them from the cage. They took off, each juggling their burden. They had to abandon hope of going back through the heating vent and went straight for the front door.

The half-breeds gave chase, and Seriana was grateful when Violent began to move. Seriana spoke over her shoulder, "You okay, V?"

The minion responded by wiggling off her back. She turned and faced the half-breeds instead of running. Seriana stopped next to her, and Mine and Dean joined the lineup. Her brother looked barely conscious, but at least he could stand. Every deep breath seemed to give him more life.

Mine growled, and Violent matched it. The battle was now unfair, and the half-breeds didn't stand a chance. The massacre was so swift it was almost funny. Mine and Violent were just so much stronger. Within moments, a handful of half-breeds littered the ground.

When the danger had passed, Seriana went to her brother. "You all right? It was dicey for a minute."

He nodded. "Mom's with him again. We can't slow down. Are you okay?" He seemed to be remembering her mating. He gave Mine a deadly stare.

"Yes, I'm great. He's been trapped just like we were. We're friends." Her brother looked doubtful.

"No, really." She looked over to see Violent now fighting an inner battle.

"V?" Dean staggered toward her, gaining balance with every step.

"Must not go. *Must* go. My king calls. Forgive me, Dean." In an instant, Violent was pulled from the group as if on a string.

One second she was there, and the next, just a small imprint in the grass remained where her feet had been.

Seriana watched as her brother turned the way Violent had been pulled. Mine did the same. Then Seriana felt it too. Deep in her core. Half her very cells were shaking, begging her to return. They began to run, as if they did not have a choice. Lucifer was calling all of his spawn home.

CHAPTER 30

EMMA

Emma flew as high as she could into the dark sky and took in the astounding full moon. The rush of the air was fantastic, and the gorgeous moon lit the ground like daylight. She tried not to cry at the thought of leaving Jack, but it was the only thing she could think to do. And Everett was the cause of it all. She circled. It was a gorgeous night — no clouds, a gentle breeze — a beautiful night to die.

Everett emerged from Hell with flames streaming from his back. Smoke hissed as he hit the open air, lighting the scene around him. She didn't doubt he'd win their battle, but she wanted to buy Jack time to get everyone out. Before Everett could reach her, Emma used her seraph powers for good. She prayed for the safety of all those in Hell, for Kate and Jason to have happiness, and lastly, she prayed for Jack's lost soul.

God,

I know I've not done You justice. But Jack's soul was the only one he had to offer. He shouldn't lose it because I had to help him. I wish I knew Your plan, because following my heart seems to hurt people. I love You, and I know I'll be extinguished soon. My soul's no good to me now, so please take it and let Jack have his back.

I love You, Emma

She felt Everett's breath behind her before he spoke.

"Praying? You are *such* a predictable whore. You'll never learn."

Emma could feel the heat from his flame wings. She opened her eyes and sighed. She was sick of him. She might even be past hating him. She just wished he wasn't such a pain in her ass.

"When I'm done with you? I'll go after Jack and all those minions and half minions. I'll kill anyone who's ever smiled at you."

And that was it. Emma decided she wasn't dying. She was going to fucking win.

She stilled her wings and dropped, grabbing fistfuls of her feathers as she fell. Then she caught herself and flew past him again, flinging her feathers into the night. They turned into dripping silver throwing stars though her only thought accompanying their release had been: *Death!*

JASON

Jason watched as Jack fell to his knees, apparently despondent over Emma's departure, and felt bad for the jerk for about a second. He quickly forgot him as he watched the minions approach. The barrier was down, and they came uninhibited. The dragon whipped its tail around the group and pulled them in close, spewing fire. Jason tried to orient himself in their flailing arms and legs as he was pressed against the dragon's scales. He felt Kate's soft skin and pulled her closer. The glow from her palms had diminished. Jack's face was close, so Jason took the opportunity to slap it. The former Devil sneered at him but did not retaliate.

"Now what?" Jason asked.

Jack was all elbows, trying to give himself more room. Nero,

Ransom, and the poodle wiggled around. "Now? Emma dies, so I could give a rat's ass about any of this. I tried. I failed. We die. Next question?" He tried to light a cigarette.

Kate gasped. "Look!"

Jason and Jack came to a mutual pause in giving each other dirty looks. He looked up to see minions climbing through the holes Everett and Emma had punched into the ceiling. Then a huge whoosh sent a bunch of minions falling back through. Everett fell on top of the pile, covered in glittering silver stars and bleeding everywhere.

"Emma!" he hollered. "That the best you got?"

Emma's voice floated down to Hell, loud and strong. "Nope. Just getting started, you asshole."

Everett's wings lit up again, and he flew back up through the hole.

Jason looked at Jack's bewildered face. "Looks like she's kicking his ass. You still want to martyr yourself? Or are you ready to nut up, cowboy?"

Jack shook his head in apparent disbelief. "If she wins, she's the Devil. Then we can be together. Shit!"

The minions had now abandoned everything and focused singularly on getting out of Hell. Jack pushed out of the dragon's grasp and grabbed Jason's shoulders.

"Listen, ride this dragon up there and help Emma if you can. Avoid the minions — they'll be crazed because Everett's freed them from their compulsions. He wants them to fight for him. It won't last forever. I'm going to find Dean, Seriana, and Violent. Does that sound right?" Jack seemed energized but a bit disorganized as well.

"I want to help you get to Seriana," Jason countered. "Kate, will you be okay?" Jason wasn't ready to rely on Jack.

The poodle came to stand by Jack, obviously not able to get out through the hole or ride the dragon.

Nero put his arm around his daughter. "Kate goes to the surface now."

With that, the dragon, who appeared to understand more English than it let on, lowered itself for the riders. Kate ran to Jason and kissed his lips.

"I feel like we were blessed or something. Please find me when this is over."

Jason didn't tell her it was crazy to even hope there'd be an after, but if there was one, he was certain he wanted to spend it with her. He held his faintly glowing palm to hers. "She did bless us. I'll see you on the other side." He kissed Kate's lips gently, aware of Nero's intense scrutiny.

Jason helped her up and the dragon took off, knocking minions out of its way, then made Emma's tunnel bigger with its head and wiggled through. All of Hell shook, as if it were trying to get into its own hand basket. Jack looked him up and down.

"Well, you're lucky I like your sister. Let's go back to the opening by Kate's house and try to get out of here before this place caves in."

Jason used his palms like a flashlight, but Jack was still faster, easily navigating the caves. So he followed Jack's cigarette and tried to let the sounds of the epic battle going on above his head give him purpose instead of panic.

EMMA

Everett had wrapped her in darkness. Emma cursed herself for not seeing this one coming. He'd had used the same trick on Jack in Hell. He flew closer to her, bruised and bloody.

"Well, this has been...arousing."

Emma narrowed her eyes at him.

"I thought I needed you under me. But I get it now. Your fighting makes your fear *much* sweeter." His hand passed through the darkness and skimmed her arm.

Emma shivered. She didn't have Jack's smoke to release her, but maybe she could call to the light. She focused on a spot in the distance where a gorgeous star did its best to decorate the sky. Emma meditated, and Everett passed both hands over her wings. Each sensitive feather protested his evil. It was just a bit of starlight, but it was coming fast. What looked white in the distance was really every color, she realized. Emma braced herself as it headed toward her heart.

Everett whispered his degrading plans as the starlight slowed. She'd expected it to hit with the force of the millions of years it had just flown through. Instead, it gently touched the edge of the dark shroud and traveled like a fire line. Rainbow sparks sizzled. Everett had slipped his hands under her wings to hold her ass, and he screamed as the starlight traveled from the dark to his skin.

Emma was free, released. She flew forward and watched as Everett writhed. The light attacked him like a parasite. She took a moment to look below her. Minions poured through the holes she and Everett had created to reach the surface. When she looked back at her greatest enemy, he'd shaken off the starlight, but it had attacked his flame wings. Gravity finished the job, and Everett began the plummet back to Earth. She took off after him before thinking. Smoosh the dragon shook the ground as he worked his way out of the underworld, and in her peripheral vision she saw Kate, Nero, and another minion on his back. She didn't stop Everett from hitting the ground.

Nero pulled his daughter from the dragon's back before they could miss their chance to be on the land. As Smoosh flew high above Emma, Ransom jumped free as well. Everett's body had made a huge crater. Emma waited on the lip, and Nero jogged over.

"You must battle him to the death," he advised. "These minions will only listen to the real Devil. They'll flow free on this unprepared world and change what humans experience."

He'd obviously taken her waiting as indecision.

"Where are Jack and Jason?" she asked, keeping her eyes on Everett's prone form.

"They were going through to help the others escape. I do not know their names."

Kate came close to her father, eyes wide. "Seriana, Dean, and Violent were waiting in my shed's entrance. The grandfather and his army were waiting on the other side."

The minions around them were losing their minds. Freedom caused some to run, some to shake, and many to fight with each other.

Emma had challenged Everett for the position to buy Jack time, but now she understood what she'd really done. She'd decided to become a murderer.

"Can you go to your house and try to help?" Emma watched as Everett began to pull himself out of the crater.

Nero shook his head. "No. My daughter stays safe."

Kate nodded at the same time and said, "Headed there now."

It was the best Emma could do. She nodded and stepped backward to prepare. She needed a second to assimilate to the changes she was asking of herself. Killing was wrong. It was a commandment. Thou shall not kill. And yet she was ashamed to find she wanted his blood. This man, this thing — he'd never stop unless he was dead. She might never spend another night in the arms of her love, Jack, and her escape from Hell had released a mass tragedy in the form of roving minions on the world she was supposed to protect.

Everett pulled himself out, flexing his muscles. His wings flamed up again. "And that's when you should have tried to finish me off. You just stood there? Shit, were you praying again?" Shaking his head, he walked toward her like they were friends.

Emma took off quickly. Everett had given her a good idea.

She prayed again: *Lord, this feels like the only choice. It also feels like I'm turning my back on You. I'm so sorry.*

With that Emma stilled and hovered. She cataloged all her seraph powers and imagined working evil with them. Everett caught up and situated himself for their brawl, once again running his mouth.

"Do you know how easy this is? You have no follow-through. You expect to be able to fight? All you've ever done is be a cock tease. In Heaven you were God's bitch. You don't have the balls to be the Devil." He cracked his knuckles and smiled.

Emma closed her eyes and dipped herself in black leather, placing swords in her hands and a black mask around her eyes. She smiled back. "You don't know me." She threw the first sword at his chest and immediately followed the strike with a numbing force, paralyzing him for a split second.

She raised the second blade above her head, ready to end him, when she finally had the pleasure of seeing fear in his eyes.

JASON

Jack and Jason could not resist fight breaks from time to time, despite their cooperative mission to get back to the portal at Kate's. One would trip the other or jab with an elbow, and they'd fall into fisticuffs, working out their dislike. Then one or the other would remember the goal and holler that they needed to keep moving.

Jason dusted himself off and gestured with two annoyed hands for Jack to continue leading the way to the entrance where his siblings were waiting. "We need to just walk, or run, or some-thing other than you trying to dry hump me every other minute."

Jack growled and proceeded down through the cave. "Even though I'm sure you have a couple of pretty, pink vaginas hidden on your body, I still wouldn't screw you."

"Let's just get this over with so I can get to Kate." He turned and slugged Jack in the face.

Jack held up a hand to stop him from landing another blow.

"The whole damn world is going to die because you can't stop touching me. Can we please just get on with it?" He stomped forward, and Jason followed.

He knew they should be out there fighting everything else but each other. "Do you think she'll become the Devil?" Jason had to ask again.

Jack shook his head. "No. Although I want to because that means she'll live. I'm stuck here, so I can't get out to protect her. She needs to fly back in here so I can fight this fucking battle with her."

The dirty pond where Lucifer lived came into view, and both men stopped, their mouths hanging open. A crowd stood around the pond, which now glowed red.

"What the fu..." Jason breathed.

"Our guys lost. The old fart vampire must have opened the stone in the shed. That's the only way these half-breeds would be in here. Shit." Jack put his hands on his knees and breathed deeply, with focus.

"Seri, Dean, and Violent? They lost?" Jason put it together. Chances are they were dead. His heart crumbled. It had been the three of them for so long.

Jack glanced at him. "Listen, asshole. It doesn't mean they're dead. I've learned you got to...believe." He stood and seemed to get purpose back into his step.

Before Jason could stop him, Jack walked right up to the pond and cleared his throat. The half-breeds turned in a daze. They seemed high from the force of the power coming from the muck.

"What happened to the half-breeds that were running from you sludge buckets?" Jack looked from one to the other.

A small girl spoke up. "We left them at the mating." She turned her head back to the pond, mesmerized as the water started to swirl. "To come here. It called." She pointed a shaking finger at the pond, which now seemed to be forming a hurricane.

Jack backed up and slapped Jason's arm to get him to come

with. Jason ignored him. The relief that his siblings were alive was suppressed by the fact that they were taken to a "mating." His grandfather's deepest wish was coming true.

Jack pulled his hair and slapped his face. "You know who lives in there. Do you want to watch as he rises after sticking his head in the sand for thousands of years? You've got discipline enough to resist his call, don't you?"

Jason backed up as Jack yanked on him again. "Now what?" he asked irritably.

"Too late to leave," Jack muttered. He and Jason managed to move a distance away while Lucifer emerged from the pond as the scariest thing in the universe. His black wings were slick, and his hot, red body was more horselike than human. The half-breeds collapsed, prostrate. Lucifer's beautiful evil coerced them instantly.

One after another began to burn as Lucifer stomped through their gathering. Everything he touched burst into the deepest red flames, punctuated by horrible screams.

"What a horrible way to die," Jason whispered.

Jack's eyes were hard when he told Jason the worst part. "They'll never die. Only burn."

Lucifer's eyes were swirls of flame, and he set them on Jack and Jason. Jason felt his knees bend of their own volition, and he shook his head in grudging respect as he watched Jack casually approach the thing that had come up out of the pond.

"Lucy, you're looking chipper." Jack held out a cigarette, and Lucifer's sheer nearness lit the end.

"Hell collapses because you fail. You're weak. Now an angel will run my home? How will that work?" Lucifer's voice sounded like a hundred men yelling in synchronicity.

Lucifer was so close now. Jason was positive his ears were bleeding from the volume. He thought about sneaking away, but Lucifer seemed able to look at one person while focusing on another — he also wasn't exactly certain he could move.

"You can't hide from this, Lucy. Now's the time to find out

exactly what you want — besides someone else doing your fucking job. You think she's winning?" Jack's hands were steady as the beast growled.

"I know she can win. I feel it. She's contaminating everything." Lucifer turned his massive head and breathed on a new crowd of half-breeds. They joined the others as flaming, living torches.

"So now what?" Jack stepped forward like an idiot, ready to brawl. Jason grabbed his leather jacket and dragged him back a step.

Lucifer flared his nostrils. "I'm going out there to decide who wins the battle."

The evil thing flew, its giant wingspan displacing enough air to knock Jack on top of Jason. Lucifer disappeared right out the exit by Kate's house. Jason looked at Jack for an answer, but he was busy recovering the cigarette that had been flung by the wind. He took a long inhale and stared into the distance.

Jason prepared to yell at him for angering Lucifer when he saw a single tear slip down Jack's cheek. He turned his head and pretended not to see. Because seeing Jack cry could only mean Emma was in worse danger than before: a hopeless kind.

CHAPTER 31

JACK

Jack knew what he couldn't do. He couldn't leave Hell. He'd given his soul to hold God in place. Then Emma's wings had held his soul in his body, allowing him to be human, but the second she put them back on, it was over. He was bound to this place. A being needed at least a soul. Hell was like his artificial heart now, its energy keeping him animated. If he stepped out of one of the exits, it'd be over.

He wished he didn't know. Otherwise he would've followed Lucifer right out of Hell to help Emma. Instead, he walked to the exit by Kate's house. He crouched as he smoked the last of his cigarette, his old motorcycle boots at the ragged edge of Hell's boundary.

Emma swooped up. Damn it, she looked amazing: covered in black, wearing a black mask. Like she'd changed. Like wearing a new outfit would make her ready to be the Devil. He knew better. Everett hit his angel, and Jack stood. Everything in him boiled. Suddenly Jason ran past him too fast to comment. Jack felt it then and almost cut the bastard some slack. Lucy was calling his beasts home — the battle must be brewing for real now — and there was nothing Jason could do to stop himself. All the minions and half-breeds on Earth and from Hell were returning to Lucifer's feet.

Returning his eyes to the sky, Jack stumbled a bit when he saw Emma take a paralyzing blow. She shook it off and came at Everett again. "That's my girl." He glanced down and realized one boot was out of Hell.

It shouldn't have happened. It couldn't happen. But he edged his other boot out of Hell and closed his eyes. He was alive. He ran before he could

comprehend the miracle of his ability to exit. He needed to get to Emma. He had to challenge Everett again. He had to get Lucifer to leave her be.

Jack skidded to a stop underneath the battle. Angel versus Devil. What a change of events. Now he would be solidly rooting for the Heavenly other side.

Emma

Everett deflected her sword, so Emma whipped around to kick him in the side. She wasn't a pretty fighter, but she channeled everything she had toward him. She began splitting his soul from his body, tearing it away with her mind while she hacked at him with her sword. Then he pulled her other sword from his chest and used it against her, engulfed in flames. On a too- close pass he chopped off half of her right wing. Mercury-colored love poured from the feathers, bleeding down onto Earth. She sliced away at his left leg in retaliation. It was harder to fly now that she was off balance, and his leg regenerated immediately. His flaming wings hissed as she threw a handful of snow tainted with prayers at him.

She watched as the love leaving her mesmerized the minions below. They stilled just to watch it splash down around them. As she turned back to her battle, she realized it had probably been ages, eons, even longer, since some of those minions had known anything resembling love. The sounds and scenes of an angel fighting to be the Devil must be a spectacular show, but the simple presence of love was what they longed for. How could she not fight for them? Renewing her focus, she pulled starlight and bits of Heaven's clouds from the sky. Everett called on darkness and fear. Above and below them, their colliding elements threw off light that put the aurora borealis to shame.

Yet when she glanced down again, many of the minions remained totally transfixed by the drops of love they'd located — and completely distracted from their fighting, which meant they weren't faring too well. And that would surely piss Everett off. If she lost this war — *oh please, God, I need to win* — who knew what horrific punishment he might exact on them. Unsure whether she acted as angel or Devil, but suddenly sure of what she needed to do, Emma pulled the dreams floating around the atmosphere into a tight bubble around her and Everett. This gave them a sealed area to fight in and shielded those below from any additional drops of love.

Everett bared his teeth at the enclosure. Emma stopped her awkward flying and landed on the bubble. She pulled out handfuls of her black feathers and was about to name them into a weapon when the whole bubble rocked. She froze as she found a huge, red horse-like monster rising before her. His eyes were horrible. Everett used her distraction to his advantage. She lost her footing when he landed behind her and swiveled her into a restraint. She waited for her eyes to adjust to the beast, or to hear more taunts from Everett, but nether happened.

Everett spoke to the thing. "Lucifer, I'm guessing. I love this promotion. Do you like what I've done with the place?"

Emma looked around and found her dragon silhouetted against the moon. At least Smoosh looked happy. She watched as it flamed up and lit the sky like a firework.

"You're a catastrophe," the thing's impossibly loud voice responded. "Everything is ruined because of you."

The bubble shook again, and Emma wasn't sure it would hold. The minions and half-breeds below had taken a knee and bowed their heads in Lucifer's presence. She felt Everett quiet behind her after the verbal blow. "Look at that. You even suck at being evil," she said with a smile. She rolled her hips a bit to see how balanced he was.

Smoosh turned and flew straight at the bubble. She wasn't sure if the dragon was helping her, coming to Lucifer's aid, or just doing a fly-by. Everett bit her ear. She pictured spike heels on her feet and sunk one into his shin.

He screamed and let go. Emma dropped to the bubble and braced herself. Smoosh hit Lucifer at full dragon speed, just like a devoted guard dog should. The bubble rumbled with the collision, and Everett fell to his knees. Emma still had a handful of feathers, so she pictured "bondage" and tossed them. The feathers restrained Everett's feet and hands, turning into leather cuffs.

Emma looked below her at the countless minion and half-breed eyes now fixed on the bubble. The dragon had chased Lucifer beyond the horizon. She pictured a dagger, and it appeared, glistening in the moonlight. The bubble of dreams hummed, a million shades of crystal. The dagger had a cross embedded on its hilt.

"Do it! Oh please. Kill me. I think I'll come when you murder me. Be just like me, whore. Do it."

Deep bruises bloomed on Everett's body, and blood seeped from several lacerations, but Emma knew that unbound, he'd be raring to fight.

The beings below her frothed at the possibility. Seeing an angel be terrible was riveting. She held the blade above his heart — or where that organ should be anyway. She'd always doubted he had one.

He began thrusting his pelvis like the sick freak he was. It was time to end him. She'd thought the mask and the black outfit would help, but they hadn't made her forget who she was, what she stood for.

The minions and half-breeds needed to see goodness, not more death and domination. Their stupefied wonderment at the love raining from her wounds had sparked her angel's compassion, and now purpose dawned on her like a thousand suns: She could teach everything in the underworld how things should be done, how they should treat each other, what love looked like. They were hungry for this message. She closed her eyes and changed her clothes back to official angel garb: a long, satin dress and silver sandals.

She watched as Jack stormed below her. Jack! It took her a second to put it together, but his presence outside Hell meant God had restored his soul. Always God surprised her with His goodness, and a wave of love burst from deep within her. In the middle of this insanity, He'd made sure a man who'd been the Devil would know redemption. A soul returned to a body was a tremendous gift.

Emma smiled. She couldn't see Jack's eyes, but she knew he was watching. She could picture him losing his mind, cursing at what she was about to do next. Whatever the outcome was for Jack in this world, she hoped he'd never forget the precious gift of his soul. And then something else made sense: it was *her* soul she was giving up for trade. She used her dagger to slice through the leather bindings at Everett's wrists. When she turned to Everett's bound feet, she could hear Jack swearing.

Everett came free swinging. He made contact with her stomach, and she folded. He pounded her on the back, yet she refused to fight. He pulled her to her feet, obviously perplexed at the change in her demeanor.

"What the fuck is wrong with you? Fight me, bitch." Everett shook her by her shoulders.

"You are a child of God, and He loves you." Emma knew she needed to say this, but she spit it out like a curse.

"Are you going straight on me? Following the rulebook? Has that ever gotten you anywhere?" Everett was spitting in her face. His horrible mouth was so close. "Fight me!" He was begging her now. Almost pleading. He needed the anger she'd been feeding him. He slapped her face as hard as he could.

Emma saw white, and her mouth filled with angel's blood. She could hear Jack screaming his head off — calling the dragon, begging the angels to come from Heaven, screaming at God. She loved him so much. Despite the miles between them, she smiled at him.

Her neck was hard to move, some of her muscles must have snapped from the blow. She clenched her fists and used all the angel power she had left to lift her face to Everett's. She looked him dead in the eyes and then slowly turned her head, offering him her other cheek.

Jack stopped screaming. A hush fell over the world.

"Oh, you're a dramatic whore," Everett seethed. "I get it. Do you want to be like God? Do you think you can be like Him?"

Emma felt tears roll down her cheeks. The next blow would certainly hurt, and might pop her head right from her neck. She hated that Jack would see that. She said another prayer for him, and Everett raised his hand.

"If you expected mercy, you were wrong. Again. Goodbye, Emma." Everett's hand sounded like thunder as it headed for her face.

JACK

Jack was stuck on the ground. He'd begged his minions to throw him, tried to get anyone able to sprout wings. It was impossible. Now he had to stand here and watch his love die. That couldn't be how love ended. What would be the point of hoping for anything at all?

Everett wound up for an epic slap, and Jack knew the red glow in his hand was Hellfire. It would be more than an angel could take, especially if she wasn't fighting back.

She'd smiled at him then — connected with *him* across all space and time. He couldn't smile back, but only held his heart.

But wait — Everett was distracted. It took Jack a beat to realize the death- blow was still in the air, and now huge, fast snowflakes fell from the sky. Soon they took shape: the fucking angels. Too little too late.

One after another they dropped. And the second they hovered above his minions, the world cracked. The most legendary battle was about to begin. Good versus bad. Evil versus virtue.

Jack could give a rat's ass. He could still imagine her gray eyes, her smile. The fighting that broke out around him was just noise. Everett was winding up again, letting the hellfire turn his hand so red it was almost black.

"Please, someone with wings, take me to her. Please." He was hoarse and whispering. His desperation had nearly taken his voice.

Jack felt her before she touched him. Then her voice came like bells and candy.

"Hang on. Guess you still have your memory?" Claudette, his former flame, lifted him easily into the air.

He didn't even let the surprise at her assistance register. "Faster."

Emma remained in the bubble of dreams. Only she could break it. He knew this from his own time as an angel a million years ago. Below there was hissing — feathers and burning. Maybe this was the apocalypse, but the whole world could go fuck itself. Jack's focus was singular.

There should have been heralds, chariots, and bursts of lights when God arrived and stepped in front of Emma. But He was understated. Claudette finally made it to the bubble with Jack, and she flew him to hover even with Emma.

Everett hadn't noticed God's entrance in time to stop his hand from flying (who knows if he would have), so God absorbed the worst blow the Devil could land. He didn't even flinch.

Instead He just put his arm around Emma. Everett stood stupidly. Everything else was meaningless when God was in front of you.

Then the Lord turned His eyes to Jack.

Overwhelmed by the gratefulness that threatened to burst out of him, Jack brought his fist to his lips. Finally he could speak, but only one thing: "Thank you."

God smiled, and Jack felt his restored soul sigh in his chest. Emma gasped and rolled her head on her neck, obviously healed.

"Thank you so much," Jack said again. If he hadn't been held aloft by Claudette, he would've taken to his knees.

CHAPTER 32

EMMA

Emma clutched God's hand. Jack thanking God made her eyes fill up.

Just living made her grateful. It was a few seconds before she realized she was in a pause. The whole world had stopped. Claudette's wings were still as a statue, and her Jack was motionless. She recognized the quiet now. Everett had frozen perplexed and unblinking. Stone Everett was a huge improvement on the moving variety.

"Was I okay? Did I follow You?" She was being too casual as she spoke to her maker, but her energy was sapped.

God turned to her and held both of her hands. "My daughter. You are the very best of me." He touched her cheek and neck. Her sliced wing was restored. "Do you have questions? Can I hold you?" God opened His arms.

Emma almost fell into them. Every muscle that had been bruised and tortured was healed. Her power as a seraph filled to overflowing.

She looked down. Below them was an army of bittersweet seraphim. They seemed to dread the fight and revel in it at the same time. "It's not just the good beings that matter to You," Emma said, thinking out loud. "The minions are your children, the half-breeds." She curled her fist on God's chest. His eyes were dark this time. Their color never mattered. Being in His gaze was home.

"My creations are my pride. Each has a place in the world, a destiny of their choice to fulfill," He said.

"Sir, in Hell there were some souls removed entirely. Is there hope...?" She trailed off, almost afraid of the answer. She thought of Tiffany, the poodles, the nameless minions who'd been killed...

"They are safe, my seraph. Thank you for worrying."

God flashed her somewhere new. Out of the dream bubble.

They were in a field. She recognized it as her horse, Feisty, cantered over. She took a few minutes to settle the horse down and pet her soft muzzle. Feisty used her lips to nip at Emma. She'd called it horse kisses when she was a girl.

"Ask, child. I will tell you what I can. You have earned answers." God petted her horse.

The sun was amazing in this pause. It touched the edges of the field grasses, and they glowed like paintbrushes dipped in magic.

"It's not my place to ask, only try," Emma said softly. "I try to listen to the part of me that feels right when I make a choice."

Feisty leaned her head down and began munching the grass. God waited. It occurred to Emma that this pause could be as long as God wanted it to be. It relaxed her to know all the people she cared about were safe indefinitely.

"Did I fail? Did I end up where you wanted me, sir? It seemed convoluted." She hoped her words didn't sound disrespectful.

"You did not fail, my pride. But you know that. You have no need to hear it from Me. When you offered your worst enemy your other cheek? Yes, my child. You were where you needed to be." God put his hand on the cheek Everett had slapped.

His kindness brought a lump to her throat. "It was terrible at times. I was so alone. I couldn't pray. I was going to murder him. Be the Devil. I just..." She wiped a tear from her cheek. God had asked a lot from her.

"I did. I asked so much. And you delivered. You were never

going to murder anyone, no matter how angry you felt. Does that help?" God sat in the meadow grass and motioned for her to join him.

Emma sat, tucking her white angel gown under her legs. She touched God's hand. Peace. She had so much peace. "It does. I just wish I could be sure of the choices I made. I love Jack. I mean, how can that be right?" Emma pictured his handsome face.

"How can it be wrong? Love picks the right path, not the one of least resistance." God's skin was deep and dark this time. The sun was warm.

"Your world is beautiful. But it's harsh as well. I can't forget Hell. Yet I think Jack tried to be a good Devil — if that's even possible." She put her hand through her hair.

"Jack. If I told you his soul was very important, would you believe Me?"

Her eyes widened. "I know it is. Was this whole journey to free Jack?" Emma hugged her knees. Shaking up the entire world to free him worked for her.

"Your journey was much more than Jack. Think about all the lives you've touched. I can't give you all the intricate details because it wouldn't be fair. The puzzle of it all is my burden." God looked weary.

She tried to ask a question a few times, but bit her lip instead.

"Say it, Emma. Holding your tongue has never suited you." God lifted her chin with His finger and smiled.

Feisty whinnied softly as if agreeing.

"I hate Everett. I can't forgive him, and I know you expect more from me. Is that why I went to Hell?" She covered her mouth after she asked, sure she was right.

"Everett. I can't disclose the state of his soul, but I never expected you to forgive him." God looked at the sky, squinting into the sun.

"Really? You put kind of a huge emphasis on forgiveness." Emma rubbed her hands together in her nervousness.

"Have you tried praying for him? You can at least do that.

Forgiveness takes time, and practice. When you can't bring yourself to forgive, you must at least pray." God waited.

"I haven't prayed for him. Never once." Guilt engulfed her.

God touched her hand. "Daughter, getting it right the first time isn't your job. Learning is."

She snuggled up to Him. God slipped his arm over her shoulder. They sat in the silence for a while. She heard Him sigh.

"That's quite a scene we're going back to." She peeked at His face.

"Lucifer has drawn this whole thing out way too long. I think I indulged him a bit. I really hoped he would choose a path that made him more of a man." God pushed her hair out of her face. "Let me worry about it, little one."

Feisty stepped closer to graze right by Emma. She reached up and petted her beautiful horse again. She loved her huge brown eyes.

"But I feel like you're alone," Emma said.

"With as many children as I have? I'm never alone. I brought you here to let you ask questions, but also to speak about what's next for you." God turned so He could see her face better.

"I still worry about you," she said. A look passed between them. She knew then that she and God were friends, no matter what happened in the world. He nodded and smiled.

"I guess I have to go to angel court again? I claimed my wings back. But Jack was out of Hell? Was it really his soul on the scale?"

"Oh, yes. I'd hoped that by refusing to doom him, I could show Jack I thought his soul worth fighting for. And, of course, there's you. He'd never been able to see how true love makes you more understanding and less angry. Emma, my wild card." God stood and held out His hand.

She took it and hugged him once she got to her feet.

"What is it you want? You have audience with God. Speak, child." God kissed the top of her head.

"Save them all. That's what I want." The warmth she felt in

His arms was the softest emotion. "And I'd really love to take Feisty for a ride."

God released her, and her horse perked her ears up at the word *ride*.

God gave her a boost and changed her gown into jeans and a sweater in the process. Emma inhaled the sweet smell of her horse. With just a nudge, Feisty took off with a buck of pep. She went smoothly from walk to trot to canter, finally settling into a gorgeous, glorious gallop. Emma felt her hair flying behind her.

God would make everything okay.

When God brought her back into the bubble with Everett, she'd lived hours: her horse, her God, and a beautiful, sunny day with no worries. It had been a vacation. And now, even though she was smack in the middle of the most momentous battle between good and evil — or, as God would put it, incorrect choices and right choices — she was grateful to see Jack's face.

She wished she had a way to convey to him that everything would be okay. She settled for a smile. Jack's face was a picture. As handsome as he was, his reverence for her sweet friend God made him positively angelic.

God slipped Emma behind him as time began to grind forward again. She peeked around him to watch. Lucifer hit the bubble just as Everett threw himself prostrate on the ground. "I'm so sorry. I'm so sorry. I'm so sorry."

Emma raged as she heard his bendable words, made of tin. Everett never meant it. God held out his hand to her while dissolving her dream bubble, save for the floor, which allowed Lucifer access. He squeezed her hand once, and Emma understood.

She prayed out loud. "Lord, please help Everett understand that being sorry comes from within, not from his mouth. Amen."

Everett looked up with a glare of pure hatred. Her prayers wounded him far more than her blows had.

Emma motioned for Claudette to bring Jack closer. She covered him in a wing when he stepped down, wincing at the lack of a visible floor to support them.

"No fear, Jack. I have wings. I won't let you fall."

He ignored the world, the minions, and God to pull her into a deep kiss.

Jason

Jason, Dean, and Seriana — who clutched Mine's hand — found each other in the stillness, with Violent still in tow. Lucifer's pull had diminished, and their love for each other was a beacon, drawing them together.

It was Violent who figured out the cause of the stillness and pointed first. "It's God!"

The terrible fighting had stopped. The angels seemed smug. They knew their weapon was the best. The minions looked shifty and unsure what to do. What was next, no one could possibly guess. Though bursting with joy, the siblings' reunion was quiet. Jason touched his brother's shoulder and sister's cheek.

"Mom?" He whispered, but it seemed horribly loud.

Seriana shook her head, and Dean mouthed, "With Vittorio."

Jason scanned the crowd as the others looked Heavenward. Rebecca was nowhere to be found. Kate and Nero, on the other hand, were just a few feet away. Kate found his eyes and pulled her father's arm as she immediately moved toward him. He reached for her, and she hugged him hard.

"What happens now?" she asked. She continued to hold her father's arm.

Jason tried to think of something comforting to say, but Nero answered her question. "Lucifer is on the horizon, God has come down. Right now is when the world could end."

All watched as the huge red beast beat the sky with its wings, moving toward a very small-looking, human-sized God. Jason felt Kate squeeze his hand and eagerly sought her eyes. How amazing to see her again.

She raised an eyebrow and whispered, "While everybody's distracted let's go get your mom."

Dean and Violent stepped closer, as did Seriana and Mine.

Violent turned to Nero and hopped on his back. At first he fought, instinctively, but she shushed him with a petting hand while she scanned the frozen battlefield. "I see him. He's scurrying back toward the entrance to Hell, dragging your mother like a dog."

Jason and his siblings instantly trained their eyes in the direction of Violent's gaze. Jason bobbed and weaved, trying to sprint, but he had to settle for fast jog-walking along a winding path. Kate stayed right at his side. The frozen bystanders around him, all eyes glued to the sky, were obstacles. Most barely registered his presence. Seeing the former Devil and a seraph kissing like they were playing patty cake with their tonsils was quite riveting.

He heard the scuffles behind him and soon saw Violent, Nero, and Mine pushing their way through as the crow flies. Jason got behind them as they passed and followed their path. He held out his glowing palm to Kate, and she joined hers with his.

Dean and Seriana joined the other minions in relocating those in their way, angel and minion alike, and finally they were back at the exit Emma had created when she shot out of Hell and dared Everett to follow. Since the dragon had ripped his way through behind her, it now looked like a seething, angry mouth yawning open in the earth. Vittorio arrived just after they did, dragging an unresponsive Rebecca, chained by the neck on a metal leash. He was missing his army. The show above must have captivated them, along with everyone else, and they'd mixed in with the crowd. He looked old, but he rallied when he saw them.

"Look at this! Grandchildren, plus my monster, the gorgeous minion, and another. We could really do some damage if we team up." He pulled Rebecca to her feet. "Your mother? You want her? Come with me. We will rule Hell. Can't you feel the power calling?"

Rebecca staggered and got her feet under her. Jason watched as Dean inched around the mouth of the hole, rocks crumbling into the abyss. He saw the glint in his mother's eyes before she acted, but it wasn't enough time to warn anyone. Rebecca pushed their grandfather into Hell, and chained to him, she plummeted as well. Her children screamed in horror, drawing the attention of the crowd around them. Seriana tried to dive in after her, but Mine prevented her.

The breeze turned into a whirlwind as a white shooting star careened past them. Moments later the smell of angel cake filled the air as Emma fluttered to the surface, cradling their mother like a doll. She hovered like a hummingbird as she ran a healing hand over Rebecca. "You raised three beautiful children. Mothers are precious," she whispered softly. Then she landed next to Jason and passed his mother into his arms. Seriana and Dean joined the embrace.

Their happy tears seemed to repel some of the gawking minions, who shifted away from them before they resumed their vigil of watching Lucifer. Emma was gone before Jason could thank her, flying back up to where she'd left Jack.

CHAPTER 33

EVERETT

Everett stared at God's feet. Lucifer stood over him like he was a doormat covered in shit. He was screwed, and to top it all off, Emma was fluttering around like a prom queen high on a crack pipe full of happiness. Bitch. She'd prayed for him in front of God — such a suck up. He'd been to Heaven and Hell to find her ass. And now he was groveling like a slug. He'd sell his soul for another chance at her.

God looked down. "You already did, son," He said, responding to the thoughts Everett had believed were private. He then resumed His conversation with the giant red beast.

Everett watched as Emma took a quick detour to save the day down below. She pulled a stupid half-breed out of the ground before coming back up to gaze adoringly at Jack. Everett looked away and noticed the conversation above him had stopped. The scene became a picture instead of a living, breathing world. Everett knew then he was in a pause with God. He stayed on the ground.

"Stand." God was seriously ticked.

Everett crawled out from underneath Lucifer. This "battle" was a farce. He could see that now. God was humoring them. It could all be over with a snap of His fingers.

227

"If I fixed everything like that, there'd be no point in free will." God crossed his arms in front of his chest.

"Um. I, ah, would like to be on Lucifer's side. So, this is sort of inappropriate — consorting with the enemy." Everett shuffled his feet.

"If I'm your enemy, Everett, you never learned. Plead your case. Tell me your side. I'd like to hear what you say."

God hadn't whisked them somewhere new. Everett could still see the motionless Emma staring into the eyes of a pleased Jack. It burned him.

"I wanted her," he spat. "She was supposed to be mine. Everything I did was to get her where she belonged." He stepped in her direction. She wouldn't move, so he could at least touch her hair...

"You will not." God didn't move, but Everett knew the tone. "Sometimes a soul can grow into the apology they offer," He continued. "That was my hope for you. But it didn't happen. Your regret when you were admitted to Heaven did not blossom into a better soul."

"So I'm your mistake? Is that what you're saying?" Everett felt a little hot under the collar. Arguing with God was a rush. There was a gripping silence as he wondered what was next.

"My child, I always assume the best of my creations. Sometimes they chose repeatedly to be less. These things were your choice." God's jaw tensed.

"Forgive those who trespass against us. Those are Your words. Do you not stand behind them?" Everett stood taller. He loved loopholes.

"They are. They roll off your tongue effortlessly but find no foothold in your heart. I have forgiven you, Everett, but that is not a free pass to continue to make evil choices. There must be a reckoning for the effect you've had on the world, on all those you've come in contact with. Are you ready to receive the bounty you've earned?" God didn't look angry anymore. He looked sad.

"No. No. No. Not today, okay? You need someone to run

Hell. I'll be that man." Everett dropped to his knees and crawled to God's feet.

His maker crouched and placed a hand on his back. "I wanted more for you, my son. And I do love you, despite what's next. In the time I'm giving you, I hope you'll come to understand that."

Everett kept his head down because this sounded promising. He thought for a minute about the effect he'd had on those around him. Flash after flash of pain came to the surface of his memories: the animals he'd tortured and killed, his mother, Emma's Sam, Emma. Oh God.

Then he was dissolving, crumbling away like ash, his soul showing its true worth. Everett screamed as he began reaping what he'd sown.

JACK

Jack held her close. His Emma was smiling, seemingly oblivious to Lucifer glowering at God behind her. Then he noticed a key player was missing: Everett. Jack pulled Emma closer and scoured the sky for the evil bastard.

She whispered to him, just behind his ear. "No. He's gone. God took him in a pause."

Jack nodded, unsure how she knew, but trusting her. Then he returned his focus to the matter at hand. Lucifer was a big, freaking, butt-hurt idiot. His meandering complaints against God were nothing but jealousy.

"Can we leave? Can we bust out of here?" Jack wanted Emma far from the red beast. It kept eyeing her wings like she was a snack. Even with God right in front of him, Jack wanted to protect Emma.

"You may," God responded before Emma had a chance.

Emma hugged him to her and took off, circling in a high arc

before plunging toward Earth. She landed softly among the angels and minions, and he felt the ground form under his feet.

"I just want to check on the others," she said. She pulled him by the hand as they threaded through the crowd to find the half-breeds and minions that had been their travel companions.

Various minions nodded respectfully at Jack as he passed. He tried to return their greetings, but there were just too many.

Emma picked up her pace as she spotted the group she was looking for. Coming up behind her, she touched Seriana's shoulder, and the half-breed jumped at her.

"Thank you! Thank you for rescuing Mom," Seriana cried. "I'm so happy you're here!"

Emma petted the woman's back, whispering prayers that fell like a veil all around her. "You did all of this," she said aloud, taking a moment to look at each sibling. "You found your mother and refused to give up. You were willing to find me? To deal with him?" She pointed at Jack and smiled. "I'm honored to know such brave souls." She stammered a bit before adding, "To love you."

Jack felt the pinch of jealousy, but he tried to ignore it. It was how his girl was. Dean and Jason hugged Emma, and then Dean spoke for them all. "We're so glad you're safe. Mom too."

Rebecca came tentatively forward and held out her hand. She showed no signs of her years of imprisonment. Emma's healing work had been flawless. "I've never met an angel before," she said, eyes wide.

Emma nodded. "You have. These kids of yours, for sure."

Jason touched her shoulder and Emma rubbed his arm, giving him her full attention.

"Kate was able to bring Nero out of Hell. Do you know what's going on? Should we leave?"

Jack tucked his hands into the pockets of his leather jacket, looking for a smoke. The minions and angels close by seemed to lean in their direction, listening. Claudette fluttered down next to the group, offering him one of his favorite hand-rolled smokes and a lighter. He waggled his eyebrows in thanks but didn't miss Emma's disapproving glance. He motioned to the battle above them and the giant mixer of creatures before lighting up. There were other things to worry about just now.

"Can you leave?" Emma asked. "It seems we're all rooted here — held by one or the other of them." She looked up at God and Lucifer. There was a decided lack of fireworks and explosions now. Just two supernatural beings in heated confrontation.

"I *must* be here," Nero confirmed. "I know it from a part that isn't my mind." Violent nodded as well.

"The angels are tethered," Claudette added. "We'd never leave God unprotected anyway."

"Looks like we're fucked," Jack said. "'Cause this crew is going to get colorful depending on how that up there ends. God may be planning to win, or He may not..." He swallowed hard. Technically, with Everett vamoosed, Emma was the Devil in angel's clothes, unless Lucifer was ready to strap on some balls. And fighter or no, he couldn't think of a being less prepared to run Hell than the sweet, kind girl in front of him.

LUCIFER

Lucifer wasn't sure how he wanted this confrontation to end. He was furious at God. He'd spent entire civilizations-worth of time underground, hiding in a hovel underwater. Because of Him.

God's patient face tortured him with its unchanged familiarity. For so many years they'd been friends. He raged that God could forget about all those times.

"You know I'd never forget, Lucifer."

He growled. He wanted his thoughts private. He lashed out at God. "You changed. The pressure of this getting so big made You *so* important," he yelled, gesturing wildly at the world around them. "You didn't have time for me!"

God glanced at the crowds below before responding. "I didn't have time for you like you wished. That's true. I also thought you'd see my responsibilities and help, not plot against me."

"You aren't the only one who can do this job," Lucifer snapped. "And you know I could handle it." He flapped his leathery wings.

"You actually proved to me you could handle none of it. And you taught me not to trust even the most devoted angel." God leveled His stare at him.

Despite his anger, he wanted to hug God. Now that they were face to face, the need of it crushed him. He hung onto the worst of his grievances so he could stay tough.

"Has being tough made you any less lonely, friend?" God shook his head sadly.

"Don't call me friend. Don't you do it!" Lucifer shrieked. The word *friend* had sounded condescending in God's mouth.

God said nothing, waiting him out, and the time broke him. Mere seconds grated on him when he'd had millennia of practice ignoring things. "We're not friends," he declared. "You wouldn't come to me. Our friendship meant so little to you that it was left to rot — like me." Lucifer turned his back on

God because he was afraid his eyes would fill with tears.

"I came to Hell to meet with the Devil regularly. But that was never you, as it should've been. If you'd done your job, I would've been with you in your lair, hearing your issues and working things out."

Lucifer knew it was true. Being thick-headed wouldn't win this battle. "I wanted to mean more to you than that," he confessed. "I wanted you to find me."

"That's a selfish answer. And after all this time I see that's what spurred you — not our perceived friendship." God sounded bored.

Lucifer whirled around, swirling his wings and steaming the

very air they touched. "After all this time you insult me? I guess an apology is too much for you too." Lucifer's blood boiled.

"Did you once seek me out, Lucifer? Did you ever wonder if I missed you? What happened when I had to deal with the world's problems without my best friend as a confidant? No. You didn't worry about me because you were too busy hiding your tail between your legs."

Lucifer was stunned. Hearing anger from God was amazing. God *had* missed him. He'd not put himself in God's shoes. Not once in all that time. "No. Instead of finding me and apologizing for trying to take over my Heaven, you hid." God drew closer, power coming off Him like lightning. "A real friend doesn't do that."

Lucifer felt as if he'd turned to stone. The scales fell from his proverbial eyes. He'd been wrong, too blind to see beyond himself. What God wanted was simple, and it was real. Perhaps they could have been partners, continued being friends, if he'd just done as God commanded.

It seemed like forever just standing there. He watched God as God watched him. The crowd below grew restless. Could he possibly be forgiven? Did he want this friendship after all this time?

CHAPTER 34

EMMA

"It's you."

Emma turned as Jack spoke to her in his sweet, sexy voice. She heard him clearly despite the chaos of minions, angels, and half-breeds around them. She'd been so certain they'd never be together again. To touch his hand was a gift.

"And it's you," she responded, but she was perplexed as he didn't smile.

"We've got to get you out of here. We'll fly. Let's go." Jack grabbed her around the waist and looked at her expectantly.

"Jack, I have to stay here. Wings and such, you know — I need to be here for God." She fluttered her wings in his face to remind him.

His voice tickled her ear as he spoke. "No, pretty child, it's *you*. You're the Devil. You defeated Everett. So any of the minions can take you on for the power."

Emma swallowed hard as she realized what he meant. "I did? I mean, God really..." She put her arms around his neck and closed her wings around them like a clamshell, creating some privacy.

"You accepted the last challenge," Jack said with a shrug. "You're the one left. You won. Do you feel different?"

Emma took a deep breath. "I don't feel different. I mean,

other than the angel stuff." It was dark in her wings, so she let some of her feathers glow, throwing soft light on Jack's face. She traced his high cheekbones.

He rested his head against her palm and closed his eyes before speaking. "I love you. So you know." He opened his deep brown eyes.

Emma willed this little cocoon to be their own world.

"You smell like sunshine." He buried his head in her hair, and she heard him inhaling.

She slipped the cigarette from his hand, dropped it, and pressed her sandal over it.

His eyes had a hint of mischief. "Really, angel? You're so stubborn."

She wrinkled her nose and hugged him. She put her head on his shoulder and parted her feathers a bit so they could see out. The crowd was restless. Instead of looking up at the sky, they were shuffling and bumping into each other now. Jack, however, was focused on God and Lucifer.

"This is going to get ugly," he said. "I'm surprised God hasn't intervened."

A chill went down Emma's back. If she was the Devil, she was in charge of the minions and their safety — and the evil they would wreak on Earth. Surely Lucifer was making Hell's decisions?

As they watched, a minion turned to face the angel next to him. There was anger and a hunger in his eyes.

"Jack?" She pointed to the brewing emotions among the polar opposites.

He exhaled loudly. "I guess we're doing something. Get us up high. I'll help with the minions."

Emma unfurled her wings and took Jack with her. She landed them both on a tall outcrop of rocks.

"Excuse me? Minions?" Her voice sounded tiny in the huge expanse of nature. From this vantage point she could see there were thousands of them, and angel wings threaded through the crowd like checkers. Jack winked at her, even though he looked nervous, then unleashed a loud wolf whistle. It was louder than it should've been from a human. Emma looked at him questioningly. The whistle was continued on the ground. Seriana and Jason had added their own.

"We all got a hit of power from Lucy," Jack explained, pointing at the sky. She'd hoped the two main players up above would ease up and help out, but they showed no signs of slowing down.

"You call him Lucy?" She rolled her eyes at his audacity.

"That's what happens when you have balls as big as mine." Jack bit his lip and looked down his nose at her.

She smiled.

"You're worth it," he said simply.

She turned to the crowd, which had finally focused on them. All eyes waited to see what they could possibly say: a fallen angel and a Devil who'd obviously fallen in love. She opened her mouth and had nothing. Not one thing came to her mind.

Jack put his arm under her wing and rested it on her lower back. He leaned in and mumbled, "I've got this. Just stand tall."

"Minions and fucking fairies, please meet a one-of-a-kind being. She's a seraph Devil. She defeated Everett." A buzz rose as the minions realized their leader was indeed gone. It was as if they were rising from a drug-induced coma — and their sudden alertness was intimidating.

Jack held up a hand, and the crowd quieted. Emma was just wowed by him. She loved how self-possessed he was. In control.

"So, angels, you have a peer to listen to and respect. And minions? You have a leader to obey." He leaned down as if listening to something Emma was telling him.

"I've not a clue where the Hell you're going with this," she whispered, keeping her face neutral.

He nodded as if she'd added something important. "Minions, you're commanded by your Devil to return to your former positions in Hell as of right now. Any delay will increase your sentences and compulsions tenfold."

He leaned over and spoke out of the side of his mouth. "Good?"

Emma nodded and pointed at the holes in the ground. There were some scuffles as the minions returned to their punishments, but Jack's words were obeyed. And she was under no illusions: the minions were listening to her man. They nodded respectfully as they passed him.

Emma followed Jack's gaze up to where God and Lucifer still remained deep in conversation. Then Jack spoke again, and Emma listened because she was curious about what she was "saying" next.

"Nero and Violent, remain on Earth for further instructions," Jack announced. "Half-breeds, kneel." Jack looked at Emma. She held out her hands and pressed them down as if directing the half-breeds' heads. They knelt. "Seriana, Dean, Jason, Rebecca, Kate, and...Mine?" Seriana nodded her confirmation. "Emma wants you to stand aside."

He turned her face to his with his hands. "Okay, the minions I knew what to do with. The angels are your business."

Emma turned and looked at her peers. They gazed smugly at the half-breeds on their knees, as if that's where they belonged, a peg lower than the celestial beings. Emma felt fury rise within her.

"Angels, kneel." There was a reprimand in her voice. She was no longer unsure of what to say. Her time with her half-breeds had changed her. Never would she think any less of another being, even if their ways were different. "Look at the souls next to you. They're even with you, as it should be. Because you use God's words against them does not make you better. It does not make you wiser. How dare you look down on God's children? By exhibiting this discrimination, you make yourselves unworthy of the wings of which you are so proud."

She glanced up at God and saw his hand move slightly. When she turned back to look at the kneeling masses before her, she could find not a one with wings. She gasped along with them. The angels immediately began feeling behind them, looking for the missing symbols of their righteousness.

Actually, one angel still had her wings, and Emma nodded and smiled at her. Claudette. "Please stand, sister. Come be with my friends." Emma motioned for Claudette to join the siblings and others behind her and Jack.

The angels began to grumble, clearly growing angry. Emma shook her head. "Oh no you don't." Silence immediately descended. "Do I have the power to remove wings? All at once like that?"

She waited while it dawned on them. God was the author of their wing removal, so they piped down. Jack nodded encouragingly. Emma looked out over the crowd and saw one angel writhing in fury. Gabriel. He was ticked off, but he couldn't rise because God was holding the angels in place. He tilted his head and snarled in Jack's direction.

Emma looked over to find Jack smoking yet another cigarette. He blew smoke in the shape of a hand giving Gabriel the finger.

"Very mature."

Gabriel was now so angry he was vibrating. "You," he hissed. "We came down to help *you* — to save you, and now we're kneeing with the likes of them. You're ungrateful and undeserving." Gabriel's handsome face looked ugly as he wore his contempt in a sneer.

Emma spoke softly, her words just for the angel who'd passed judgment on her in Heaven. "Maybe *I'm* helping *you* now. To not see the worth of a soul is blindness a seraph can't afford. I've learned that. You should too. But thank you for coming to my aid as soon as I had a set of wings."

Emma closed her eyes. She'd let a little bitterness slide out with that last statement, and she tried to rally her thoughts. She caught Jack looking into the opening to Hell.

"What's up?" She turned from the crowd and touched his tattooed chest.

He looked down at her hand and back up at her. "Hell needs someone in charge. It gets crazy down there." He covered her hand.

As if his words had decided the battle above him, everyone's attention was instantly turned skyward. Lucifer took to his knees in front of God. He inched closer and closer until he was at God's sandals. A collective gasp floated up from Earth as the crowd watched Lucifer kiss God's feet.

CHAPTER 35

KATE

Kate was grateful her father and Violent were a vocal twosome. They'd made it their job to explain things as they happened. The minions returning to Hell was a huge relief, as apparently they'd been on the verge of running wild. And the angels kneeling with minions would have been about as likely as ice catching on fire. Violent laughed dryly as she wondered aloud about the Heavenly force it must have taken to get them to kneel with the half-breeds. And yes, Lucifer had appeared, but this didn't seem to mean he was the Devil. He and God were still deep in discussion, and at the moment it seemed Emma remained between Lucifer and his dark throne, if he finally decided he really wanted it.

Despite the unrest, as Kate stood with Jason, who wouldn't let go of her hand, and felt her father's hand on her shoulder without any shaking, she was the happiest she'd ever been. She even felt happy for Jack, who seemed a whole lot less like an asshole with Emma next to him.

When Lucifer kneeled before God, Kate had a stunning thought. She scanned the faces of the crowd, looking for one in particular. When she saw her mother, she looked so healthy Kate hardly recognized her. Then Jenny smiled, her eyes sparkling. In that moment, the child in Kate cried out to be held, and her desperate need for her mother's love came rushing back. Kate tried to run, to get to her, but her feet were fixed, her knees on the ground. She clutched her father's hand without taking her eyes off her mother. "Dad, do you see her? Do you see her?"

Kate watched as her mother changed her focus and gasped. She could read her lips clearly: "Nero." Tears wet Jenny's cheeks.

Nero's voice was so small and full of tenderness. "Jenny. My Jenny."

Kate looked closely at her mother's outfit. Jenny was missing her wings, as all the angels were, but the soft white gown and glittering hair gave her away. Jenny had come from Heaven. Her father gripped her shoulder, his prayer whispered out loud. "Oh please, let me go to her. Please."

With everyone's attention on the groveling Lucifer, Jenny stood, somehow released from her forced bow. Kate gasped, realizing God must have heard her father's prayer — and her own heart's dearest wish. Kate waved at her mother, begging her closer with her hands.

"Please." Kate added her own prayer to her father's.

Jenny began to run, and Kate could hear her sobbing their names as she ran angel fast. Yet the time seemed endless, and Kate was so scared the world would change, that something would happen to her mother before she could get to them.

But Jenny skirted the rocks and grabbed Kate so hard it hurt. "Baby, baby, baby. My beautiful baby." Kate gave up everything in her mother's arms.

"Mommy!" She broke down completely, gasping sobs that sounded like torture instead of happiness.

Her mother touched her back, her hair, her face, kissing her again and again.

"My girls." Nero's voice was so proud, it sounded as if he were commanding an army instead of watching two women he adored. Jenny reached a hand out to him as if she were drowning and pulled him closer. Then Kate could finally stagger, her feet free.

Nero's huge arms engulfed them both. Family. Kate had her family.

LUCIFER

Lucifer kissed God's feet in a full-on grovel. He wanted to make things better.

"Stand, Lucifer."

He did as he was told, noticing that the minions below him had drained from the field like water from a tub. All that remained were the angels, sans wings, and the muted half-breeds.

"Here is what I ask of you: Run Hell. Learn from your predecessors — the ones who earned respect. Know that my children dwell in all the levels of the world. Can you do that, Lucifer?" God waited.

Lucifer knew God, even after all these years — the way He held his shoulders, the tone of His voice when He meant business. Right now He meant business. But God asked too much. Lucifer wanted a pardon from Hell. He wanted out. He also knew better than to ask. God's word was law, and really, by offering him Hell again, God was giving him an extension on the End of Time, when everything in Hell was supposed to be reduced to formless awareness.

"I accept, my Lord. I will run Hell." Lucifer's voice held no pride, and very little resolve, as the task was set before him again. But he didn't have it in him to fight anymore.

God nodded. "Let us go below and make it known."

Lucifer bowed his head. Inside he felt restless and unfulfilled.

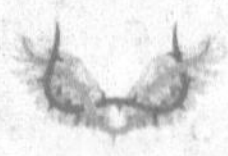

Jack

Jack stood riveted as his former shoveling minion was made whole by the women he loved. He wiped a tear, trying to pass it off like he had a bug in his eye. The crowd all around them now watched this most unlikely reunion, and Emma was flat-out weeping happy tears, her wings tinged with gold.

He looked at Violent and found her purple eyes glowing. He watched her face as she put it together. Then she began to struggle. When she could finally move, he knew she'd freed herself from her fixed place on the ground using sheer love. God had allowed Violent to move as well. She scaled the rock he and Emma stood on and pushed them aside.

She scanned the crowd, whispering at first. "Giovanni?" She moved to shouting as her desperation grew.

Jack looked out on the crowd. There was one angel way in the back working diligently at tugging himself to his feet. Jack tapped Violent and pointed him out. "That your guy?"

She nodded and slipped down from the rock, her eyes never leaving the angel. She moved toward him as if afraid he'd disappear.

Jack smiled as he realized the man she was desperate for was small and unremarkable — not much like the ruggedly handsome Dean at all. But he was clearly as desperate as she. Both walked until they got close enough to run. Then they did, clumsily, stumbling and tripping over the half-breeds and angels on their knees. Finally they were within arm's reach.

He spoke first in thickly accented English. "Thousands of years, my love."

She returned the sentiment in his own language. *"Migliaia di anni, amore mio."*

Instead of a hug, he bowed. Violent moved like a dream as she curtsied. Giovanni began singing softly as he stepped toward her, pulling her into an old-world dance. She mouthed the words with him, but let his lovely singing voice carry. The song was one of deep love. They danced in the small space they had, and in his white angel's garb, with every step and every word, Giovanni became more beautiful. More spectacular.

Jack turned to Emma. "Look at that. Never thought I'd see V so happy.

Amazing."

She seemed to have a hard time looking at him, and when she did, she had tears brimming. "I'm going to have to run Hell, aren't I?"

He shook his head. "No, sweetheart, Lucifer's gonna man up. You watch." He pulled her closer, her wing covering his shoulders.

Maybe it was a false sense of security, but with all the love cropping up around them, Jack couldn't imagine he'd ever be without her again. He watched Giovanni dip Violent dramatically, then kiss her sweetly.

EMMA

After God's command, Lucifer flew, and God simply rematerialized on Earth. God's presence brought all to their knees, even those no longer forced to be there.

After a few moments Emma felt God's attention and lifted her eyes. He motioned for her and she pulled Jack along as she came. She didn't use her wings, not wanting to add insult to injury for all the angels around her that were without.

"My sweet. So you're the Devil Seraph now? That's quite a title." God smiled a bit.

Emma shrugged, unsure what to say. Lucifer looked fairly tame, and the minions were back where they belonged — well, most of them anyway — but there were a lot of loose ends to tie up before God left.

"Children, I've already interfered too much," He said. "I can't choose your destinies without restricting your free will. I leave you to settle your differences. Know that I love you."

God was gone so quickly, it was as if all the air had been sucked right out of the atmosphere.

Jack instantly furious. "*Now* he leaves? For crap's sake. That solves nothing. No fucking thing. Come back! Come back!" He shouted into the dark night.

Emma touched his arm. "Hey, it's okay. It'll work out." The peace she'd been given in the pause with God still encircled her.

"Really? What about the angels' wings? And Nero and Violent? And big ol' Lucy here?" Jack held out a hand to Emma. "Fuck it. We're blowing this joint. I'm not hanging around." He was insistent.

But Lucifer's voice stopped Jack. "I'm not in charge of Hell — yet," he said. "I do believe I have to lay a challenge at the feet of the current Devil."

"No. You're the ultimate Devil," Jack snapped. "The position is yours whenever you want it." Jack pulled Emma behind him.

Then Lucifer's voice became a million men screaming at once again. "I groveled at God's feet, and yet I have to *earn* my role as the leader of the worst place. That's the rule, right? And unless something's changed, that starts with your girlfriend. I do believe I'll tear her apart."

Emma felt the ice-cold IV drip of fear slide through her veins. God left? How could He leave her now when she was so close to happiness? This couldn't happen. Not here. Maybe Lucifer didn't know what power she had in this maybe-transitional phase. Who was she, anyway?

She used the seconds before the fight as best she could. "Half-breeds and remaining minions, I command you to run as fast as your legs can carry you. Angels wings, return. Fly to Heaven." She watched as a swarm of bodies that included Dean, Violent, Seriana, Jason, Kate, and Nero — all those she'd come to care about — bolted from the scene as the angels took off for Heaven.

Her next command, for Jack to leave as well, was swept away

with her breath as Lucifer grabbed her wings and swung her into the sky. It was disorienting to see the stars and Earth twirling so violently. When she was finally righted, she was face to face with the first fallen angel. She gulped down her tremendous fear. Lucifer's eyes danced with flame, and his red skin pulsated with thick veins just beneath the surface. Almost everything about him conveyed movement, unease, unrest. The power within him was a hurricane, trapped and barely contained. And as he reached for her, Emma realized that compared to what lay ahead, her tussle with Everett had been like parlor tricks. Facing off with Lucifer would be like trying to push over a skyscraper, but she had no choice. She'd go down fighting no matter how brief the battle. She owed it to Jack and to God. And to herself.

CHAPTER 36

JACK

Jack was alone and screaming when he saw Emma's life begin to be squeezed from her. Something had gone incredibly wrong. Horribly wrong. Jack looked around, but there was no one. No angels, no half-breeds, no friends. He screamed for the dragon, he screamed for God, but before his eyes Emma went limp. He still had hope, even when her head lolled at an impossible angle. Even when Lucifer let go and Emma fell.

Jack rushed to get underneath her. He could catch her. But she was going so fast. Emma transformed into what looked like a falling star before she got to his arms, and Jack was impossibly stunned when instead of an armful of angel, he felt pieces of white-hot rainbow scatter around him. Some fell on his outstretched arms, and Jack hugged the pieces to him. They scorched his chest, burning his tattoo of her name.

Lucifer landed with a thud, seething.

Jack stood and raised reluctant eyes to the massive killing machine. "What changed?"

The synchronized chant bled from the Devil's mouth. "I told God I'd run Hell. I needed to make sure my path was clear. That foolish girl could never have lived that life. It was a gift to her."

Jack swayed as Lucifer brushed past him, and his leather jacket caught fire. He didn't brush at the flames. He let them engulf him. Before Lucifer could crawl back into his home, Jack uttered the only sentence he could think of: "I formally challenge you to a battle to the death." Things had happened fast, but Jack's heart told him unequivocally that it should only beat when Emma was around. "This is a winner's crusade to become the Devil."

He looked at his feet as he felt the flames reach his back. Without her, there was nothing. He would be nothing. There was no point. As Lucifer stalked over to end him, Jack closed his eyes and let his energy dissipate out into the universe.

VIOLENT

Violent stood in the shadows, watching as Jack ceased to exist. He didn't even fight, and she didn't blame him. Having the love you'd been reunited with so briefly disappear into thin air made a being numb.

She knew this firsthand. Giovanni had been in her arms and then just... gone. She watched, disheartened, as Lucifer stalked back to his hole. He hadn't seemed joyful or triumphant when he killed Emma and Jack. And the magnificent dragon that had bravely fought for them was surely dead as well.

Once Lucifer disappeared, the exits to Hell sealed. The ground repaired itself as if there'd never been great burrowed holes in the soil. It was oddly quiet. No noises from the wildlife, who were surely scared and far flung. Like the half-breeds. Like the angels.

She looked to her left and saw Nero, the other minion so briefly reunited with his love. She sighed and he met her eyes. "Would you want her here again?" Violet's voice was a whisper, but it seemed to jolt him.

Finally Nero shook his head sadly. "Holding her was…" He tightened his mouth into a line.

"I know." She didn't know what to do. She certainly didn't want to go home. Nero and Violent stood separately, their hearts dreaming of people in Heaven.

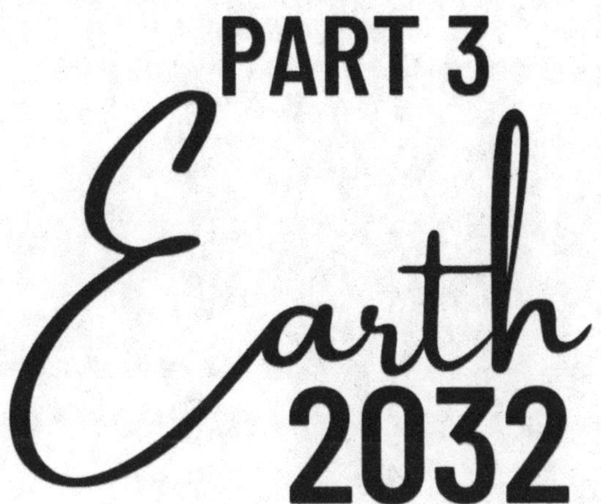
PART 3
Earth
2032

J ason felt warm, inside and out, as he sat in his house with Kate and the rest of his family. He hadn't asked her to marry him yet, but she was part of him. It was Christmas Eve, and he'd found yet another tree in the woods — this time not to cheer his siblings, but to celebrate love redeemed, love found.

Trimming the tree was a riot of laughter and music. Mine had finally learned to navigate furniture, rather than plowing right over it, and after copying Seriana's movements for so long, he had almost a feminine walk, which Dean and Jason loved to tease him about on occasion — such as now when he pranced back and forth carrying ornaments. Rebecca, finally healthy again, glowed in the center of her children's joy. She seemed to soak it all up. It wasn't until they unwrapped the angel for the top of the tree that the room got quiet.

In that instant, the news that Emma was gone punched them all again. It had been twenty years since Violent and Nero tracked them down to tell them: Jack and Emma had perished. But at least they had answers to their questions. They'd searched for them to no avail until the minions came to their door.

Kate's father was going to stop by again tomorrow. He made regular appearances to be part of Kate's life, sometimes with

Violent, sometimes without, and they'd mourned the loss of Jenny again and again. Jason often wondered if the glimpse of their loved one had been more of a punishment. But Kate told him it gave her peace to know her mother wasn't in Hell and her father had finally stopped shoveling. Nero and Violent wouldn't speak about what they did between visits, or where they stayed. They certainly didn't act like a couple.

Tonight as the silvery decoration angel topped the tree, Jason felt thankful he didn't remember his relationship with Emma. Just the loss of what he'd come to know of her was deeply sad. She'd brought all of them together so many years ago. In a way, they owed her everything.

Nero could never stop wanting Jenny, but he and Violent had forged a partnership after the big battle. They were in a similar position: their loved ones were angels, although Nero rejoiced that he still had Kate to visit, and Violent saw Dean occasionally. She referred to him as her "walking photograph" of Giovanni, but he didn't really ease her loss, and she'd thankfully stopped trying to make him Giovanni's replacement. Nero and Violent had made their home base her house, telling no one where to find them. They didn't converse much, but he'd been happy to help her in her gardens with anything but shoveling. It had taken about a year to decide what to do.

A comment from Kate had sparked Nero's first semblance of a plan. "Dad, you're an angel to me, even if you don't have history on your side," she'd said one night as she hugged him. He'd believed she was right. Yet when he mentioned his idea to Violent, she thought for weeks before responding.

Finally, one clear night, Violent nodded after spending quite some time petting a tree. "Yes," she said. "We need to make more history so the balance will tilt in an angelic direction."

Nero had cleared his throat. "That could take a very long time, at least for me."

"For me as well," she said. "I've corrupted a whole species. But we *have* a very long time either way. Even if it's delusional, it's better than the alternative." She knelt and brushed her hand over the grass.

"I can't go back to Hell, and living here is full of wanting anyway." He made fists out of his hands.

"At least we'll have something to live for." Violent stood and held out her hand.

Nero had gripped it firmly, and they shook.

Since their pact that evening, they'd gone out every night looking to better the world. Her focus was, of course, nature. She tried to sniff out toxins and eliminate whatever polluted the natural world she loved.

Nero had focused on people. He found the evil ones and used his strength to intimidate them into a better life, hoping they'd seek good and continue down a better road on their own. He'd stopped muggings, robberies, and rapes. The saved victims' gratitude felt worthy of his Jenny. He wore his scrap of her nightgown around his throat and lifted it to his lips after each night.

Violent and Nero wanted no less than to become angels one day.

With the tree finally decorated, Kate watched as Jason and Dean played cards with their mother. Jason was amazing. He was devoted to her and so kind, so generous. All her time waiting in the cabin had been lonely. Her mother had set such a solid example of being in love with mostly a memory, Kate often thought she'd be broken when it came to connecting with a partner. She hadn't been herself for a long time after freeing her father, so it had taken some work to get here, but finding this little unconventional family was everything she wished for. And Jason was so patient. All these years later, they were still just dating. He liked to take her to the movies and bring her flowers. She saved the stubs from the tickets and pressed at least one bloom from every bouquet. She was almost positive their love would make it. They'd be fine.

Kate smiled and left them to their game, going into the backyard for some fresh air. In the dark she turned over her palm. Its glow was subdued now. She'd told herself over and over again that she'd done what she had to to free her father, but on this side of Hell, having a tiny bit of Lucifer inside her body was alarming. It seemed to have slowed her aging — the years were liquid now — but she sometimes felt it had exacerbated her quick temper, which she was always working to control.

The screen door squeaked behind her, and she smiled as Jason came out to visit.

"Hello, gorgeous. Have any plans tonight?" He slipped his arms around her.

Kate tilted his palm up and compared their glows. His was diminishing more quickly.

"You know, maybe it clears out of my system faster," he said, as if he'd read her mind.

"Mmm..." Her fears were a little too real.

"That doesn't sound encouraging. Tell me what's going on up here." He kissed the top of her head.

"If it stays in me longer, does that mean I'm a better host?" She leaned back against his chest, looking up through the leaves to see the stars.

"I'd stay inside you as long as I could." He leaned down and nibbled her ear.

She squirmed away and rolled her eyes. "You're so comforting."

He spun her around and tilted her chin with his finger so she was forced to look at him. "We're going to get through this. I know we will. Together. I'd take all that glow if I could. I know it bothers you."

"I know. I wish I wasn't such a baby about it. Those first few years..." She trailed off thinking about the dreadful arguments she'd had with Jason. She'd said things she'd regretted. Jason had too.

Nero had pointed out their trouble one evening. "You've brought Hell to Earth in your hands," he said. "To stay here, you must fight against the seven deadly sins. For they will always try to gain hold."

Kate still didn't really see a correlation with the seven deadly sins, but these days when she was being a bitch, she tried to step outside herself and calm down.

Jason hugged her close. "You know that was Lucifer and post-traumatic stress all rolled up together. We're both doing better now."

She shrugged and sighed. When he took to his knee and turned over her hand, Kate had thought he was just getting a better look at her palm.

"I had a romantic plan — you know me — but you look so sad, and this thing is burning a hole in my pocket so..." Jason reached in and pulled out a pretty little box.

"What?" Kate's mouth dropped open.

Jason looked nervous then, but he soldiered on. "Kate, would you do me the tremendous honor of becoming my wife?"

He used his leg to help him pop open the box. Inside, a gorgeous diamond sat in the center of black velvet, looking a whole lot like the stars in the sky she'd just been looking at.

Her palm illuminated his knee as he slipped the ring on her forsaken hand.

She lifted it to her face. "Maybe we can put this on my other hand?"

He shook his head. "No, your hand reminds me of our first kiss. I'm proud of it."

She curled her bejeweled hand into a fist.

"Is that a yes? I'm kind of dying here." His eyes were wide, and his smile tentative.

"Of course. Of course." Kate pulled him into a deep kiss. She hated the dread that settled into her chest as she agreed to marry Jason. She hadn't yet told him she thought she was pregnant.

"I expected a bit more happiness. I mean, I'm not too bad, am I?"

He knew her so well. She put more effort into the smile. But with her fairly pure linage, she feared the twentieth generation might actually be what the old coot had wanted. She hugged Jason hard, maybe a little too hard because she was afraid of what kind of life they would bring into the world.

CHAPTER 38

EMMA

Emma petted her horse, Feisty, in the barn. It was shimmery cold out, so she slipped into the stall to adjust the horse's blanket and make sure her window was locked tight. Feisty nuzzled her and almost knocked her over.

"Silly." She laughed as the horse lipped her pocket, looking for treats.

She loved this animal so much. Her foster parents had bought her the pony years ago, giving in to her constant pining. She'd worn horse T-shirts as a child and plastered her walls with pictures of bay-colored ones, in particular.

The birthday she'd woken up to find a saddle at the end of her bed was her happiest childhood memory. She'd discovered a corresponding horse, named Feisty, in the barn. The name stuck, as did the excitement. Together they'd won ribbons at all the county fairs, and Feisty had listened to Emma's deepest fears and most horrible dreams. Nightmares of a torturous hallway woke her up in a cold sweat so many nights. But she'd make her way to Feisty in the dark and cuddle with her until her heart stopped pounding.

Emma's cell phone vibrated in her jacket pocket. She smiled, knowing her friends were on their way to pick her up. Tonight, Christmas Eve, was her twenty-third birthday. She'd spent the day with her parents, and they'd given her a silver angel pendant. She smoothed her fingers over it and smiled. Soon she heard honking outside the barn, and Shannon and Karen started right in when she got in the passenger side.

"You old whore!" Karen greeted her.

"Finally time you caught up to our asses," Shannon added.

Emma gave them the finger.

They cranked the radio as they headed to the only bar in town. At school, they had a selection of drinking joints, but here, when the girls converged for the holidays in their hometown, they had to settle for Hades.

At least they were all legal now, and Karen had agreed to be the designated driver, but the bar was going to be lame and sad on Christmas Eve. They'd taken bets on how many actual people would be there. None of the guesses topped out over ten. Nevertheless, Emma wore the gift she'd received in the mail yesterday: a soft white sweater with silver wings threaded in the back. There'd been no card, which was odd, but the top was a perfect fit.

They spilled into the bar, laughing as they decided to use their fake stripper names tonight. An online quiz had revealed Shannon to be Lola, Karen to be Marilyn, and Emma to be Butch. A glitch in the test had mistaken her for a man, which doubled them over giggling all over again. When they stopped laughing long enough to find seats, Emma realized the bar contained more than ten people, which was shocking. Most looked liked regulars, and some were townies they recognized. The music was anything but Christmassy, and it was loud.

The girls screamed back and forth, insulting each other and cracking up. Emma was to be treated to drinks, but she insisted on buying the first round. She headed for the bar and turned back to give her friends the finger when they loudly suggested she was wearing her lucky granny panties. "Well, I borrowed them from your extensive collection, *Shannon* — I mean Lola!" she screeched. Shannon/Lola stuck her tongue out in return.

Smoke covered her shoulders like a shawl from behind her. A

low, sexy voice sent shivers of recognition across her skin. "Nice sweater."

She whirled to stare at the bartender's chest, taking in a leather jacket before reaching his long brown hair, high cheekbones, and smirky white smile. By the time she found out his eyes were deep brown, she had the distinct feeling she knew him, but from where? Suddenly she remembered her manners. "Thanks."

He bit his lip and seemed to be waiting for her to say more, make a connection.

"Do I know you?" She had to sit on her hand on a barstool so she wouldn't touch his face.

He took a long, slow pull on his cigarette and exhaled in her direction, making a circle with the smoke.

"Look, now the angel has a halo." He gestured to the mirror behind him, and sure enough, for a split second the smoke ring hung above her head.

"I guess I don't know you. I don't hang around with smokers." She teased him as if they were old friends. His face danced just on the edge of her consciousness, frustrating her.

"ID?" He took a defiant inhale of his drug.

She had to think hard to remember how to show him her driver's license. She pulled it out of her back pocket and handed it over. His finger brushed hers as he took the card. It was like touching a live wire to her lady business. He watched her instead of looking at the license, as if he knew what was happening to her body.

"Heard your friends calling you Butch. That's a Hell of a name."

"Butch is my stripper name." The words were out before she could consider them, and now she wanted to throw herself under the bar. "Online. For a quiz. Oh, God, I'm not a male stripper."

He watched her trip over her words with an eyebrow raised. "Well, Butch, what can I get you?"

Emma knew her cheeks were red. The bartender was so goddamn hot. She didn't know what to do with her hands, her tongue felt like it was made of glue and cement, and she totally forgot what to order.

"Um. Three Old Fashioneds?" She tried tucking her hands into her pants. She'd meant to order a pitcher of beer and three cups. Instead she'd selected her father's favorite cocktail.

"Old Fashioneds? Really? Did I miss the part where you turned into a fifty-five-year-old dude?" He flipped three glasses onto the bar.

"We like them," she insisted.

He looked her over knowingly. "I don't believe you, Butch."

She was backed into a corner now. "No, really. We guzzle them like cowboys."

One side of his mouth lifted in a smile. He put his cigarette in his mouth and began filling the glasses with a healthy dose of whiskey.

"Okay, tell you what, you drink this glass in front of me right now and drinks for all you fine-looking ladies are on me." He added the bitters.

She futzed with her hair and glanced back at Karen and Shannon. They pretended to fan themselves and made obscene hand gestures. No help at all. "No problem. That's a bet you'll lose." How bad could it be? It had cherries. As he slapped a very full glass in front of her, Emma tried not to look alarmed.

He set his elbows on the bar and smiled. "Bottoms up, Butch the stripper."

She tried to seem nonchalant as she lifted the glass to her lips, keeping her gaze on his. He exhaled his smoke and licked his lips distractingly.

She took a healthy mouthful and pulled the glass away, covering her mouth and willing herself to swallow. The bartender smiled like the winner of the bet. She choked it down and idly wondered if her dad had any taste buds left at all. "Water."

He pulled out a hose attached to a nozzle. "Open up."

She stuck her tongue out as he gave her a mouthful. She was grateful as the burning and taste subsided. She opened her mouth again, leaning toward him. He paused for a split second, eyes turning carnal, before giving her another mouthful.

"Thanks." She wiped her mouth with the back of her hand.

"You do love Old Fashioneds so much. Really amazing to watch you sling that back like a pro." He hooked the hose back under the bar where it belonged.

"I couldn't get it down because you obviously suck at making them," she countered, trying to save face. "That tasted like gasoline."

Karen and Shannon were rowdy behind her, scream-singing a porno-style theme song: "Bow-chicka-bow-wow."

She rolled her eyes at them without turning around.

"Never mind. Just give me beer in bottles. That way you can't screw them up." She pushed the drink in his direction.

The bartender stood looking at her for a moment before taking her glass and purposefully turning it to drink from the same side she did. He gulped the drink with effortless ease before sliding the other two drinks down in front of two lucky patrons at the bar. "How these taste to you, boys?"

He walked back over to Emma and continued to smoke while the men sampled the drinks.

"Great, Jack."

"On the mark as usual." "They like 'em."

"Fine. You win. I never tried one before. Why don't you give me something I'd like?"

He nodded as he accepted her challenge, already lining up three more glasses. He filled all three with an assortment of colorful liquids. He added various girly frills, like umbrellas, paper parrots, and fruit garnishes. "You'll *love* these," he purred. "Especially since I'm giving them to you."

Holy crap. He was sex in a bucket. The way his mouth moved was sin.

"So what do I call these things?" Emma asked. She waved a hand over the drinks, then stuffed it back in her pocket when she realized it was shaking.

"This one is the Buttery Nipple." He ran his index finger across the rim of the glass. "The pretty one is a Screaming Orgasm. And this last one, especially for you, is a Long, Slow Screw in Jack's Bed."

"The first two I know I'd like," she said, praying for a poker face. "That last one sounds chock full of diseases." Emma juggled the drinks and left her money on the bar. She could feel him watch her walking across to her friends. They clapped when she put the drinks on the table without spilling any.

"Can a girl get a little help next time?" She sat and pointedly selected the Buttery Nipple. Jack's attention was like another person at the table.

Shannon leaned over to Karen. "I think she did fine. You know, Butch, I'm getting the impression this isn't your first time drinking."

"It's not mine either," Karen declared as she selected the Jack's Bed drink. She took a small sip and groaned. "This is the best drink I've ever had. Too bad I'm driving tonight."

She slid it over to Emma. But Shannon intercepted it and sampled, moaning. "Holy shit, I think that's made from liquid lust. I love it."

She offered a sip to Emma, who shook her head. She focused on trying to ignore Jack the bartender, still feeling his gaze on the nape of her neck. She was hyper-aware of every move she made.

Shrugging, Shannon finished off the Jack's Bed and shared the Screaming Orgasm with Karen. Karen slipped Emma more money.

"Go get more of those." She pointed to the now-empty Jack's Bed drink. "And also, I need a Coke or something."

"Really? I have to do it?" she protested, searching their faces for mercy.

"Yep," Karen said. "That way you'll get exactly what you want. It's your birthday!"

Emma rolled her eyes and went to the bar. Jack was smoking again and laughing loudly with three bleached blondes. *Loose whores*, Emma thought. Then immediately followed with, *How dare I? I don't even know them.* She was stupidly, unfoundedly jealous. She waited a few minutes while Jack took his sweet time flirting as he replenished their drinks.

When finally he turned to her, her happiness was ridiculous. The way he looked at her made her mouth go dry. She grabbed one of the empty glasses and sucked an ice cube out, trying to get some moisture before he made his sexy way over to her. The cube slid down her throat, and all at once she was choking on it. She tried not to let her eyes bug out, totally mortified as she began to flail.

Jack vaulted the bar, set one hand between her breasts, and whacked her back with the heel of his hand, hard. The ice cube shot out like a rocket. Emma began coughing, doubled over with an excellent view of Jack's tremendously beat-up motorcycle boots.

In an instant he hopped back over the bar and poured her a glass of water. Emma wanted to drown herself in it. Had she really just tried to die a most undignified death in front of the wickedly gorgeous bartender? The sluts at the end of the bar were snickering. Shannon and Karen appeared her sides.

"You okay? Damn, girl."

Emma nodded.

Karen rubbed her back, making a fuss. "Can't have your birthday be the day you cork off on us!"

"I'm fine. Really." Emma coughed a little more and sipped her water. She shot a look down at the bitches, this time forgetting to chastise herself in her head.

Shannon gave their drink order, and Emma recovered enough to help carry the drinks back to the table. She wanted to be stubborn, but now her only drink option was the Long, Slow Screw in Jack's Bed. And, okay, it was amazing. She had no idea where he'd hidden the alcohol, but the liquid tasted just like salted caramel. It instantly became her favorite drink of all time.

Jack

Jack leaned down to catch his breath. He wiped up the small puddle of water from her ejected ice cube and couldn't believe his adrenaline rush. Saving her had felt like so much more than knocking her on the back. He stood and watched her. When that girl had found her way into Hades, the whole room changed. Such a rush of déjà vu. He knew what color her gray eyes would be before she looked at him. And he was positive what her lips would taste like.

It made no sense at all. She wasn't his type. He liked his ladies dirty and rough. She was all sunshine and goodness. Her friends kept calling her Butch, and it frustrated him. Her name was... was...just at the tip of his tongue. He made himself scarce so he could settle his nerves. He went to the storage room behind the bar and crouched down, wiping his hands on his jeans. Something poked him in the hip as he bent, and he pulled the girl's ID from his jeans pocket. He remembered asking her for it, but had no recollection of putting it there.

He knew her. She was so important. He just didn't know why. He scanned her ID, and her name was Emma. Of course it was. This couldn't get any weirder. He dreamed of that name nearly every night, waking up screaming it as if it were his last breath. He'd lost quite a few girlfriends because they were sure he was cheating on them with "Emma."

Just now, when she'd been choking, he panicked. There'd been such a splitting pain in his chest when she couldn't breathe, he barely remembered what to do. He'd been operating on instinct then. Goddamn if he didn't do the Heimlich at least twice a year. Drunk people sometimes forgot to chew. He kept his first aid and CPR current for precisely that reason.

And now he wanted to dash back out, hop the bar, and cuddle her to his chest. It made no sense. He held her ID up to a light so he could read the rest of it. She lived an hour away and was in her early twenties — explained why he'd never seen her before. Her regular haunts must be good distance away. Her friends made her laugh, and they'd been on it when she started choking, so she had good people, it seemed. He looked at the picture again: Long blond hair, gray eyes, and something familiar he couldn't put his finger on. But he wanted to desperately. He stuffed the ID back in his pocket and tried to steady himself as he returned to his spot behind the bar.

The front door opened and a cold rush of air charged in. Jack groaned. The local rich boys were home from college. They were all self-entitled pricks, and of course, they made a beeline for the table of pretty girls. Shit.

The tallest was also the loudest — their names were interchangeable: Brad, Dom, Breck. They sucked monkey nuts.

"Hey, old asshole! Get us a pitcher over here, stat!"

Jack was immobile as he watched one sling an arm over Emma's shoulders.

"Get a move on, wouldja?" from the peanut gallery was enough to get him moving again. He filled the pitcher with beer and let the foam slop around as he slapped it on the bar. He looked their way and pointed at it with both hands before folding his arms over his chest.

"Come on, bar monkey, earn your tips!" one of the inter-changeables taunted. Sighing heavily, Emma stood and came to the bar. "Sorry about them." She picked up the pitcher.

"Interesting friends you girls have." Jack suddenly felt a bit of shame at his less-than-professional job. He mostly enjoyed bartending, but he now had an overwhelming desire to impress Emma.

She sighed. "You know what? We hardly know them, but now we're big buddies...I think they're already drunk."

He just wanted to keep her. It was insane. "They're lucky to sit with you," he said.

She blushed, and it killed his balls, but the blonde bimbo crew catcalled him again so he left her to her peers and whipped up some Midori Sours for them. He pretended to listen to their chatter while keeping an eye on Emma. The men were trying their best to impress, but it was rather clear the girls not enjoying their company.

Jack refilled the pitcher once but determined he wouldn't do it again. He didn't like how loud they'd gotten. Emma went over to play pool, and the tall loud one jumped up to follow her and stumbled. Jack couldn't listen to the bimbos anymore, so he moved to the center of the bar. He watched as Emm plucked a pole from the wall and chalked it up. The tall one tried to put his arms around her.

"Let me show you how to play! Come on!"

Emma shook her head and racked up the balls instead.

"You're going to choke that rag to death, I think," noted a voice in front of him.

He kept his eyes on Emma while he released his grip. "You need a drink, princess?" Jack glanced at his knuckles, which had been white, and then at Shannon.

"You have a few roofies back there I could slip these guys? If these crotch lobsters would just leave already, we could get back to having some fun." She tapped her glass. "I'd love whatever you gave us before — the salty caramel one — and one for Emma too."

Jack whipped up two more and handed one to Shannon. "I'll deliver this one." He carried it out from behind the bar.

Emma's mean game of pool was pissing off the tall one. He tried harder and harder to get her attention — and then gave up. As Jack crossed the room, he began accusing her of cheating. She sank one after another, and when she sunk the eight ball, he had a full-out fit.

"Son of a bitch! I want a rematch. That's just fucked." He came closer and closer to Emma, spitting with his words.

Jack set the glass down on the pool table and staggered a bit — a flash of Emma lying on top of it, her arms reaching out to him, was so real he was momentarily blind with the vision.

Emma tried to back away from the tall one, but the wall stopped her. "No. I'm good. I want to get back to my girls."

"The Hell with that. You've got to rack them again." He pointed at her with the pool stick.

The man hadn't really been violent — yet. But something deep within Jack began to burn. Only later, when he was explaining the situation to the police, did Jack realize he'd had no real reason for teaching the tall one what his teeth tasted like.

Jack pushed on the tall guy's chest and slid between him and Emma. Jack was smaller, but he'd never lost a fight in his life. And there'd been a shitload of them. Besides, standing in front of Emma felt like the most important thing he'd ever done. Jack didn't warn the guy or threaten him, he just punched him so goddamn hard he went down like a sack of bricks.

He felt Emma grab his shoulders. "Stop, Jack. Don't kill him!"

He turned, knowing it would be a while before the guy was able to stand.

He wanted to apologize, to double check that she was okay, but standing this close to her, he could only do the most amazing thing. He leaned down to kiss her lips.

Emma had never felt a kiss in her toes before. But damn if her knees didn't go all weak. He wrapped his arms around her and made sure she stayed standing, splaying his hands across her back.

She needed to breathe a moment — and find out if this desperately good kisser was also a murderer — but instead she grabbed two fistfuls of his long brown hair. For a moment she saw him in the sunlight, in some sort of drink-inspired daydream. He was tan and smiling in a bed in the middle of the woods. It made no sense at all.

She pulled away to make sure she was still in the bar. The mirage had been so lifelike. His sexy eyes were half closed, and he gave up a deep, grumbly laugh.

"Do I know you?" she asked. It felt like she was missing something vital, just out of her reach.

"Feels like we should, doesn't it?"

Emma felt a flash of panic as Breck's pals made their drunken way over to the result of the fistfight — or beat down. "Brad and Dom, get Breck and take him home," she instructed. "He was being a bastard."

Jack turned around lazily, and he made sure Emma stayed behind him. Brad helped Breck to his feet as Dom promised to call his father the senator, the chief of police, and God. Jack scratched his nose with what Emma believed was his middle finger. At that point the bouncer, who had kept to himself until now, came and stood next to Jack.

"Hey," Jack said casually to him, but his eyes never left the rich boys as they stumbled out of the bar. Once they'd gone, Jack nodded at the bouncer as he called the cops.

Then Shannon and Karen were once again on either side of her, prattling on about the fight and her amazing, f-ed up birthday. They pulled her out of the bar before she could exchange another word with Jack, though she did manage a meaningful parting glance. Police lights decorated the parking lot as Karen hustled them all into her car.

Chapter 40

Emma

Emma was disoriented being in her parents' house instead of her apartment in the city. It was stupid o'clock in the morning, and all she could think about was the dirty-sexy bartender. She worried he'd been arrested after punching Breck. Talk about a twenty-third birthday to remember. Considering all she'd drunk, she should be sleeping off the alcohol in her system. Instead she had a little trouble breathing every time she thought about the kiss Jack had planted on her.

There was just something about him. She kicked off her covers and twirled her long hair into a bun. It smelled like the smoke from his cigarette. She opened her old bedroom's balcony doors and stepped out in her bare feet. She shivered in her flimsy sleep T and low-slung flannel pants.

Ignoring the cold, she leaned on the railing, touching her lips again. The flashes of him were what didn't make any sense. Like they'd been that way before. Which was impossible — she'd remember him. A lot.

An orange, glowing firefly caught her attention. Then she clearly heard someone exhale. He stepped out into the light seeping from her second-story bedroom. Jack.

Her heart dropped its panties.

"Hey, stalker. Not in jail?" She loved teasing him. His smirked response let her know she was onto something.

"Not yet. Am I a stalker if I'm returning your ID?" He reached into his jacket pocket and held up her driver's license like a winning poker card.

"Yes. I don't even remember leaving without that...It doesn't even have this address." She wished she sounded even a little offended instead of delighted.

"Googled you. Figured you were at your parents' for the holidays. Happy birthday, by the way." He gave her body a deliberate onceover.

"Whatever. Are you okay? Did the cops come?" She shivered and rubbed her arms.

He slipped her driver's license in the pocket of his jacket, put his cigarette in his mouth, and tossed the jacket up to her. She leaned over and caught it. As she retrieved her license, her fingers brushed a box, and she pulled out his smokes.

"You can wear the jacket for a minute, if you're cold." His brown eyes sparkled.

"Thanks." She slipped it over her shoulders and held out his cigarettes.

"You can toss those down. I'm assuming you don't..." He held out his hand.

"Smoke? Never. Hate the habit. It kills, you know." She held the railing as a wave of dizziness swept through her.

"One can hope." He seemed to tense as he watched her wobble. "You all right?"

She nodded and shook her head. She'd already choked in front of sex-on- a-stick here. She wasn't about to pass out.

She pulled a few cigarettes out of the box and crumbled them, letting the dried leaves fall to the ground like snow.

"Knock it off," he growled.

But when she checked, his face was playful. She pulled out another handful. He stubbed out the smoke he'd been nursing and eyed the tree next to her balcony. When he grasped the first branch and pulled himself up easily, she knew she was in trouble. She grabbed another batch and crumbled them.

"That's almost a full pack!" He climbed the tree like he'd done it a million times.

"I'm doing you a favor!" She was laughing and squealing now. When he hopped onto her balcony, his presence was palpable.

"Be careful," he told her. "You might just need to be spanked for this, pretty child."

His mouth and that pet name exploded in her brain like a gunshot. They were someplace smoky and desperate. She was chained to something and very afraid of him. Her balance left her, as if her body were trying to recreate the scene in real time.

Before she hit the decking, he had his arms around her and eased her to the floor.

"Come back to me, Emma. Come back." She opened her eyes and groaned.

Super handsome was so worried. She wished she could stop feeling like a fainting pansy, but the words he strung together were haunting. She flailed against him.

Wings, tattoos, God? None of this made any kind of sense.

She felt something cold on her forehead and fluttered her eyes open, horrified to find she was crying — and back on her bed.

"What's going on? Do you get seizures or something?" He was holding a hand towel from her bathroom on her head. She could feel its ruffled edges.

She shook her head. "It's you. Your words."

"I'm sorry. Do you need me to leave?" He stood, looking so sad.

The thought of Jack leaving made her cry harder. Her heart was blazing. She sat up and pulled the wet towel from her eyes.

"Come here." She patted the bed and held his rough hand. He touched her cheek. "Quit passing out, please."

Threading her hands behind his neck, she pulled him against her chest. He hugged her awkwardly at first, but then melted into her as she hugged him hard, trying to pull him into her body, let her heart touch his to put its fire to rest.

"What is this?" She needed to know if he felt it too.

"Is it long and hard?" He pulled back and winked at her.

She slapped his arm. "Not that — these flashes I'm having. Did you put something in my drink?" It was the only thing that made sense.

"No." He seemed offended. "Are you seeing me, but it's not something you can remember?"

She nodded.

"It's happening to me too." As if to prove his point, his eyes fluttered a bit, and he leaned heavily on her chest.

She pushed him back to touch his cheeks. His face was so dear to her. He was everything.

"Case in point," he said after a moment.

"Where were we? What did you see?" She searched his face.

He actually blushed a bit, and it was the cutest damn thing. "Um..."

"Were we horizontal?" She winced because everything in her flannel pants seemed to think that would be awesome.

"You were mine, and I was grateful," he said carefully.

They were so close now, it was as if they were trying to occupy the same space. He licked his lips. But then they both turned toward her door. Someone was clearly coming upstairs.

"My dad!" Emma whispered. She sat up and pushed Jack off of the bed, grabbing his jacket from her old comforter.

"I don't want to leave." He was stubborn as she pushed on his chest to make him back up.

She looked over her shoulder. "My father will kill you. No joke. Go." She tossed his jacket over the balcony. "Get."

"I'm not leaving until I know when we can see each other again." He was still as a statue, not looking the least bit alarmed by her father's heavy footfalls.

She leaned up and kissed him quickly. He kept coming at her. He wanted more. She put up a hand and stopped his sinful lips.

"Today. On the other side of this field. I'll meet you there this afternoon at two!" She turned to face the door that would open any a second.

He pressed his lips to the back of her neck, and the thrill almost took her legs out.

Her father swung open the door. "What's going on here?"

She heard the rustle of the leaves behind her and smiled. "Just a bad dream."

"Close the doors. Are you crazy? You'll catch your death."

Her father was an amazing man. She adored him and would hate for him to think she was slutting it up under his roof. She quickly grabbed the doors, swinging them closed behind her.

"I thought I heard voices." He backed away and switched her bathroom light off.

"Just me. Singing." She closed one eye. What a stupid answer.

"I hope you didn't drink too much." Her father went to the door.

"No, I'm good. Just a bit to celebrate, you know. I love you, Daddy." She got in her bed and laid it on too thick. "Just seeing you makes everything better."

He squinted as if he could tell what she'd been up to. She batted her eyelashes and blew him a kiss. He shook his head and closed her door. She waited until his footsteps had carried him away before she hopped up to peek out the window.

She was too late. Jack was gone.

Chapter 41

Seriana

Seriana could scarcely remember her life before Mine. She'd wanted desperately to teach him the unconventional ways their mother had instilled in her children. It had been a horrendous struggle, but with the help of her brothers, she'd kept him from killing anyone.

It was one thing to connect with each other in a cage, but it had been a whole separate situation to adjust to living together. He'd been fascinated with watching her do everyday tasks and seemed intent on doing anything portrayed on TV as manly. He watched football, and Seriana tried to explain the game. It didn't help that she'd never been a fan.

But the bedroom sexcapades were her favorite. The ridiculous chemistry between them was outrageous. Although at first, she'd been a little concerned. Mine's foreplay had included telling her she was cheating on him and ripping her clothes off. Their love was passionate, but always affectionate, so it was puzzling why he would think she was cheating. The only time she was out of his sight was alone time in the bathroom. Seriana solved that mystery one day when she forgot to bring her new shampoo in from the kitchen where she'd unpacked their purchases. Clutching a towel around her, she slowed as she walked behind the couch where

Mine sat. He was intent on the TV screen, watching a rerun of an old soap opera. She burst out laughing when she saw the tumultuous relationship being portrayed.

"You laugh? This is...silly?" he questioned. He was still experimenting with new words.

She rounded the couch to him quickly when she saw her giggles had wounded his pride. "You are never silly. How could you be this sweet? Are you trying to make our life like that?" She nodded in the direction of the screen.

"The commercials say this man, Drake Hardweather, is every woman's dream." Mine pointed at the shirtless Romeo onscreen. "I want to be a dream for you." He was so serious.

"I'd take you over Mr. Hardweather every damn day. You're *mine*." Seriana had kissed him and taken him *and* her new shampoo into the shower.

She'd realized years ago that she had a responsibility. She had to expose Mine to things so he could become his own person. After spending his years in a cage, it was almost as cruel to force everyday life on him. So Seriana made it her life's work to watch him and gauge his reactions. She took him golfing, water skiing, and rock climbing. Mine was drawn to abstract art in the museum, so she got him paints and an easel. At the lake, she taught him to read, write, and swim. He was so patient with himself, and with her. It killed her over and over again inside to know that this spectacular man had been kept like a dog.

Doing all these things in the name of love, Seriana felt content. And there was nothing special about the day she realized she was all he'd known. It was a regular day, actually. They'd been cleaning together. She just suddenly stopped wiping the Windex off the window. She let the stream of blue bubbles drip down and turned to watch Mine vacuum. He loved her because he'd had no choice. She'd been forced on him by her grandfather all those years, just like the bars on the cage. She dropped the Windex and held the rag to her chest. Her heart crumpled in a ball.

Mine sensed the change, somehow, and locked eyes with her,

shutting down the vacuum and cautiously approaching. "Seri? What's wrong?" He took the rag out of her hand and hugged her.

She leaned back until she could see his beautiful eyes. When they'd met, his hair had hung in thick, matted ropes. He liked it short now.

"You don't love me." The words put tears in her eyes.

He shook his head as if she was speaking a different language. "You are love. My love." But he looked concerned now too.

"No, I know. But I'm all you've had. All you've been forced to be with." Her tears fell.

"You are scared? Show me what to fight." His eyes blazed with an unfought battle.

"If I keep you, I'm no better than him." She didn't need to say Vittorio's name out loud.

It was unfair, she could tell. She watched his face scroll through emotions, trying to pick one that would fix the situation.

"You are not like him. We are happy." He grabbed her face. "We are happy?"

How did a simple housecleaning turn into something so horrible? It was easy to see it now. He needed other opportunities, other experiences.

"There are ways you could be happier." She pulled the rag out of his hand and wiped her eyes with it. The smell of Windex would always remind her of this moment.

He waited her out, never moving his hands.

"If you were away from me, you'd get to pick your life instead of having me choose for you." She took his hands off her face. "I think you should get that chance."

He was quiet for so long, and Seriana just cried. Mine finally wiped her tears and scooped her up so quickly she gasped. He sat on the couch and put her on his lap.

"I am not sure if I will say this correctly. Please hear me." He searched her face, and Seriana nodded. "In the cage? I had no sunshine. I had nothing to hope for. And then he started with the pictures. Of you. You were my daylight. I looked forward to your face — like when we open the windows at night? That feeling on our skin? When you get the bumps and shiver? That was your face for me. Chilly and happy. I had someone to dream about. I hoped every day that he would find you and bring you to me. I feel bad about that now, because that wasn't your hope."

He pulled her harder to his chest, and she could feel him inhale the scent of her hair.

"When you were brought to me, it was my dreams coming to life. I know this life must be hard — teaching me, it's hard."

She shook her head, freeing more tears. "Never hard."

He put a finger on her lips. "And if me..." He seemed to search for her words in his head. "If me giving life a chance frees you in a way you need, I will do. I will not like, but I will do." The potential loss played out on his face before he added, "For you? Anything you ask."

She twisted and kissed him until she could finally tell him. "Anything?"

He nodded, solemn as a knight.

"Then stay with me. Always stay. You're my night air too. Just like that, with the chills. I love you in such a greedy way, I'm guilty about it." She tilted her head back as he moved his lips to her throat.

"Guilty is for crimes. Always is for love."

Mine was on top of her before she knew he'd moved. He was desperate, reminding her of their first time, in the cage, as if being inside her was all there could be. He growled as her jeans held tight to her skin, finally ripping them up the seams with his almost-full-minion strength. She pulled her own shirt off in response.

"In my cage, I had this, like this." He held her breasts roughly. "But you ran — sometimes you ran in my head. And I took you anyway. Does that scare you?" He crawled over her, biting and kissing and licking.

"Should I run?" Her chest heaved with excitement.

"Just once." He lifted himself off of her, and she bit her lip. His pants were around his hips, and he was ready for her.

She twirled quickly and scrambled off the couch, intent on running up the stairs. He was staying, and damn it, if he wanted to pretend she was running, she could do that for him. Her torn jeans flopped around her like a ragged skirt. Topless, she bolted for the stairs, and he ran after her.

The only reason she got anywhere at all was because he'd paused to divest himself of his clothes. He followed her up the long flight to the top floor of their house, catching her easily when she was halfway up. She stopped smiling and giggling when she saw his face. It was so carnal it was murderous. She almost came.

His mouth dropped open as he felt her strung tight for him. "My daylight."

She let him have her however he wanted. Mine wasn't controlled or trying to practice some move he saw on TV now, he was once again a beast in a cage. He used the slim stairway to find every way he could to enter her. They braced themselves as he found new ways to make her melt for him. She kneeled, trying to use her mouth on him, and Mine jumped over her and took her from behind. He pulled her hair a bit and twisted her nipple as he pounded the rhythm of a trapped man.

When he was spent, they lay on the stairs, gasping for air. He brushed her hair from around her damp face and looked into her eyes. "Always?"

She cuddled into his chest. "Always."

CHAPTER 42

JACK

Jack stilled his motorcycle at the far end of the field Emma had pointed to early this morning, cursing himself. "You pussy-whipped ass-muncher. Sure. Come meet the sweet, pretty lady after knowing her just a few hours. That's perfectly normal."

He pulled off his helmet and tossed his riding gloves inside. *And* he was a good ten minutes early. All his personal rules were shot to shit: Never come to the girl; let her come to you. Never show up on time. Never get invested.

Jack ran a hand through his hair. At twenty-six, he'd had his share of the ladies. Okay, fine. He'd had ten guys' share of the ladies. There was just something about him — mostly it was in his pants. He was like the pied piper of pussy and loved every goddamn minute of it.

He'd been on the streets since his drunken old man had tossed him out at sixteen, telling him he'd never amount to much. Jack had gotten his degree because he was a stubborn bastard, and he'd started work at Hades around the same time, cleaning dishes and mopping up the kitchen. He'd paid his dues and worked his way to being totally badass, which in his crazy opinion was pouring the drinks out front. And, of course, covering himself in permanent ink.

He lit a cigarette, using the extra time to get his nicotine fix. He actually punched himself in the leg when he realized he was trying to get done with it so Emma wouldn't have to smell the smoke. He was *so* done.

One girl, two kisses, and he was a mushy fucknob? Figured. The dreams of her had messed with him, making him weak. He decided to leave right then, give himself some freaking space and clear his head. He was just taking the final drag when he heard a horse galloping its ass off. *Crap!*

He tossed the smoke and tried to settle into some sort of cool stance as she came into view on her damn horse. *Oh, fuck.* She was gorgeous, riding bareback in jeans and a white sweater. She hung on to the animal's mane like some sort of horse whisperer.

After a cutesy little wave, she shouted, "Race me, Smoky!"

They ran right by him. He slapped his helmet over his head and pulled the face shield into position. All his intentions to leave blew out of his mind. His balls would have driven the bike by themselves to follow her. He felt the odd lump of his gloves in his helmet, but left them there as he started the engine and began to give chase. She ran the horse along the road and was way the Hell in front of him. But he slapped the bike up a few gears and was almost to her.

Then the fence came to a neat ninety-degree angle and closed off the back of her property. She didn't even seem to consider slowing down. His heart leapt into his wussy-assed throat, and he hollered. Paying him no mind, the horse leapt gracefully over the fence like it had a part-time job as the cow jumping over the moon. He almost crashed his bike. She looked over her shoulder and gave him the finger.

I'm so done. This chick owns me. He pulled over to the side of the road and got off his bike, kicking the stand into place. She was laughing, and he wanted more of it immediately.

"Do you always ride like that?" He felt relief as she slid off the horse and landed on her feet.

"If it's a good day I do." She tucked her hands in her pockets. Her giant horse got down to the business of munching grass. "Merry Christmas."

Her hair hung in two long braids, and he wanted to wrap his fists around them. He watched as she approached him. She bit her lip before smiling in a way that made him think she was trying to hide it, and finally Emma stood right in front of him.

The impulse to tuck her on his bike and drive her to the ends of the earth was so intense he could hardly keep still. He wanted to save her, even though she was clearly fine — and pretty capable of taking care of herself.

"Was everything okay with your dad?" He folded his arms in front of him so he wouldn't do anything drastic that might scare her.

"Oh, yeah. You cut it kind of close though." She looked over her shoulder to check on her horse and then back at him quickly, like she couldn't wait to see his face.

"Sorry." He had to hold her. He opened his arms, and she stepped in and grabbed his jacket's lapels. Finally, he could take a deep breath. "Emma."

She shivered. He rubbed her arms and back to try to warm her.

"All night, it was dreams with you in them," she breathed. Her fists clenched harder, and the leather in his jacket crinkled.

"Did you see the dragon? I mean, really? What's up with the dragon?" Jack looked at the sky. The clouds seem to glisten.

Emma nodded. "It was crazy. Smoosh? And then there was a man named Everett."

"I wanted to kill him in my dream. So much." Jack felt her look at him, and he glanced down into her eyes. The answer was just on the tip of his mind.

"I hated him, yet I was...praying for him?" He could see her trying to sort it all out.

"And I was missing you, mostly," she said. "And you were...powerful?"

Her pink lips called to him. He leaned down and touched them with his before speaking against them. "Well, I'm am wildly powerful."

She kissed him back, and he had to stop himself. He grabbed each of her braids and wrapped his wrists in them so he wouldn't reenact his favorite part of the dreams on the side of the road.

His voice was raspy as he attempted to do things right. "Can I take you to dinner? We could go to my place afterwards...just to talk."

She wiggled her head, and it made his hands move. "If I have you alone I'm not responsible for what I do to you," she countered.

"Agh. Um. Holy shit." It was dangerous here for him. He felt like he was coming home from a war he'd not even known he fought until this moment. And he'd fought it for her. Emma belonged to him. She was his wife, his responsibility, and his prize. He knew it.

"I think I have to stop trying to understand this," she said. "Because it might make me lose my mind."

"Dinner tonight? What time?" He was barely speaking in full sentences anymore. He unwrapped his hands from her hair.

"Six. Pick me up at six." She staggered away from him, and he stepped back slowly until he could rest against his bike.

Watching her pull herself up onto her horse was sexual and gripping. He wanted to stop her.

"Next time, give me a boost!" she said by way of goodbye.

She talked in clicks and tugs to her horse, who gave up munching after a few moments. She picked up speed and launched the pony over the fence again. The whole encounter had been just a few minutes, and he already craved more of her. Needed her.

Jack had to settle himself down before getting on his motorcycle.

EVERETT

Everett supposed he was still in existence. He was aware, at least — aware that the punishment for all of Hell had been given just to him. At the moment he was floating on top of a bubbling hot spring in a forest. The water around him was brilliant blue. Colors he'd seen previously only in Heaven were now here on Earth. But to say time passed slowly was an understatement. He could only think and watch. And boil. No mouth to scream with, no arms to pull himself out. He was a speck. An anomaly. A type of organism that could survive in impossibly high temperatures.

Everett wondered what this was supposed to teach him. Maybe that having power is overrated? He knew now he'd taken a lot for granted — like breathing, and closing his eyes. Endless awareness was a bitch.

At first he'd tried counting the sunrises, but then they all got pushed together. Now it was either hot from above and below, or just from below. Sometimes he floated near the edge of the spring, and he yearned to get washed up on it so he could dry out, but that never happened. He just came tantalizingly close. Once in a while wildlife would walk by, and that was something.

This was his life. He looked forward to passing squirrels. So he watched with great interest one day when a hiker came by with a test tube. He seemed to be some sort of scientist. The man was nowhere near Everett as he collected a sample from the water and capped it tightly. But periodically he came back. Everett estimated it was about every three days, and each time he wished desperately to be chosen. Wherever that scientist went, Everett wanted to go too.

CHAPTER 43

EMMA

Emma put on her third outfit. She was trying way too hard. And why? She had just two more days home before she, Shannon, and Karen headed back to the city. Maybe she should just forget all this. Life was not supposed to be spent having horrible nightmares about some fantasy.

After opening presents with extended family, she'd napped for an hour on the couch while her parents watched the Yule log burn. When she woke up screaming in a cold sweat, they were understandably alarmed. Her father didn't like the rash of bad dreams she'd been having, and he'd wondered aloud if she was having an allergic reaction to something. After assuring them she was fine, Emma took a long shower. The only thing her body was allergic to was not being around Jack. She could never forget all this.

She brushed her hair one more time and hoped her outfit was okay. She'd settled on her favorite jeans and a long-sleeve top. Jack was a low-fuss kind of guy. *How do I know that? I shouldn't.*

Emma spritzed on her favorite perfume, which smelled like cotton candy and cake. It felt very high school to get picked up at her parents' house for a date, but her dad had seemed pleased to get the opportunity to intimidate a suitor.

A loud motorcycle pulled into the driveway. *Crap.* Her dad was *not* going to be thrilled to have his daughter ride off on the back of a bike. She heard the doorbell and forced herself to stay in her room so Jack could face the awkwardness on his own for a minute. She smiled — couldn't even stop herself — when Jack's grumbly voice drifted up the stairs.

"Emma! Your date is here!" Her mother was obviously doing her best to put Jack out of his misery.

Emma had to hold the handrail to steady herself. His brown eyes were waiting for her, and he nodded as she began her descent.

Her dad handed Jack back his driver's license. "Ever been in an accident, son?"

Emma winced. Jack surprised her by answering politely and with respect. "No, sir. I've been on two wheels more than I've been on my feet. I tried to rent a car for the evening, but Hew's was all out. I promise to drive with extreme caution." He slid his license into a money clip.

He'd dressed up a bit. His jeans looked fancier coupled with a tucked-in white button down. He still wore layers of necklaces and his leather cuff, but his hair was pulled back.

Her mother whispered in her ear before pushing on her lower back. "Woof."

Emma's heart felt like a rabbit's from sheer nervous energy. She went to the closet and selected her fancy jacket.

Jack clucked his tongue, and she looked at him.

"Sorry, darlin'. It's a little cold tonight. Have anything warmer?"

Emma pulled out her riding jacket, which was thin but really warm. Jack motioned for it and held it out to her. He wasn't smooth at all, which made her laugh.

She turned and mumbled, "First time being a gentleman?"

He shook his head and rolled his eyes for her benefit. After a few more threats from her father and an exuberant goodbye from her mom, they were out the door. Jack grabbed a helmet and forced it on her head.

"Whose helmet is this?" she asked before he could slap down the face shield. He seemed embarrassed. "I have an extra."

"For girls. I get it." She fixed her purse to be secure across her body.

Jack zipped his jacket and straddled the bike. "Get on."

Emma settled behind him, and the seat forced her close to his back. Having him between her thighs made her moan, just a little.

"Don't. Don't make that noise or I won't be able to drive." His voice was muffled by the helmet.

Emma gave him her loudest moans and pretended to thrash around behind him.

"You're a wise ass." He started the bike, and it was freaking loud and vibrated. "Hang on."

She slid her arms around his waist and pulled in closer as he accelerated. The ease with which he commanded the bike was ridiculously hot. She watched as the dusk settled around them. He was right — it was chilly. She scrunched down to stay out of the wind.

When they pulled up to house instead of a restaurant, she knocked on his helmet like it was a door.

He pulled off his helmet, looking supremely annoyed. "What the Hell?"

She tried to take off her helmet and failed. Then she tried to lift the face shield and failed again. She pouted at him through the acrylic. "I'm trapped!"

He laughed at her, and it was like a massage. God, his laughter touched every part of her body.

He helped her get the helmet off and his fingers traced her throat. He nodded toward the house. "I felt like we couldn't talk at a restaurant because of, you know, discussing dragons and stuff, so I'll make you dinner here."

She gave him a skeptical look.

"What? I can cook. If you're not comfortable — "

Emma got off the bike and headed for the door as he rushed to put the bike in a more permanent position. It was kind of a sweet little house. The bushes and grass were dormant for winter, but they were trimmed and neat. Jack unlocked the door and stepped in to hold it for her as he flipped on the lights. His place seemed freshly cleaned.

"Did you do some panic cleaning in here?" She unzipped her jacket, and he draped it on the couch.

"You have no idea," he confessed. "I busted my ass today."

He took off his leather jacket and set it next to hers. Then he lit a few candles and put on some music. Emma tried to make a smart remark, but she couldn't help smiling at the thought of him bustling around. The kitchen smelled fantastic, and he set a pot of water on to boil.

He poured her a gorgeous, ruby red glass of wine and held it out. His high cheekbones and sharp jaw were captivating. They locked eyes, and she reached for the glass, but took a knee instead. It was a flash again. She and Jack in a smoky bar. Emma felt illegal and happy. She wasn't afraid *of* him in this daydream, but *for* him. He was bare-chested with her name written on his skin. "God-damn it. Angel cake dipped in wine. Girl, you will kill me." He was kissing her so deeply...

She opened her eyes and saw the same face, except he was worried instead of lusty in the real world.

"Again? Was I there?" he asked.

She was in his arms, his white shirt covered in red wine. He must have splashed it all over himself trying to catch her. She nodded and tears came to her eyes. "What's going on? This isn't normal."

"Where were we?" Jack pulled her even closer.

"A smoky bar? You had a tattoo of my name. I was happy." She tried to sit up, give herself some space from his face.

"It was a pause. We were there illegally." Emma was shocked. "You know?"

He nodded.

"You know why we're having similar dreams? Why I'm falling all over the place?" She pulled away from him. "Tell me. Tell me right now." Instead of a date, this night seemed to be tinged with horror.

"I can't. You need to remember on your own. I don't want you overloaded with information." He rubbed his hand on the back of his neck.

"Stop, Jack whatever-your-last-name-is. Tell me right now or I'm leaving." She pointed at him and snarled.

"I drove you here." He tried to lighten the mood with his words, but his eyes showed only concern.

She felt like she was choking.

"Just after I left you, I remembered everything," he told her. "Damn near killed myself on my bike." He watched her.

His words burst a dam in her.

He must've thought she was going down for the count because he quickly grabbed her up. She had her head against his chest, listening to his regular, soothing heartbeat as it all came back to her: her first life, Feisty, Everett, and dying in the fire. And then she was an angel. God was her friend, and Everett was evil. Jason...Seriana, Dean. And Jack, dear heavens, Jack. When she'd died again as an angel, her last thought had been of him. She opened her eyes with a gasp.

"I love you."

He had tears running a path down his face. He nodded. "Back at ya, pretty child. So, so much."

"This...This..." She couldn't make her words make sense, but he understood. She was frantic for his mouth. He kissed her for what must have been hours, their tears mingling and interspersed with hugs as they sobbed together.

Life. They had life.

JACK

Seeing Emma remember was a tidal wave of emotion — relief, ecstasy, amazement. Jack had hoped, of course, but he wasn't positive she would come around. Then he'd fretted that she wasn't meant to think about her previous lives.

He'd cleaned like a hopped-up mom and cooked to let off steam. Not running to her the instant he knew had been the hardest thing he'd ever done. He was panicked, horrified at the thought she might be in danger. But she was in his arms now, safe and not cringing at the fact that he'd been the Devil.

Emma yanked off his shirt, buttons flying. "Don't want this, looks like blood. Are you okay?"

She stopped assaulting him to hold his face. She was so...*present* in her eyes. His Emma. Not just a body that looked the same, but her light, her courage — it was all there.

"Yeah. I was...not sure if me being the Devil would be a thing now." He looked from her mouth to her eyes.

"I think I was the Devil last, right? So how do you feel about that? No. *This* is our reward from God. Don't you see what He did? We get to start from scratch! I was wondering how it'd work — if we'd be in Heaven, on Earth, what would be next. And here's our answer." She finally got his shirt off completely and hugged him again.

They were tossing around on his kitchen floor. She deserved a bed, a nap, worship. He stood and pulled her to her feet. "See, I thought it might be more of a punishment because as humans we eventually — "

"Die? I've done that a bunch. We'll be okay if we just love each other."

"A human life isn't enough time." He already felt rushed about the minutes they were wasting.

"Oh, hey," she said, smiling brightly. "We can probably have kids. Can you imagine?" She pulled him closer and kissed his whole face.

He smiled through her affection. "We can do whatever you want." "It's you." She started to cry again.

The lump in his throat made his voice faulty. "It's you."

He lifted her off her feet and had every intention of taking her to his bedroom when he remembered the stove was on. Now it all mattered. Keeping her safe was everything. No accidents, no fires, no nothing. He could already feel himself getting paranoid.

He nuzzled her neck. "Can you turn those off?"

She reached down and twisted the burner's knobs. "Damn, this smells good."

"You want to eat?" he asked. She'd need health care and food and retirement. The desire to provide for her welled up in him. She should want for nothing.

"Not until after." She traced his lips with her fingers.

"After?" Jack glanced at the door to make sure it was locked. It was. He carried her up the stairs, remembering their time in the pause, in the sunshine. He'd been stronger then, but he still managed to get her on to his bed now.

She was already shimmying out of her jeans, and his mind shut down at the sight of her panties. She was so ready for him. He crawled onto the mattress, and theirs was a wickedly paced — as if they were racing against time — love making session. He hit the right spots, and her moans put him over too fast. He was embarrassed immediately.

Emma pulled him to her naked chest and laughed. "I think we rushed."

"I'm so sorry. That was supposed to be epic. Kill me." Jack kissed her soft skin, hiding the blush he knew was forming.

"No, thank you. I was totally afraid something bad would happen before we could — like a meteor tearing through the house." She pulled the tie out of his hair, and it all fell across her pale skin.

"I will do that again properly. I'm just...yeah."

She didn't seem to care. "My love, I'd volunteer to live a thousand lives if I got to spend any part of them with you." She buried her face in the bedding, and her short inhales told him she was crying.

He uncovered her head and looked at her luminous eyes, sparkling with tears. "And I'll kill as many assholes as I have to to make sure that happens."

They were serious now, and hearing her speak like an angel made everything better.

"Let's go shower." She smacked his ass hard.

Jack widened his eyes with surprise. "You little tart."

He tickled her until she begged him to stop, and finally Jack let her off his bed, determined to make more of an impression between her legs. He tried not to mourn the loss of all his fancy Devil tricks. The vibrating fist... his extra-long tongue...

She stood stark naked with no shame, like a woman already married to him, as she set the temperature of the shower. She slipped behind the curtain, and he realized he still wore his socks and motorcycle boots, his jeans around his ankles. *So fucking suave.* She was wetting down her hair when he finally got in the shower with her.

"How can I miss you when there's just a curtain between us?" She wiped the water from her eyes.

Jack looked at her skin, slick with water. She was all he'd ever need. He didn't answer her question, just pulled her against him and twirled them both under the spray. He'd promised to take his time, but his hands were greedy. He touched every part of her that made her gasp or shiver, and as he watched the reactions play across her face, he tried to memorize them. She began exploring him as well, and he tried batting her away. She was about to unman him, again.

He grasped her wrists and held them behind her back. "You need to just take for a few fucking seconds. I've a reputation to uphold."

She laughed at him, and he bit her lip gently to punish her. She moaned. With his other hand he felt the weight of her breasts, her body so very much his. When he found her nipples, she bit his lip in return.

He slid his hand between her legs and found the heat there. Now, with her held still, he could prove he knew exactly what to do. She was already tensed and forgetting herself, saying his name again and again. As she spread her legs wider, he dropped to his knees and let go of her wrists. She grabbed handfuls of his hair and urged him on. With both hands, he could be everywhere she needed. He wasn't delicate with her, yet she begged for more.

That, he could do. Jack pushed her out of the shower, never stopping his hands until he had her, sopping wet, on his bed. He grabbed a chair. He was going to be between her legs so long he'd need it. Jack pushed her legs apart and leaned down to taste her. His tongue may have been longer as the Devil, but nothing was trying to kill them at the moment, so he made up for it. When she came she thrashed, yanking his bedspread so hard it ripped. But he didn't stop. He insisted on more. Her muscles relaxed, and he could tell she thought she was done. He knew better. He wound her up in a frenzy again, his hands more insistent and adding fingers and teeth to take her where she could explode again for him.

"In me. Get in me!"

Emma spoke her first coherent words in quite some time, and Jack complied. He slipped her knees over his shoulders and kept pressure on the spot he knew would give her the most release. He pounded into her like the Devil he'd been and the man he wanted to be. Having her convulse against him was better than any power he'd ever possessed.

She scratched his back and slapped at his ass with her feet, laughing and gasping at the same time. At her ultimate joy, Jack gave in to his own need. She clenched just for him, and he saw stars. He landed next to her, barely trusting himself, his muscles twitching.

"Well." She turned his face to look at hers.

"Well," he replied, a huge smile on his face while he panted with her. "Sex that good should be illegal."

Her smile was so satisfied. Jack felt the most masculine pride of a job well done. *Thank God.*

"I love you, Emma the human angel." He put a possessive arm across her chest.

"I love you, Jack the sweetest Devil." She patted his arm and sighed.

CHAPTER 44

JACK

This time Emma was driving. She'd complained that the throbbing between her legs made it impossible for her to ride Jack's bike.

He'd simply blown on his fist and winked. "By the time I'm done with you, you'll have calluses like a runner down there."

"That's gross." She tried to listen to the GPS over the music.

"You love me anyway." Jack slipped a hand under her shirt.

She let him grope for a while before pushing him away. "Let me concentrate." "This is a shitty idea. Just putting that out there. Again." He lit up a cigarette. Emma hit her window so it would open a crack. He knew what was coming and tried to take evasive action. She'd thrown quite a few of his smokes out the window.

"You don't quit that soon and I'm withholding sex."

Jack took one long drag and tossed it out the passenger window.

"Great! That's horrible too. Now you've probably lit up some squirrel's tail," she protested. "The whole forest will burn down Bambi-style thanks to you."

"You're too addicted to give up the sex."

Even on four wheels, Jack preferred to drive, and she saw him tense up as she approached the stoplight.

"I prefer you alive to anything else," she said. The interior of the car went from playful to serious. Mortality sobered them both. They'd talked about it every day since they remembered who they were. Emma wasn't scared to die, but she definitely wasn't ready.

She'd moved in with Jack because she didn't have a choice. Her brain almost convulsed with the loss when he wasn't in the room. Her family had taken to him despite his sudden appearance, which was good because they were now inseparable. Jack stopped by on the weekends to help her dad with the lawn or sit and talk with her mother.

She smiled at him. He was amazing. And he also thought going to check in with the half-breeds was a poor choice. She wasn't sure if his concerns were about jealousy or being afraid they might become a snack, but he'd been very vocal about his dislike of this trip. But when she'd remembered the location of the Parishes' house, she'd told him she was going with or without him. She wanted to go, needed to go. Jason's soul was still her job, in her mind.

When she pulled into the driveway, the place looked the same. Only the cars out front were different. A ridiculous Ferrari glistened in front of the modest house. She prayed as she opened her door. *Please, God, let them have found peace.*

"Last time I saw a car like that, it was Violent's ride," Jack commented as he got out of the car. "This may be more of a reunion than you've anticipated."

Emma took his hand, for once ignoring the fact that he'd lit a cigarette.

The door opened before they knocked.

"Emma? Jack? How? What?" Seriana threw her arms around Emma, who squeezed her back, hard.

Looking past Seriana, Emma saw Jason round the corner of the hallway.

He stopped and his mouth dropped open.

"You're alive? You're alive?" Jason pulled Emma into a hug as Seriana hugged a fairly angry-looking Jack.

She patted Jason and kissed his cheek.

"I don't understand. You're human?" Jason held her an arm's length away.

"Yeah, Jack and I found each other, and then we remembered who we are. I'm so glad you guys are still here. Your mom? Kate? Dean? How's everyone?"

Seriana and Jason pulled Emma into the living room. She smiled at all the familiar furnishings and Dean's countless books.

Dean appeared next, and after he was thoroughly hugged, Emma was reacquainted with Nero and Violent, as well as an intense man named Mine who couldn't take his eyes off Seriana.

It was a nice, if slightly confusing, reunion. The half-breeds and minions all looked exactly the same, young and beautiful as ever, but Emma knew the time must have worn on them. These past decades, she'd been a human in her head, unaware of all that had come before. But they'd had to pick up the pieces and move on.

Rebecca fussed over everyone, insisting on sending Dean and Seriana out for the makings of an impromptu grill party, despite Emma's protests. "Really, Rebecca. Don't go to all this trouble. Jack and I are the only humans here."

Jack did his best to be surly, but he was clearly happy to see Nero and Violent. The minions and former Devil immediately began to talk shop. Emma smiled at them over a glass of wine, and Jason came closer, pulling Kate behind him.

"So, you're alive," he began. "With…him. I guess if that's the price you have to pay to be with us again, it'll do."

Kate touched her stomach and looked worried. Rebecca called for Jason to help her prepare the chips and dip. Emma patted his arm as he excused himself.

"How long have you known you're pregnant?" Emma asked gently once he'd gone. She just knew — the way the woman held her body, the fear in her eyes.

"I've only just told Jason. Did he tell you?" Kate assessed Emma again.

"No. I can just tell. Some sort of holdover from angelhood maybe? For a while I was a labor and delivery angel before I was promoted to seraph." Emma took a sip of her wine. Behind Kate, she could make out the silhouette of Jason whispering the good news to Rebecca. There was a certain look to a woman when she found out she was going to be a grandmother. It was beautiful, and Rebecca had it. She refocused on Kate.

"Not sure how many angels will be at this birth." Kate rubbed her arms with obvious alarm.

"First, congratulations," Emma told her. "Second, there will be an angel. There always is. It's such a moment, the meeting of parent and child. It must be witnessed." Emma wanted to drag the nervous mother-to-be to a room and comfort her until she smiled with her blessed news. She left out the part about how God himself comes down to Earth for any child who doesn't live through labor. Now wasn't the time for that information. Kate was scared enough.

"Okay, Emma, not to be rude? But none of this is your business. I really don't want advice from my man's ex-girlfriend." She looked around for an out.

Shocked, Emma shut her mouth and in the same instant felt Jack's hand on her lower back. He never missed a trick.

"Kate? What's up?" he said by way of greeting.

Rebecca burst out of the kitchen, crying and sighing. She looked longingly at Kate's belly.

"You told her? Jason!" Kate was ticked, but Rebecca immediately wrapped her arms around her.

Emma stepped back so the family could have a moment, and Seriana, Mine, and Dean came through the front door holding grocery bags, clearly puzzled at the emotion in the room.

Jack and Emma watched as the family expanded. He spoke close to her ear. "What was that about? She was angry with you?"

Emma nodded and stupidly wanted to cry. It had been a crazy

assumption. She was human now. She had no right to try to be an angel. "I left him for you. I forget that, I guess."

"Something's up. Kate's a sweet girl. She'd never hold that against you." Jack left Emma to sidle up to Kate.

Trying to find something to do, Emma gathered the grocery bags from the floor where the uncle- and aunt-to-be had dropped them. Seriana broke away to help.

"I can't believe we're going to have a little one running around. So cool." Seriana kept hugging Emma and leaned over to tuck a strand of her hair behind her ear.

"I'm so happy you're okay," Emma said. "All these years I didn't know to be worried, and now it's crashed in on me all at once." Emma stilled Seriana's busy hands and held them. "Tell me about Mine."

"Oh, I don't even know where to start with that one." She shook her head and smiled.

"Well, then tell me how it ends. Are you happy?" Emma wrinkled her nose. "So, so happy. He gets me and loves me. I'm crazy about him." Seriana did a little wiggly dance.

"And Jason? How has he done?"

"He had a time for a while. Kate and he had, you know, pure Lucifer running through them, and they had to...I guess...detoxify? They're better, though. I bet the baby will settle things for them. Maybe a wedding? Wouldn't that be amazing?"

Emma's mouth dropped open. She knew damn well what Kate was afraid of now. Rebecca and Dean came into the kitchen to pour some drinks to toast with.

Emma scurried into the living room. "Jack? I need you outside."

"Done." He stopped mid-conversation with Nero and followed as she left the house in a hurry.

She turned toward him on the front lawn. "Jason and Kate both got juiced from Lucifer. Can this affect their baby? I bet that's why Kate's off her rocker. I would be too."

His face flooded with regret. "I don't know. Honestly? Lucy

rarely made appearances, and the whole kissy face thing was a new one to me. I mean, *I'm* fine."

"You kissed Lucifer?" Despite her worry, Emma couldn't help but smile a little.

"Don't even. No. You will *not* taunt me with this." Jack looked murderous.

"Oh, yes I will. A lot. Often." Emma leaned in close and kissed him. "Seriously. Let's think about this. I'm coming up with a vague reference about Lucifer being unable to procreate. Am I making that up?"

Jack lit up a cigarette, and after exhaling he shook his head. "I wasn't exactly hitting the history books back in the day."

"How can we help them?" Emma slid under his arm so she could put her hand over his heart.

"Not sure we can. Their problems might be their own." Jack tapped the drug so the ashes fell, glowed, and extinguished.

Emma went in for a kiss and snagged the butt at the same time. She dropped it and stomped it out as he tried to get her to stop.

"We're going to go through all our money if you keep wasting shit." Jack hugged her to his chest.

They stood looking into the dark woods.

"I refuse to do nothing. I have to figure out a way to ease her mind." "How did I know you'd say that? Come on, let's go get something to eat."

Jack held out his hand and led her back into the house.

She loved him because he'd help her help them, even though he hadn't wanted to be here in the first place.

CHAPTER 45

JACK

On the way home Jack drove, stealing glances at Emma, who sighed on occasion. At least they'd gotten out of the Parish house alive. Emma had assumed they'd still remember not to kill, but Jack had watched people's convictions change enough to have a gun in his pocket.

Emma broke the silence. "I guess it'll be okay. God wouldn't put life where it wasn't meant to be." She reached for his hand.

He smiled at her, but disagreed in his head. Evil was out there, and it could thrive. When he pulled her car into his driveway, he was nervous again. Now wasn't the best time for his question. She was thinking of everyone else.

He kicked off his old motorcycle boots and followed her upstairs. She twisted her hair into a knot and pulled off her bra, throwing it off to the side. Jack rolled his eyes at her back. She hated wearing bras and pulled them off the second she could. He'd find her bras in the living room behind the couch or lying on the kitchen table next to the mail. He snagged the lingerie from the floor as they made their way to the bedroom. She was harping on one of her concerns for Jason and Kate, but he wasn't listening. Folding his arms behind his head, he just watched her.

As Emma tugged on her favorite pajamas, Jack had a flash of

her falling from Lucifer's arms again. His heart became pain. It must have shown on his face because she stopped lotioning up her arms and crawled onto the bed next to him.

"What's wrong?" She put a hand on his face.

He leaned into her touch and turned his head to kiss her palm. "I watched Lucifer kill you. You fell from the sky, and when I caught you? There was nothing left but glitter."

"I'm so sorry." She put her head on his chest and clenched his shirt, right above his aching heart. "I can't even imagine."

"Here's the thing, you keep wanting to do that to me again."

She pulled her head up, startled. "What? Never."

Shaking his head, he looked sadly at his angel. "With this whole Jason and Kate thing, you want to take that burden from them, get involved, visit them, see if Jason's soul is in a good spot."

She watched him, swallowing. What he said rang true. It was who she was. "But I think you did your part. I think you get to say a prayer for them and live your fucking life for you. For us." He touched her lips.

The bedroom was quiet for a while, and Jack was scared. What if telling her this made her leave? Was being a version of an angel more important than being in his every day?

"You're right." She rolled off of him and flopped on the bed. Absently she pulled out the knot in her hair.

He was afraid to breathe, paralyzed by the hope that she'd just live with him, for the time they had.

"You know, *we* were brought together, but I had to seek them out." She watched their fan loop circles on the ceiling. "You are my gift, my prize for lives well lived. And I'm here trying to borrow a situation I surely can't fix."

Exactly. He didn't want to say it out loud. She had to see this on her own.

"What should I do? I can't ignore them now that I know where they are." The light from the hallway lay on the bed with her, making two slices of illumination at her sides, almost like wings.

"Really? I think a Christmas card and a few visits a year should suffice. Could you do that? It might keep me sane." Jack flipped onto his stomach and hushed his opinionated mouth.

"Yeah. I owe it to you, after all." Her hand threaded into his hair, gently tugging.

"Nope. It has to be for you, not me," he said.

Jack loved her lips, they were so pink. She fidgeted.

"You feel guilty because it's a relief," he said. He twisted her hand and placed a lingering kiss on her wrist. "They've been at this for over twenty years. We're *humans* now. What the Hell are we going to be able to do if they have a demon baby? Can we help? Can *you* breastfeed it fire? Who the Hell knows what Kate's going to pop out. You and me. That's it."

"But to just write them off? I don't know." Emma let her hand fall from his lips and touch his leather necklaces.

"I'm not saying write them off. I'm saying we should do what we can. Which is nothing." He held his breath again. This was asking her so, so much. He knew it.

She sighed like she was getting ready for a painful procedure. "Okay. Fine. I'm not going to try to fix it, or get involved. I'll pray, and we can stay friendly, but I'll live this life for you, for me. For us." Her smile was genuine.

"Really?" He raised an eyebrow at her.

Emma's voice was soft, but she answered with conviction. "Really."

"Well, hot damn. Did not expect that." Jack covered her quickly, hugging and kissing her as if they had forever.

EMMA

A small bark from outside woke them, partially clothed and tangled together, as the sun slanted into the bedroom. They looked suspiciously at each other, then went to look. Jack popped open the window, and Emma gasped at the small puppy squeak-barking at their window.

Emma slapped Jack's bicep. "Don't just stand there! Go get me that pile of cute!"

Jack shook his head. "No way, baby. It's someone's. They'll be around to get it."

It took a few more barks from the puppy and a few more moments of silence from Emma before Jack sighed in exasperation. "Fine, damn it."

Even he had to smile when he came back into the room. "You'll never guess what this little bastard's name is. He's got a collar and everything."

She shook her head as she took the correct guess. "Smoosh?"

Jack nodded as he passed the little puppy to her. Their dragon had come, sent by God to be part of their family in this life. Emma smiled. Jack pulled another puppy from behind his back. Smoke looked just like his brother. The puppies' timing was perfect because it confirmed the meaning of her dream the night before. She had to share.

She watched Jack for a few moments. He was clearly losing the battle to avoid falling in love with Smoosh, who nipped at his fingers relentlessly. She tucked her hair behind her ears.

"So, last night I had a dream, and I believe it was a message."

"From my dick saying how much it loves you?" Jack flipped Smoosh onto his back to rub his belly.

"Well, that and from Claudette. Your old angel flame? She was laying out the plans for Kate and Jason's baby. She told me the child would become a great peacemaker. I really wish..." Emma trailed off. She'd made a promise and didn't want to go back on it.

"You could go deliver the news?" Jack picked up her foot and rubbed it in a way she particularly loved.

Emma waited him out.

"Why don't you send Kate and Jason a nice, old-fashioned

letter? I'm sure that would fulfill your angel requirements as a messenger without getting tits-deep in their drama."

The puppy began play-fighting Jack's hand. He growled back at him, then leaned in to find her lips.

His mouth took away her cares, the running lists of things that needed to be done, the lingering doubt that she should be living differently — all of it faded until she could only feel him. His lips, his relentless hands. This go around would be for their love, she promised as she lost herself in his skillful touch. And when they were both exhausted, naked, and spent, she thanked him.

"I know if I'd decided to stay all up in Jason's business you'd have supported me."

He was having a cigarette. She ran her hand through the smoke.

"Darlin', I'd follow you off a cliff riding a horse with its tail on fire." His face glowed orange as he inhaled again.

"I know." She hadn't asked him yet, but it was far beyond time. "How did you die, after I did?"

"Let's not." He shifted uncomfortably.

"You have the burden of knowing how I died." She pulled a blanket off the floor and covered herself, suddenly chilled. She covered his bottom half as well.

He glanced at her and gave her the smile she loved by way of a thank you.

"Doesn't mean you deserve the same knowledge." Jack stubbed his cigarette in the ashtray he must have rescued from the trash.

"Did you have anyone else?" She bit her lip.

He tsked at her and gave her a look of disbelief. "Of course not. You really want to know?"

Emma nodded, eyes wide.

"I simply challenged Lucy for the position of Devil and refused to fight back. It was over in minutes." One of his hands began to tremble.

He was right. She didn't need that knowledge. Her imagination put her right back on Earth's battlefield, picturing her love cut down. Minutes could feel like forever. She started to cry, the sadness a sudden punch.

He cuddled her to his chest, rubbing her back. "Hey, I'm here. I'm here, and I'm fine. Actually, I'm great. I've got my girl, a huge dick, and my girl. What more do I need?"

She laughed a little and understood more of where his overwhelming need to keep her safe came from. "A little modesty might serve you." She pinched his nipple.

"Ouch! For fuck's sake, that's not even fair." He got out of bed and went to a dresser drawer. "Hey, can I ask you something?"

Emma shrugged. "Of course."

Jack opened a small box and pulled out what looked a Hell of a lot like an engagement ring.

He kneeled, naked at her side, and she sat up, covering herself with the sheet. "No." He pulled on the sheet so she was topless in front of him. "I'm

proposing to your tits too."

She gave him the middle finger. Jack trapped both her hands in one of his.

He slid the ring on the pert nipple on her left breast.

"Left breast? Will you be mine forever?" Jack spoke to her chest.

Emma wiggled a shoulder while speaking in a high-pitched voice. "Sure, unless we have a kid. Then you're shit out of luck for a few years."

"That's how your boob talks?" Jack's smile was huge, his eyes dancing with laughter.

"It is now." She wiggled the ring from her breast, and he caught it before it hit the ground. "You're really screwing this up," she said. "I think this might be the worst proposal in the history of the world."

Jack pulled her to the edge of the bed until she straddled him.

He slid himself inside her, and she sighed despite their joking mood.

Connected, he sobered up. "Okay, how's this? I've been to Heaven and Hell. I've seen the whole world, but the only thing that makes me want to live is this: being inside you. Say yes, pretty child. I love you so much. You're all I see."

She nodded then, smiling while she held out her hand.

"That's your right hand. Let's do it on the other one, yes?" He slipped the beautiful diamond on her hand. It wasn't the biggest, but it was crystal clear.

"I will be your wife, no matter how many lives we live," she declared. She took his face in her hands and kissed him while he rocked her back and forth on his lap.

"Wait now, I just asked you about this one." He held up his hands as if offended.

"All or nothing, Satan." Emma kissed Jack hard and long.

When he finally came up for air, he answered easily. "All, pretty child. I want it all."

The next time Emma kneeled before God with Jack at her side, she'd be able to tell Him her heart was pure, baptized in love.

ALSO BY DEBRA ANASTASIA

Angst with Feels:

CRUEL PINK

DROWNING IN STARS

STEALING THE STARS

Mafia Romance:

MERCY

HAVOC

LOCK

Silly Humor:

FIRE DOWN BELOW

FIRE IN THE HOLE

Funny Humor:

FLICKER

BEAST

BOOTY CAMP

FELONY EVER AFTER

BEFORE YOU GHOST (with Helena Hunting)

Paranormal:

THE REVENGER

FOR ALL THE EVERS

CRUSHED SERAPHIM (BOOK 1)

BITTERSWEET SERAPHIM (BOOK 2)

Acknowledgments

I'd like to thank, as always, my gorgeous husband and children. Thank you for sharing me with the computing deadlines. I love you all so much. My parents and in-laws, you are fantastic role models and friends. My sister, you're the best librarian in the world. Jessica Royer Ocken Carol Oates, thank you for making my books into visual art. Jack, Beckett, and I love you. Jo and Ted, I'm writing you into the next one! Karen, I adore you. Believe in impossible things. Shannon, let's share a bed again. Nise, Patti, Alicia, Jillian: tat privileges! Thanks to Rhonda, Tamie, Elena, Ashley, Autumn, and all the great blog girls who let Jack in! Mad4hugh: I'm missing you. Helena and Tijan I love you guys

ABOUT THE AUTHOR

Debra creates pretend people in her head and paints them on the giant, beautiful canvas of your imagination. She has a Bachelor of Science degree in political science and writes new adult angst and romantic comedies. She lives in Maryland with her husband and two amazing children. She doesn't trust mannequins, but does trust bears. Also, her chunky tuxedo cat talks with communication buttons. So that's fun. DebraAnastasia.com for more information.

Pretty please review this book if you enjoyed it. It is one of the very best ways to support indy authors. Thank you! (Plus, anyone that reviews is granted three wishes by the first vampire they meet.)

Scan the code below to stay connected to Debra:

tiktok.com/@debraanastasia

facebook.com/debra.anastasia

instagram.com/debra_anastasia